*For the brave ones who dare to
sit, stand, and kneel
for the cause of
equality*

PROLOGUE

When I went to the river that day in 1959,
I didn't expect to meet a colored boy
who loved birds like I love my cow.
I didn't know what all I'd learn from him
or that a mean old drunk would come along
and force me to see myself as I never had before.

I didn't realize I was face to face with a muddy wide river.

I didn't think when I went into eighth grade
that a teacher would name my strengths
and inspire me to be even stronger.
I didn't know that I'd learn
to speak up while measuring my words,
to hold back when I wanted revenge,
or to imagine an enemy as my friend.

1

AUGUST 1959

"Daddy," I said, "wanna go to the river? We could catch a few fish for supper."

"And leave this lonely woman all by herself?" Daddy said. "Nah, I'm gonna keep your momma company, but you go right ahead."

Oh, of *course* he would stay with Momma. She was always lonely after family dinner on Sundays. She'd start moping the second my sisters headed for home with their husbands. Later she'd watch television with Daddy, and that would pull her out of her sadness. But it seemed like once in a while Momma could watch television without Daddy there holding her hand.

Couldn't he see that I was lonely sometimes too?

I dug some worms and grabbed my fishing pole and a bucket for bringing fish home, just in case I had any luck. I wasn't much of a fisherman, but the sight of the river rippling by and the smell of the woods always made me feel better. I figured maybe if I went downstream I'd find a good spot. So I followed a trail by the river and rounded a bend, and there on the riverbank was a colored boy pulling in a good-sized fish. I stopped in my tracks and watched how he let his pole curve and tip practically into the water before he pulled back and then leaned in again. When he landed that bass, I couldn't help but let out a "Woo-hoo!"

He turned real fast to see who was sneaking up on him, and when he caught sight of me his big old grin sort of slid off his face. Maybe he thought I was trouble. But puny as I was, I shouldn't have worried him none. He looked to be about my age, maybe older. Taller and broader for sure. And with bigger muscles.

If he'd claimed that fishing hole for himself I'd have gone on my merry way. But I reckon he wasn't taking his chances on starting something up with a strange white boy. I was pretty sure I'd seen him somewhere, but I couldn't quite place him. Figured I might as well introduce myself. "My name's Jackie," I said.

And before I could tell him my last name, he said it for me. "Honeycutt."

"How'd you know?"

"I keep my ears open."

"Evidently *I* don't. On account of I don't know who you are."

Turned out he was Thomas Freeman, and he lived in the brown house on the back side of Garland Abernethy's farm. My school bus had been driving past his mailbox for years. So I'd seen him plenty of times—just not up close. I told him where I lived, and wouldn't you know, he attended the little colored church along the road that leads to my lane. All those years we'd been going right by each other and I'd never once looked him in the eye.

Now, here we were on the riverbank, getting to know each other. School was fixing to start up the next day, and I'd be going into eighth grade. He'd be a freshman in high school. But even if he wasn't older we'd go to different schools. After all, he was colored.

I told Thomas about my family and how I was raising a heifer for the dairy contest at the fair. "That's just two weeks away," I said. "But Lucy's ready. I named her after Lucille Ball, in case you're wondering."

He shook his head a little, which I took to mean he wasn't wondering.

"Mr. Nolley—that's our 4-H agent—says Lucy's in fine shape. I think we've got a chance of winning."

Thomas gave a little snort then. Not much—just enough to let me know he wasn't taking my word for it.

"What?" I asked.

"Nah," he said. "Nah. I wasn't saying nothing."

"No, you didn't say a word. But I can tell; you think I'm crazy. How come you don't think I can win?"

"You never heard of the Lutzes? Over in Startown?"

"Yeah, sure I have. Mr. Nolley even took us to a Lutz farm to learn about cattle judging."

"Then I guess you saw their fine barn with all the latest equipment."

"We got a tour. But that's the barn. We're talking about cows here."

"Hmm," said Thomas.

"What?" I demanded. "Say what you're thinking."

"I'm thinking the Lutzes breed cows. They own the best in the state. That's what I'm thinking."

"I got Lucy from Arnie—that's my brother-in-law. He's a dairy farmer. Lucy's mother and sire were both prizewinners." I could hear the edge in my voice. I mean, who did this guy think he was? Judging my cow, sight unseen?

To be honest, my pal Wayne had told me the same thing about the Lutzes, and he'd tried to talk me into raising a pig for that very reason. But Wayne was raising a pig, and who would want to compete against his best friend? I'd lose that contest for sure.

"How do you know so much about all this?" I asked Thomas. "Are you in 4-H?"

Thomas shook his head. "Colored school don't have 4-H. But my buddy works for the Lutzes. I've been to his house and helped him on their farm even."

"Oh, I see. Well, maybe you should come to *my* farm. Meet Lucy. You'd see just how fine she is."

Thomas didn't say anything at first. He was busy pulling another fish out of the water. Then he focused on putting a fat worm on his hook and throwing his line back in. "That an invitation?"

"Uh . . . well, sure."

Thomas laughed. It was like he knew I wasn't expecting him to take me up on it. If he did, he wouldn't be impressed. After all, two sheds, a garden, and a pasture didn't exactly qualify as a farm. We didn't even have a barn, just a lean-to that Daddy helped me build for Lucy.

Then again, now that I realized where Thomas lived, I knew his little farmstead wasn't so fine and fancy either. Sure, he had a barn, a saggy one. But there wasn't any point in arguing, so I changed the subject. "What are those for?" I pointed to a pair of binoculars on the ground beside him.

"Birdwatching."

That sounded boring. But he proceeded to fill me in on the particulars.

"I've got seventy-five birds in my record book. That's how many species I've seen."

"Oh," I said. "Well, I guess you know that the Lutzes in Startown have at least a hundred in their record books."

"Huh?"

"They probably even *breed* birds. The best in the state."

Thomas snorted, figuring out I was trying to be funny, and then went on. "I can do twenty-three bird-calls."

"You brag about something, you might have to prove it."

"Listen." And just like that, he gave out a raucous call.

"Ha!" I said. "Even I know a crow when I hear one."

"What about this?" He made a shrill sound.

"Blue jay."

"Bingo. And blue jays make other sounds too."

I have to say he lost me after that. Lots of the bird songs sounded familiar, but I'd never really paid attention to which birds in my yard were making which sounds. I saw cardinals all the time, but I didn't know they had four different calls. Thomas could do all of them.

"Now sit there real still," he said, "and I'll talk a cardinal into dropping by for a visit." And wouldn't you know, he actually fooled a cardinal into thinking he was a bird. I wouldn't have believed it if I hadn't heard him talking back and forth with one. Finally a flash of red swooped down and landed right across the river on a low branch. It was a beautiful male. Cocking his head from side to side and looking downright confused, he held a conversation with Thomas.

It was real comical because Thomas was not the lady bird that the cardinal was hoping for. "He's not exactly in love with you," I said.

I guess I moved or something because the cardinal flew away. Thomas watched without a word until the bird was out of sight. "But I sure do love *him*," he whispered.

While he gazed at that red bird, I stared at him—the way his eyes followed its flight, the look of pure gladness on his face. It was an ordinary bird that I could see practically any day, and yet, for Thomas Freeman, it was so much more.

A little breeze kicked up and brought the smell of pine needles with it. The river flowed past almost as quiet as Thomas, who had settled into fishing again. I knew I should probably be heading for home and leftover dinner, but I wasn't in a hurry. There was something real peaceful about being in the woods—even if I hadn't got so much as a nibble on my fishing line.

But Thomas? Maybe he knew fish talk too, because he soon landed another big one. I wondered whether I might learn a thing or two if I hung around long enough.

2

AUGUST 1959

On Monday morning, the first day of school, Momma walked to the bus stop with me—well, not actually to the bus stop but to our neighbors' house. The Hinkle sisters lived at the corner where the bus picked me up, and Momma looked after them on weekdays. I'd known those ladies for as long as I lived. In fact, I was born in their fine brick house. Evidently I was in a hurry: I came in the middle of a supper there one evening!

I could see Miss Dinah now, sitting by the living room window working on a jigsaw puzzle like always. I knew she wanted me to come in and say hello, but I couldn't because the bus was almost there. So I just waved and got on.

About a mile after my stop, we passed by Thomas's house. There he was, heading out his lane with an older brother and two sisters. I'd seen them plenty of times before, but not up close, because they always stood a distance from the road. Thomas and his brother and sisters mostly kept their backs to us.

After yesterday Thomas knew *I* was on that bus, but this morning he didn't so much as glance my way. A few minutes later, my bus met the one coming to pick him up. It rolled right on by with both drivers staring straight ahead. How many years had we done this and I hadn't thought a thing of it?

According to the Supreme Court of the United States, public school segregation was unlawful. The old law of "separate but equal" wasn't working, because Negro schools didn't have equal money or textbooks or desks or anything else. At least that's what my sister Ellie said. And I'd seen talk about it on TV too.

But television news also showed what happened when schools tried to integrate—anger and violence. Bombs even. A few schools in Tennessee and Arkansas actually had to shut down. Evidently some parents figured no education at all was better than having their kids go to school with Negroes. Momma and Daddy would never admit to such a thing, but they sure weren't pushing for integration. They didn't want trouble.

This morning, like in past years, there were only white kids arriving at Mountain View School. I stepped into the hallway and stopped for a second to take it all in, the shiny wood floors and the smell of wax. Fresh colors on every wall and smiling teachers standing in the doorways. Mrs. Cunningham was waiting for us at the eighth-grade classroom door.

One by one she stopped us. She put her hands on our

shoulders, looked us in the eyes, and said our names. From the way Mrs. Cunningham held me there for a long moment, I felt like she was memorizing something about me. "I'm glad to have you here, Jackie," she said. She had a twinkle in her blue eyes and a big smile on her face.

But friendly as she was, she set *me* straight first thing. I made the mistake of flashing my new Davy Crockett comic book at Wayne while she was taking attendance. That started us whispering.

"Jackie," said Mrs. Cunningham, "do you and Wayne have something to share with the rest of the class?"

"Uh, no. I mean, no, ma'am."

"Wayne?"

"No, ma'am."

Somewhere in the back of the room Dennis Aiken snickered. He was always itching for a fight. Mrs. Cunningham pounced on him next. "What about you, Dennis? Did you want to add to this conversation?"

And just that quick, Dennis said, "No, ma'am."

That almost made *me* snicker. But I wouldn't dare. I could tell already that Mrs. Cunningham was a no-nonsense kind of teacher. She sat back against the corner of her desk where she could keep her eye on every last one of us.

Now that she had our attention, she reminded us that this Friday, August 21, 1959, Hawaii would officially become the fiftieth state in the union. We'd be follow-ing current events this year, she told us. "So let's celebrate!" she said. "And we'll learn some things about Hawaii at the same time."

We broke into small groups, and Mrs. Cunningham gave us topics to report on. Wayne was in my group, and so was Pamela Davis. Our topic was plants, and we had a *National Geographic* magazine and a travel brochure to help us out. I started sketching coconuts and palm trees.

Mrs. Cunningham came to our group, took one look at my palm trees, and snapped her fingers. "Oh, Jackie, you're an artist." She crooked her finger at me. "I need you over here."

She put me at a table in the back of the room. "See that empty bulletin board? Help Norma and Jimmy make it look like Hawaii—maps, flowers, volcanoes . . . You know what I'm getting at."

Hot dog! Decorating a bulletin board sounded good to me. We joked around while we worked, and Mrs. Cunningham played Hawaiian songs on the record player.

On Friday we had a party—a *luau*. But first, each group had to give a report. I volunteered to explain the bulletin board.

When our class went to lunch Mrs. Cunningham stopped me at the door. "Jackie," she said, "you have a flair for speaking in front of a group. I'd like to see you develop that. Channel your gift for gab in a useful direction—know what I mean?" She gave a little wink and nudged me out the door.

Honestly, I didn't even know what a flair was. But I could see that she was paying me a compliment. *And* she was telling me to watch my mouth, all in the same breath.

The worst part about school was Dennis and his pal Tony sitting at the same lunch table with Wayne and me—three days in a row. If we talked about Lucy or Elmira, the pig Wayne was raising for 4-H, Dennis would start mooing and oinking. He thought it was downright hilarious that I'd named my cow after Lucille Ball.

Then on Friday afternoon I caught him at the back of the room with my Davy Crockett comic book.

"Where'd you get that?" I asked.

He glared at me. "You're not the only one who owns comic books."

"That's mine," I said.

"Maybe it is. Maybe it's mine. Or will be."

"Will be, my *foot!*" I tried to snatch it, but he held on. I wasn't about to rip it, so I let go. "All right then, read it. But if you don't want trouble, it'd better be on my desk by the end of the day."

Evidently he didn't want trouble, because he dropped

it on my desk on his way out to the bus. I waited until he was out of the room and stuck it in the very bottom of my desk. I'd have to keep my comic books tucked out of sight from now on. Mrs. Cunningham wouldn't be happy if I got into a fight with Dennis Aiken.

3

AUGUST 1959

The Hinkle sisters didn't usually come to our house for Sunday dinner, and Bessie Bledsoe didn't either, because even though she lived with her son, Junior, who was married to my sister Ann Fay, Bessie spent nights and weekends looking after the sisters. But Miss Pauline was going stir-crazy riding her wheelchair from one end of the house to the other, and lately she'd become obsessed with fears about Russia and bombs. Bessie said Miss Pauline needed to get out and about.

So there we sat—the Honeycutts, the Bledsoes, and the Hinkle sisters—just like it was Christmas in August, but without presents, of course. I straddled the table leg at the corner between Miss Pauline and Miss Dinah. My sister Ellie was on the other side of Miss Pauline, because that's where Miss Pauline wanted her. Ellie was home from Winston-Salem for the weekend—another reason for us to get together.

It was hot and crowded, but nobody was complaining. Ida and her husband, Arnie, were there. And of course

Ann Fay, with Junior and their two young'uns, four-year-old Bunkie and Gerianne, who was two.

Ida asked Ellie to tell us about her new job. I didn't realize Ellie had a new job, but of course Ida would be the first to know. She and Ellie were twins—alike in looks but different in almost every other way.

"I'll be working for Maribelle's father," said Ellie. "As a volunteer—so I can get some experience in the field."

"What field?" I asked. "And who's Maribelle? Is that your roommate?"

Ellie frowned and shook her head. "No. I met Maribelle at a passive resistance workshop."

"What in the world is that?"

"Good grief, Jackie. If you'd just listen you might learn a thing or two," said Ellie. "Passive resistance, for your information, means bringing about social change with nonviolent action. Like when Negroes stopped using the city buses in Alabama until they gained the right to sit at the front of the bus. Dr. Martin Luther King helped organize that movement."

"Oh," I said. I started to ask if Maribelle was a Negro, but I stopped myself and took a bite of roast beef instead.

"Maribelle's father is a lawyer in Winston-Salem," said Ellie. "He's working on civil rights issues. This is an amazing opportunity for me." She reached over and touched Miss Pauline's arm. "And it's all because of you, Miss Pauline. You're the one who encouraged me to go

21

to college, and you even set up that scholarship fund. I'll always be indebted to you."

Miss Pauline frowned. "Civil rights? Reverend McIntire says communists are behind the civil rights movement. I wasn't expecting you to indulge in questionable pursuits."

Miss Pauline was once a teacher, and sometimes she forgot she shouldn't still be bossing people around. One thing about Ellie, though—she had a mind of her own. Besides that, when she went away to college, she met all kinds of people and latched onto new ideas.

"But Miss Pauline," she said, "do you ever think maybe that radio preacher has forgotten what he learned in Sunday school? Wouldn't Jesus want my Negro friends to get a good education? And I know how *you* value schooling. I've met with a committee that's working to get Negroes admitted to Wake Forest College. I thought you'd be proud of me."

Miss Pauline set her fork carefully on the edge of her plate and took a deep breath. "Americans need to take the communist threat much more seriously," she said. "Nikita Khrushchev is winning the space race, and that means he's winning the arms race too." She shuddered and hugged herself like she was worrying about Russian bombs finding us in Hickory, North Carolina.

I guess we all worried about bombs. Seemed like you couldn't go to the movies or even watch television without hearing that if the big flash ever came, we should duck and cover.

Bunkie piped up then. "I can beat Uncle Arnie in an arms race," he said. He put his elbow on the table and puffed out his puny little muscle—ready to arm wrestle.

That cracked us right up. Even Miss Pauline giggled.

"What's so funny?" asked Bunkie.

Arnie ruffled Bunkie's hair. "Not that kind of arms race. Sometimes, 'arms' mean *weapons*. This race is about who has the biggest bombs and who can make the best rockets to shoot them at each other."

"Can we *not* talk about this in the presence of children?" said Ann Fay. Then she rolled her eyes toward Daddy so we'd know she was protecting him too. Talk of bombs agitated him. Sometimes they brought on nightmares from when he served in World War II.

Bessie hustled over to the kitchen counter for her lemon meringue pie. "I hope you saved room for dessert." She handed the pie to Momma to serve while she and Ann Fay removed the meat platter and vegetable bowls.

After everybody left, I pondered whether to go to the river—in case Thomas Freeman would be there again. I wanted to see him but I couldn't explain why. Maybe it was on account of those birdcalls and him collecting so many birds in his record book.

I had a few collections myself—an insect collection from back when I was younger, some baseball cards, and a whole bunch of wooden toys Daddy had made for me. But my favorite collection was comic books. Thinking about that gave me an idea. Thomas might like to see my Jackie Robinson one. I tucked it in a paper bag and headed for the river. I didn't even take my fishing pole.

Sure enough, he was there. His fishing pole was on the bank, though, and he was peering through those binoculars.

I gave out a crow's caw, just checking to see if I could fool him. He lowered his binoculars, turned, and frowned. I cawed a few more times, and he sat there shaking his head. Finally, when I was a few feet away, he said, "That was pitiful." He laughed, but I didn't let it bother me.

"Yeah, maybe I need some practice. You not fishing?"

"Fish aren't biting." He eyed my paper bag.

"I brought you something to look at." I pulled out the Jackie Robinson comic book and held it out for him to see. For some reason I expected him to be impressed—maybe give out a little whistle or ask how in the world I got my hands on that.

Instead he said, "I got that same one."

"Oh."

"Wasn't expecting *you* to be owning a comic book about a Negro baseball player," he said.

"Are you kidding me? Jackie Robinson was the best!"

"There've been plenty of great white players," said

Thomas. "Joe DiMaggio, for instance. Or Yogi Berra. Babe Ruth."

"Yeah," I said. "I got a Babe Ruth book. But this one's special on account of Mr. Bedford sent it to me." Of course Thomas wouldn't know who Mr. Bedford was, so I explained. "He lives in Connecticut and we went to see him when I was little. That's when he gave me my first Jackie Robinson baseball card. He still sends me things every now and again. Like this comic book."

"Connecticut?" said Thomas. "That's a far piece."

"Yeah. But my daddy wanted to meet the Bedfords because their son was his war buddy."

"Was?" asked Thomas. "Then I reckon he didn't make it out alive."

I shook my head. "But thanks to him, my daddy did. He was sick one night, so Jackie took his patrol. He got killed. Jackie Bedford was a war hero. And Daddy named me after him."

Thomas gave out a long, low whistle.

"What?"

"I reckon you got yourself something to live up to."

"Uh, yeah. I guess so." I hadn't thought about it like that. I just knew I owed my daddy's life to that man. Mine too.

Thomas reached for that comic book then, and I gave it over to him. He leafed through it, pointing out facts about Robinson's batting average and stolen bases. "Look at that," he said. "There was a death threat if Jackie played in Cincinnati. White boys might admire him now, but it wasn't that way when he started playing with them."

"Wish he was still playing," I said.

"Doing important work now," said Thomas. "Fighting for civil rights."

"I guess so," I said. "You know who else is fighting for civil rights?"

"Yeah," said Thomas. "Dr. Martin Luther King. You watch. He's gonna leave his mark on this world."

"My sister Ellie sure thinks a lot of him. She's working for civil rights too."

"Really?" asked Thomas. He sounded like he wasn't taking my word for it. "And how's she doing that?"

"Well, for one thing, she goes to Wake Forest College, and she's trying to get that school integrated."

I thought maybe Thomas would be proud of my sister, but evidently he wasn't impressed, on account of he snorted a little—kind of like when he heard that my cow would be competing with the Lutzes' cows. If you asked me, Thomas could be a downright snob.

"What're you snorting about now?" I asked.

"Nah, I'm not snorting."

Yes, he was so snorting, and now he was denying it, just like he did the last time. "Well, I know a snort when I hear one," I said. "And it's gotta mean something."

"I'm just thinking, how's your sister going to integrate a college?"

"Well, not by herself, that's for sure. But she's on a committee that's working on it—negotiating with the college or something. And besides that, she works for a civil rights lawyer. And he knows what he's doing."

Thomas grunted. "Well, good," he said. "I reckon a couple of white people in Winston-Salem gonna fix everything right up."

This time I was the one who snorted. "Who said that? And besides, how do you know those people are white? My sister's got Negro friends."

"Oh, I see," said Thomas. "So I guess you figured you'd get yourself one too. Is that why you been coming down here? Or maybe you're trying to relieve a guilty conscience. Making up for things you might have done in the past." He shrugged. "Course, I don't know," he said. "I'm just guessing."

I sure wasn't expecting him to say that! But still, I wasn't stupid. Slow, maybe. But when someone gave me a hint that was wide as the river, I could take it. So I reached for my Jackie Robinson comic book and put it back into my bag.

"Making stuff up is what you're doing," I said. "I don't have anything to feel guilty about. And what would you know about my past?"

Thomas shrugged.

27

"Look," I told him. "I didn't mean to get in your way. I'll leave you with the birds. And the fish—if they decide to start biting."

I left him sitting there on the riverbank, and I didn't even look back. As far as I was concerned, the birds could have Thomas Freeman. At least *they* seemed to understand him.

4

SEPTEMBER 1959

I'd spent most of my school years steering clear of Tony and Dennis. Tony was big for his age, so I never wanted to tangle with him. By himself, he seemed decent enough, but for some reason he'd do whatever Dennis wanted him to. This year Dennis evidently wanted the two of them to sit at the same lunch table as me and Wayne.

On Monday of the second week of school, Mrs. Cunningham showed up there too. Every day she sat with different students. She was the first teacher I ever had who did that. "How come you sit with us?" I asked. "You could be eating in peace right now. Or talking to another teacher."

"Yes," said Mrs. Cunningham. "But then I wouldn't get to know *you*, would I? So tell me, what do you boys like to talk about at this table?"

"Pigs," said Tony. "Oink, oink."

"Cows," said Dennis. "Jackie's in loooooove with his cow. She's going to win a blue ribbon at the fair. Be a big star!"

I had the pepper in my hand, and for about two seconds I thought I might give it a good shake over the vanilla pudding on Dennis's plate. But with Mrs. Cunningham sitting right there, it didn't seem like a smart move. So instead I pretended not to hear him.

She ignored him too. "Jackie," she said, "you and my husband would get along just fine. We live on a dairy farm, and sometimes I am positively jealous of his precious cows. He's a quiet man and doesn't have so much to say. Then I catch him out in the barn, carrying on conversations with those cows! And he knows them all by name. Does your cow have a name?"

"Lucy," said Dennis. "After Lucille Ball." And just like that he started whistling the theme song from the *I Love Lucy* show.

"Good grief!" I said. "She wasn't asking you, Dennis."

I guess Mrs. Cunningham figured that Dennis was bound and determined to take over the conversation, but before she let him she said to me, "I have an idea. You like comic books, so why don't you make one about Lucy? Use at least half of this week's spelling words in the story and you'll earn some extra credit. I'd love to hear about Lucy from *your* point of view." She gave me a little wink, and then she turned to Dennis. "So tell me, what do *you* do when you're not at school? For fun, I mean."

What I learned about Dennis was that he lived down the road from Tony, but then I quit listening to him and started dreaming about making a comic book with Lucy as the main character. That night I pulled out my spelling words and got started. I drew Lucy with red hooves and ribbons in her hair and red-and-white-polka-dotted underwear. Silly stuff like that. I made her a talking cow who called Mr. Cunningham on the telephone, and together they dreamed up goofy sentences using this week's spelling words.

The next morning I handed it to Mrs. Cunningham. She read the whole thing and giggled all the way through. Then she hugged it to herself and said, "Oh, Jackie, I *love* this. May I please show it to Mr. Cunningham?"

"You can *keep* it," I said. "I'll make another one for me."

"Oh, *may* I? That's wonderful," she said. Then she whispered, "Next time, don't give Mr. Cunningham so much hair."

On Thursday, Mr. Nolley came for our first 4-H Club meeting. The fair was coming up, and we had to fill out registration forms and go over last-minute instructions. Mr. Nolley reminded us that not everyone would come home with ribbons, but we should congratulate the ones who did.

"We'll both win," I told Wayne. "Your stinky little pig and my sweet heifer will be the stars of the show."

On fair day I ran all the way home from the school bus. Arnie was at the house already, waiting to load Lucy into his trailer. He'd brought Ida with him so she could ride to the fairgrounds later with Momma and Daddy. She carried in two drawings of barn cats and one oil painting. The painting was of a Jersey cow sticking her head through a barbed-wire fence and nibbling on the grass. "How do you like it?" she asked. "It's called 'Greener Over There.'"

The cow was so realistic I wanted to reach out and give her a scratch behind the ears. "You'll win a prize with that one," I told Ida.

At the fairgrounds we had to wait behind four other trailers of livestock. "Got your registration handy?" asked Arnie.

"Right here." I fished it out of my pocket, unfolded it, and smoothed the edges. Arnie handed our papers to the man in overalls waiting at the truck window. The man signed his name to the paper, wrote something on his clipboard, and pointed toward the barns.

The Lutzes were there already. I couldn't miss their big banners with professional lettering. W. R. Lutz & Sons, Charles Lutz, Philip Lutz. The Sigmons had a fancy banner too. Personally, I liked Arnie's and my wooden signs. Ida had painted Arnie's and I'd made mine with my wood-burning pen. But those other banners—you could tell they'd had them printed up special.

The barn was a long, open-air building with low walls dividing it into sections. After I settled Lucy in her stall I took a little walk around. A Lutz boy about my age was setting up a fan. A good idea, because sweat was pouring down my neck. I tried to catch some of the air moving around, but I knew the fans were actually for keeping the animals comfortable.

Arnie saw me watching. "That's Rusty Lutz. You know his family will be hard to beat." He pointed to the other end of the barn. "And the Sigmons are tough competitors too. But just do like I trained you and have fun while you're at it."

I was lucky to have Arnie, a real farmer—one who had won prizes even—teaching me what to do. "Yes, sir," I said. I went over it all in my mind. *Keep a firm grip on the halter. Lead her to where the judge wants us to line them up. Stay calm. Ignore everybody except Lucy and the judge.*

I told myself not to worry about the Lutzes and the Sigmons. But the Lutzes were hard to ignore. They were everywhere, taking up most of the barn spaces with their heifers, bulls, and milk cows. They seemed to know exactly how everything worked. In fact, they could probably run that place if they wanted to.

"Hey. Wanna look around? Come say hello to Elmira."

I turned and there was Wayne. "Hey, Wayne. Uh, sure. But I don't know if I should leave Lucy."

"Go on," said Arnie. "Have a little fun. I'll look after her."

I gave Lucy a last handful of oats and went with Wayne to the swine barn. "Look at Elmira," he said.

"Tell me if she isn't prettier than a bouquet of flowers."

How Wayne could admire that bristly haired pig was beyond me. He reached over the stall and took Elmira's face in his hands. He stared into her eyes and scratched her cheeks. "Don't you wish you were showing a pig?" he asked.

"I've got news for you," I said. "Pigs stink. Compared to them, cow poop smells like wisteria flowers."

"Pfft!" He grinned. "You're just jealous. Come on. Let's go check out the exhibits while we wait for the rides to open."

People were still setting up exhibits. Blanche Shuford and some other women from the Home Demonstration Club were there, making a display on preserving garden vegetables. A construction company was just about finished building a model bomb shelter. People stood around and watched. Two men argued about whether the shelter would actually survive an attack. Someone else said, "What's the point if you come out alive and all your neighbors are dead?"

A guy from the construction company looked up from his work. "That's why every household should have one."

Just listening to them was giving me goose bumps— and not the good kind like you get from riding a roller coaster. I grabbed Wayne's arm and pulled him away from there. "These people are trying to scare us to death,"

I said. "I thought we were here to have fun. Let's see if the rides are open."

Before we got to the ticket booth we ran into Nancy Hatley. She was in a different 4-H club, but I remembered her because she raised bees. Nancy had a handful of tickets and was giving them out to her friends.

"Wow! Somebody's rich!" I said.

Nancy laughed. "Not me. Aren't you in 4-H? Want some tickets?" And just like that, she ripped off two strips of tickets and gave one to each of us.

"Gee, thanks! What'd you do?" I asked. "Rob the ticket booth?"

"Ha-ha!" said Nancy. "No. My mom works for a doctor, and he gets them for her. Wanna ride the Tilt-A-Whirl with us? Let's go."

We followed her, and next thing I knew we were whooping and hollering with the 4-H hotshots—Nancy Hatley, Carolyn Lutz, and Barry Sigmon. They were all older than us, but they treated us real decent. It made me feel like I *was* somebody in this world. Even if I wasn't a Lutz or a Sigmon.

5

SEPTEMBER 1959

Sweat poured down the inside of my shirt. The latest group of winners was coming out of the ring. Most of them were Lutzes.

The sight of Rusty Lutz, who was about my age, leading a bull made me feel downright stupid. Why was I showing a heifer? They were for babies. Beginners. But that was exactly what Arnie had emphasized. "Start with a calf," he'd said. "She'll learn to trust you from the beginning."

There were about nine heifers, and Lucy was the best looking of the bunch. For the last two days I'd been whispering in her ear how great she was. I hoped she believed it.

But what if we couldn't beat the Lutzes?

We just *had* to, because Wayne and Elmira had taken the blue ribbon in the swine contest. I couldn't let Wayne outdo me.

It was time to go. "Hold your head high, Lucy," I

said. "They might be Lutzes and Sigmons, but you're a Honeycutt. That's nothing to be ashamed of."

Still, for some reason I felt small. That little Lutz girl ahead of me was only a kid—probably not even ten years old—but you'd never know it from the way she held herself. *I* could see she had a leg up in this world. Her green 4-H uniform was clean and starched. She stood so still and calm that just watching her made *me* feel shaky.

I straightened my new green necktie and forced myself to be still—like she was. I watched how she held her heifer, and I moved my hand on Lucy's halter just enough to do it the way she did. That's when I realized that my hand ached. *Relax, Jackie. Stay calm. She's just a kid. You can beat her easy. And all the others, too.*

The line moved forward. I gave a tiny tug to Lucy's halter. "Here we go, Lucy. It's your time to shine."

I followed the group into the ring. We paraded around the sawdust floor, past our families in the bleachers. I could feel Daddy's eyes following us. I straightened my shoulders and tried my best not to look at him, and to remember his encouragement in my ear—about how ready I was. He expected me to bring home a blue ribbon.

But suddenly I wasn't so sure.

The first competitor set his heifer, and the rest of us began lining up beside him and his cow like cars in a parking lot. I turned and walked backwards, facing

Lucy, keeping a tight grip on her halter. She balked a little. "Lucy, girl, come. It's okay." I tried to say it without moving my lips, since I knew Arnie didn't want me talking to her during competition. We needed to have a quiet understanding, Lucy and I.

She tossed her head a little, and I moved my hand up closer on her halter. But this pulled her head up even more. I looked at the judge. Uh-oh! He was watching. I took one step back so I'd be lined up with the little Lutz girl. I could see all the way down the lineup, and every other competitor, except one, appeared to be a Lutz. And I think that person was a Sigmon, which, as far as I could tell, was just as bad. All I could think about was how good the other contestants looked. So quiet and sure of themselves. So in charge of their heifers.

I heard the judge asking questions as he came down the line. I didn't hear much, just the murmur of his voice and the low replies of the contestants. I glanced up at the stands. Mr. Nolley was there with all the spectators. He smiled and pointed toward the judge—reminding me where to keep my eye.

The judge was getting closer. I tried to keep my focus on him. But it was hard not to glance at my family in the bleachers. Daddy nodded and grinned, but Arnie squinted hard and frowned a little.

Yes, Arnie. I know. Watch the judge.

Then, just before I turned away, I caught sight of

somebody else. Dennis Aiken. And Tony. What were they doing here? But I knew. The show was open to the public.

Ugh! I should've never mentioned my cow and this show in Dennis's presence.

Now that I knew Dennis and Tony were watching, it was harder than ever to focus on the judge. I looked at the Lutz girl beside me. She held herself real proper and steady. And she answered the judge's questions without batting an eyelash.

Watching her and waiting on him and thinking about Tony and Dennis was really making me sweat. Finally the judge was there, talking to *me*. "Tell me about your heifer. When was she born? Who was her sire?"

Dennis hollered out then. "Go, Lucille Ball! After all, you're a big star!"

I could feel my face turning red and my mind going to mush. I answered the judge's questions and he nodded, but his face didn't show whether he thought I was doing okay. "What are her weaknesses?" he asked.

"Weaknesses," I said. Suddenly I couldn't remember what I'd planned to say about weaknesses. So I said the first thing I thought of. "Um, well, actually she's might near perfect. Look how filled out she is."

I knew I was only supposed to answer his question. I was saying the wrong things. But I needed the judge to understand how good Lucy was. "And she listens to me,"

I said. "Did you see how she followed me in here?"

The judge nodded and grinned a little. He moved on to the next cow.

After he talked to all the contestants, he walked past each of us, eyeing every animal carefully. I kept a firm grip on Lucy's halter, and she held her head still and watched me. I looked from her to the judge. He headed toward me and pointed to the entrance gate. "Take your heifer over *there*."

"Yes, sir."

He was singling me out. And I had a feeling that wasn't good. I led Lucy away. One by one more contestants joined me. Soon there were more standing with me than were left in the lineup. Then I knew for sure that Lucy and I were in the losers' group. But why were *we* the first ones the judge threw out? Okay, so maybe I talked too much. But Lucy was perfect.

He began announcing the winners, starting from fourth place and moving up to first. That little Lutz girl was in the winners' group, and next thing I knew they were announcing her name. Beth Lutz had actually won the blue ribbon! How had I just lost to a kid who probably wasn't even ten years old?

According to Mr. Nolley I'd have to go over later and shake her hand. But what I really wanted was to wipe that happy grin right off her face.

6

SEPTEMBER 1959

I didn't notice when Arnie left the bleachers, but as Lucy and I led the other losers out of the ring, I heard his voice. "It was a valiant effort," he said. "And Lucy's a fine heifer. They're both getting good practice."

And another voice. "But the poor kid will never stand a chance against the best in the state."

The poor kid? He was talking about me. I glanced over and saw Arnie nodding—like he was agreeing with that guy. So he never expected me to win? He lied to me—telling me that Lucy was so well-bred because she had two prizewinning parents. That she could be a winner.

What had Lucy's parents won? Consolation prizes, probably. Because if Arnie had competed against the Lutzes, he'd surely lost too. Thomas Freeman was right about how great the Lutzes were. I should've listened to Wayne and raised a pig.

Except I couldn't have beat Wayne and Elmira. Besides, I didn't like pigs. I liked cows. Especially Lucy.

She could feel how upset I was. We were halfway back to her stall and she kept nuzzling up against me. I didn't stop to snuggle, though. "Come on, Lucy, let's get out of here," I told her. I couldn't wait to settle her in the stall so I could escape this barn and all the people who'd watched me fail. Suddenly the stupid things I'd said to that judge were loud in my ears. Probably everyone in the stands had heard me. Including Dennis and Tony. I'd never hear the end of it.

Back at the stall, I reached for some oats. While Lucy licked them from my hands, I whispered how good she looked and that she behaved just right and that it was too bad nobody noticed. "The judges have stars in their eyes," I told her. "Startown Stars. Mountain View Rangers are just not good enough and we never will be."

But I knew that wasn't exactly true, because Wayne was in the same 4-H club I was and he managed to be a Ranger and a winner at the same time.

I heard Daddy's voice then. Next thing I knew, he was in the stall, pulling me up against him and saying how sorry he was. "Lucy did just great," he said. "And you did too. Nothing to be ashamed of."

But I *was* ashamed. Ashamed of being the worst in the bunch because I talked too much, and ashamed of crying right this minute on my daddy's shoulder.

I heard Mr. Nolley's voice coming through the barn, congratulating the winners and encouraging each competitor. I didn't think I could face him just then. And I sure didn't want to be there when Dennis and Tony came snickering by.

"Will you comfort Lucy?" I asked Daddy. "I need to get out of here."

I took off through the dairy barn and out into the blinding sunshine. From behind me I could hear the judge announcing the next class of cows going into the ring, but I shook his voice out of my head and focused on the Ferris wheel, sitting there waiting for nighttime so it could light up and start spinning.

Just a few hours ago I was fingering the money in my pocket, imagining a night of celebration. But now I didn't care. What were a few measly dollars good for anyway? Especially when you knew that Nancy Hatley had a handful of tickets and could ride forever if she wanted to. Her and her uppity friends.

Someone shoved a stick of green cotton candy in front of my face. "Ten cents," he said. I didn't even look at the man who was trying to sell me his stupid candy. But then I heard a voice saying, "I'll take it."

Arnie.

I walked faster and slipped around the corner of a hot dog booth, but Arnie grabbed my elbow. "Here," he said, trying to hand me the cotton candy—as if a pile of sugary fluff could make me feel better.

"I don't want that." I swatted at the candy and knocked it to the ground. But Arnie didn't give up. He fol-lowed me past the exhibit hall with people wandering in and out and sometimes stopping to talk. Two men in overalls were laughing at something—probably me. Everyone seemed to be having a perfectly good time. How could they?

"I'm sorry," said Arnie. "Losing hurts. I know all about it."

"Oh, yeah?" I shouted. I kept walking, not even glancing at Arnie. "That's not what you told me. You said both Lucy's parents won prizes." He grabbed my elbow and I jerked it away. I turned and looked into his face. I could see his concern there, but I ignored it. "What'd they win anyway? Last place? Because that's what Lucy won. You knew all along I didn't have a chance. Didn't you?"

"There's always a *chance* of winning," said Arnie. "Something can go wrong with other contestants, or your cow could honestly be the best in class. Or third best, even. But not getting a ribbon is no shame. Ask me how many times I competed and didn't win a thing."

"I don't *care* how many times you lost. You told me Lucy was a winner, and I believed you. Now I look like a stupid fool."

"If you look like a fool," said Arnie, "it's because you're standing out here having a pity party when you should be in there congratulating the winners. That's what you're supposed to do, Jackie. You smile and shake hands and you pick yourself up and try again. Lucy *will* be a winner. Maybe next year or maybe not. Maybe in

44

three years. You just keep working at it. You've got to pay your dues."

I tried not to hear what he was saying. Instead, I stared into a fenced area nearby with ducks racing inside a wire maze. Yesterday it would have been funny. But right now the whole entire fair seemed dumb—wagonloads of ridiculous amusements. Who cared which duck found its way through a maze first? Or whether anyone could catch the greased pig or even which cow won a blue ribbon?

Not me, that was for sure.

But just then, I saw that little Lutz girl walking toward me with two friends. The first-place ribbon was pinned to her 4-H uniform. I glanced away because I didn't want her to catch my eye or recognize me. But she did. "Good showing," she said. She smiled real sweet like the perfect lady she probably was. She could win a prize for her manners, too.

Maybe she thought I would thank her or reach out and shake her hand and tell her how good she was. I knew what a loser was supposed to say to the winner, but I couldn't make myself say it. I turned away. What did she need from me? She had everything she wanted already.

7

SEPTEMBER 1959

Ida's cow painting won Best of Show. "I knew it would," I said. I tried to be happy for her, but mostly I felt sorry for me.

My family told me there'd be other years and I had a great start and someday I'd bring home a blue ribbon. But of course they couldn't know that! Every one of them was getting on my nerves. So instead of pushing Gerianne on the tire swing or playing hide-and-seek with her and Bunkie, I took off through the fields and hiked up Bakers Mountain.

Later, after they went home, I didn't even consider going to the river. The last thing I was in the mood for was Thomas Freeman. Hearing him say "I told you so" about the Lutzes winning all the ribbons would be more than I could take. Besides, he'd made it clear as glass that he didn't actually want me around.

I pulled out my sketchbook and took it to the back porch and sat there mindlessly drawing whatever was in front of me. The sandbox I never played in except when

I was entertaining Bunkie. Momma's clothesline. The woodshed. And the outhouse, which really ought to be torn down. We never used it anymore.

The mimosa tree.

There was a grave under that tree, although you'd never know it unless someone told you. My brother, Bobby, had died of polio before I was even born. Daddy was off at the war when it happened, and Ann Fay said they were poor as dirt. Burying him in the backyard was the best her and Momma could do.

After Daddy came home, he'd offered to make a marker, but Momma wouldn't have it. She didn't want to be reminded of her baby's death every time she went to the clothesline.

From what I could tell, the main reason Momma and Daddy had *me* was to take Bobby's place. But I could never replace him. I knew *that* from the way Momma's voice wobbled and her eyes teared up whenever she talked about him. There was no way I could live up to the memory of Bobby Honeycutt. He'd be a cute little four-year-old forever.

While I sat there drawing with quick, dark lines, I caught the sound of blue jays squawking to beat the band, way out on the other side of the pasture. Normally I wouldn't pay such a thing any mind. But since meeting Thomas, I'd started noticing birdcalls.

Then it hit me. Thomas. Blue jays. Wait!

I left my sketchbook on the porch floor and walked

out to the fence. Sure enough—there he was on the far side of the pasture, right at the edge of the woods. What was *he* doing on our property? I didn't want to talk to him. He'd ask about the fair, and I'd have to admit what a loser I was. And how he was right all along.

No. I would *not* admit that—wouldn't give him the satisfaction. But for some reason he was waiting out there, so I opened the gate and started across the field. Lucy saw me and headed my way, like she did any time I stepped into the pasture. When I reached her I wrapped my arms around her neck and gave her chest a good scratch. "Hey, Lucy girl. Looks like you and me got company. We could ignore him except he's squawking like a blue jay and that's gonna get on our nerves."

Lucy walked with me to the barbed-wire fence along the tree line. Thomas was just on the other side. "Hey," I said. "I wasn't exactly expecting you."

He shrugged. "I thought to myself, 'Jackie invited me to visit his farm. Maybe I'll find out if he meant it.'"

"So," I said. "There it is. Our *magnificent* farm." I swept my hand back toward our property. "House, sheds, lean-to. Not exactly Garland Abernethy's place. Doesn't even have a silo." I made sure not to mention the Lutzes. "Did you see my cow? This is Lucy."

Lucy had stuck her head between the strands of barbed wire, trying to be sociable.

But Thomas stepped back a little and looked her over.

"Like you said, she's a beauty. I just came to say I hate she didn't take a ribbon."

"What? How do *you* know?"

"Like I told you before, I keep my ears open. My eyes, too."

"I reckon your pal who works for the Lutzes told you?"

"Newspaper."

"Oh." Of course. It was there for the whole county to read. The names of the winners at least. And mine wasn't on the list.

"Like I said. I hate it for you."

Was he kidding? I thought he didn't want anything to do with me. I looked into his eyes then, and he looked back at me real steady—like he actually meant what he was saying.

"Thanks," I said. I looked away, staring toward Lucy's lean-to. "You were right. I didn't have a chance against the Lutzes. Those people got a leg up in this world. And there's so many of them. How is that fair?"

Thomas shrugged. "It's not. You going fishing?"

"I'm not in the mood. And besides, I'm not looking for a Negro friend. That was your imagination."

Thomas nodded. "I'm sorry about what I said. I'm just not used to white boys coming around looking for me—unless they're up to no good."

"I'm not interested in starting trouble," I said.

"Maybe I'll see you around somewhere. Come on, Lucy."
I turned to go.

"Well, I reckon you can sit home and feel sorry for
yourself. If that's what you want."

Oh, now he was getting all preachy on me. But he
was right. I *was* having a pity party about the fair. And
maybe even about how he treated me the last time I went
to the river. It still burned me that he said I had a guilty
conscience. I wasn't about to admit it, though. So I told
him to wait while I went back to the house for my gear.
While I was there, I hollered in the backdoor that I was
going fishing and not to hold up supper on my account.

"I'll have to dig for worms after I get there," I told
Thomas.

"Don't you worry. I got worms."

We walked most of the way without saying much.
Normally I'd have plenty to say, but today my mind was
in a tizzy. One minute I was kicking myself for messing
up at the fair, and the next I was wondering why Thomas
actually showed up at my house. Was he really sorry for
what he'd said to me? And why *was* I going to the river
with him?

But there was something about him I couldn't shake
off. Maybe it was because I'd never been around Negroes
all that much—even with that colored church less than
a half mile from my house. I'd heard plenty of opinions
about them, good and bad. But I wouldn't mind finding

out for myself what they were like. What Thomas was really like.

Maybe he was right about me looking for a Negro friend. Maybe I just didn't know it.

Ellie would approve. Ann Fay too, on account of her having a colored friend back when she was in the polio hospital. My brother wasn't the only one who got polio.

Momma and Daddy knew I'd bumped into Thomas at the river. But I hadn't actually mentioned seeing him a second time. They always told me God loved everybody the same, but I knew they worried about integration. According to Momma, Blanche Shuford, the president of her Home Demonstration Club, had been keeping the women riled up about that for the last two years. And for some reason Momma cared about Blanche's opinion of her.

When we got to the fishing hole, I saw that Thomas had tucked his gear out of sight, under some thick rhododendron bushes, along with a bucket holding two fish he'd already caught. He pulled it all out and set his can of worms on the ground in front of me. "You get first pick," he said.

"Oh man, you got some doozies in here." I took out a huge wiggly earthworm and put it on my hook. "No wonder you catch fish."

"They come from Momma's flowerbed." Thomas baited his hook, and we both threw our lines in the water.

But we had barely settled down and caught our breath when we heard a voice coming through the woods on the other side of the river.

"Wonder who that is," I said.

Turned out it was a man—a stranger—with a liquor bottle in his hand, and he was talking to himself. When he saw us, he stopped dead in his tracks. Then he came to the edge of the bank, which was high above the river—higher than on our side. His eyes shifted from Thomas to me and back and forth a few times until they landed on me and stayed there. "What's *your* name?"

Jackie—it was on my tongue and ready to ride right out of my mouth, but Thomas whispered, "Don't tell him."

"Whatchu say, *boy*?" He said *boy* like he wanted to make good and sure Thomas wouldn't like it. I saw Thomas flinch just the teeniest little bit. "What do you think you're doing?" the drunk asked. "Sharing the river-bank with a white boy?"

Thomas didn't answer. He just tilted his bucket to show him the fish he'd caught.

"And you," said the drunk. Now he was looking at me again. He leaned in so far I thought he might fall into the river. "I reckon you know race mixing is communism. And communism is godless."

I stared at that sorry old man in his overalls with no shirt underneath it. At his muddy boots and his face that hadn't seen a shave for at least a week. And at that whiskey bottle. Who was *he* to talk about godlessness?

"Don't just sit there," he bellowed. "Whatcha got to say for yourself?"

If that old man wanted somebody to speak up, I could do it.

"*We're* just minding *our* own business," I said, meaning that he should do the same. I reckon he took my meaning because he scowled like an old bulldog. He tried to take another swig of his liquor, but it was empty, so he raised that bottle in the air and aimed it toward the ground like he was going to smash it on the rocks. But then, just that quick, he turned and threw it hard as he could. Right at Thomas.

8

SEPTEMBER 1959

The man's aim was low, so when Thomas ducked, he was right in the line of fire. I saw it hit just above his ear, and I heard the awful *thunk*. Thomas hollered and grabbed at his head. Even with his hand over it, I could see how—just that quick—a knot had popped up.

"Thomas, you're hurt." I jumped up and reached for him, but he shrugged me away.

So I ran along the bank. "Who do you think you are?" I hollered at that ugly coward of a man. But he had taken off downriver, fighting his way through the bushes. "I'm gonna report this!" I yelled after him.

I figured since he was drunk and the river was shallow I could catch him. But Thomas might need help. I'd always heard if you got hit on the temple, it could kill you. That hit was too close for comfort. I turned and ran back to him, but he was picking up his gear, fixing to leave.

"Thomas, are you okay?"

"Yeah, I'm fine. Just dandy." I could hear the anger through his clenched teeth.

"You didn't deserve that."

"No. But what's *that* got to do with it? I'm shoving off. You can have the fish."

"Wait! Let me see that knot you got there." I reached for him, but he jabbed his elbow at my face. "What?" I said. "Let me help you."

"You've done enough already." He stalked away, head high. Showing me he could handle a little pain. And he was mad at *me*. But what did I do?

"I'm gonna find out who did that!" I hollered. "My daddy or Junior Bledsoe will know who he was. We'll go after him."

Thomas stopped. He stood there in the trail with his back straight and stiff, and then he turned and stalked back toward me. He stopped about ten feet away, and that knot on the side of his head looked bad. I saw the twitching in his cheek and the set of his jaw and how he flexed his hand around that fishing pole like he could break it with one hand. "Leave your precious daddy out of this," he said. "I don't need *him* meddling in my business. Or your sister's husband either. Don't you dare breathe a word."

"But Thomas, we should report him to the sheriff."

Thomas stepped closer. Maybe he was fixing to hit me.

"Okay, okay! I won't say a word. I promise."

"Good." And just like that he turned and stalked off.

I watched until he disappeared behind a stand of holly trees. "Well, okay," I muttered. "I know you're mad. I would be too. But what did *I* ever do to you?"

I stomped back to the riverbank and stared at those fish he'd caught—two of them swimming circles around each other. Going nowhere. Trapped. Confused. There was no way I could enjoy eating them. "It's your lucky day," I said. And I carried the bucket down the bank and dumped them into the river.

I tucked Thomas's bucket under the rhododendron bushes and then headed for home—practically running because I had so much energy building inside. Anger at Thomas for not letting me help him. At that old man with all his hate. At me for talking back to him. I should've listened to Thomas. But how could I have known the man would do such a thing? How could either of us have known?

I tromped through Garland Abernethy's pasture and crossed the highway into the cornfields leading toward my house. The closer I got to home, the more I sorted it out. Thomas knew to be quiet. And he tried to tell me. But I didn't listen.

I was almost home and fixing to bust if I didn't talk this out with somebody. I couldn't, though. I'd promised. The only thing I knew was to let it all out on Lucy. So when I got to our pasture I told her the whole terrible story. The more I talked, the guiltier I felt.

"Lucy," I said, "I'm the one who sassed that old drunk. If he was going to throw that bottle at one of us it should've been me. But he didn't because I'm white and he don't hate me. He hates Thomas for being a Negro. How is that fair?"

9

SEPTEMBER 1959

All night I dreamed about glass bottles flying through the air. I'd hear the *thunk*s of them hitting someone's head—was it mine or Thomas's? And I'd jolt awake. But somewhere in the middle of it all, one of those bottles changed into something else—a half-eaten apple. I was the one throwing it—at Thomas.

I shook myself awake, and I knew right off that it wasn't just a dream. It happened. I was a bully throwing things out the school bus window. Except I didn't think I was a bully. I *never* yelled out the window at the colored kids or did anything mean to them—until one day in fifth grade. I was eating an apple on the way to school, but halfway through I ran into a worm. So of course I didn't want the rest.

I was thinking about what to do with it when an older kid across the aisle dared me to throw it at one of those colored boys when we went by their house. I told him no—until he reached into his pocket and pulled out a dime. And just that quick, I thought how, if I had that dime, I could buy myself a comic book.

The bus rounded the curve just before their house. The older kid pushed me toward the window. I could see the Negro children waiting for their bus. I threw the apple at one of the boys. The shorter one. He wasn't looking my way, and it hit him square on the back of his head.

Now I knew exactly who I'd hit with that apple. Thomas. Now I remembered sitting down fast, trying to get out of sight. The kids around me hooted and cheered, and the big kid dropped the dime into my hand.

I didn't remember buying a comic book with it. In fact, I didn't remember anything else. All I knew, lying there in my bed and staring into the darkness, was that this was not a dream. It happened. And I did it.

Somehow Thomas knew too. And I was sure that *he'd* never forgotten. But I couldn't figure out how he could know it was me. When he said I was trying to relieve my guilt, he was baiting me. Wasn't he? I rolled over and told myself I wasn't a fish and I wouldn't take the bait. I couldn't. That had happened a long time ago. I'd grown up since then.

I never did get back to sleep—not with my mind racing and me kicking my fifth-grade self. I was glad when morning came, even if it meant going back to school and putting up with Dennis ragging on me about losing at the fair. Maybe that would take my mind off that apple. Sure enough, Dennis followed me into the school building. "Mooooo," he said. "I guess Lucille Ball isn't such a big star after all."

I walked faster, but since we were heading for the same room, I didn't exactly get away from him. Just inside the classroom door he put in one last dig.

"Got beat by a *girl*," he said. "A *little* girl."

I turned and looked at him, and I could just feel my fists clenching. I wanted so bad to hit him. But I'd caught a glimpse of Mrs. Cunningham watching as we came through the door. "Go jump in the lake," I said. As I walked away, the rest of that rhyme sang itself in my head. *Swallow a snake and come back up with a bellyache.*

I settled in at my desk and tried not to see the blue ribbon Wayne was showing off to the people around him. But I did notice Mrs. Cunningham asking Dennis to step out in the hall with her. I had a feeling she knew exactly what he was up to. I figured she was putting a lid on it. When they came back I gave him a smirk just in case he looked my way. But of course he didn't.

If it wasn't for Dennis taunting me, I wouldn't be thinking much about the fair. Mostly my mind was turning over what happened at the river yesterday. About Thomas getting hit on account of me running my mouth. And about me being real stupid. Not just yesterday—but especially in fifth grade.

Mrs. Cunningham read a newspaper article about Nikita Khrushchev, the Russian premier. His visit to the United States was only a week away. The class got real fired up about that. Some students, including Dennis, thought it was downright stupid for President Eisenhower to invite him just like he was our friend. "You can't trust Khrushchev," he said. "Everyone knows he's a communist dictator trying to take over the world."

Pamela raised her hand. "Doesn't Khrushchev say he wants peaceful coexistence? That's better than being in a cold war. It's better than both sides racing to have bigger weapons. Maybe we'll find out he's not so bad," she said. "Maybe the United States and Russia could actually become friends."

Dennis booed and hissed, and a few other people did too. I saw Pamela's shoulders sag a little. Personally, I liked what she had said. Maybe it *was* an impossible dream, but I hoped she was right. If Russia and the United States decided to be friends, we could live without the constant fear of bombs hanging over our heads.

Mrs. Cunningham put her hands out like two stop signs and waited for everyone to get quiet. Then she walked to the blackboard. She picked up a piece of chalk and wrote in her perfect longhand:

Do I not destroy my enemies when I make them my friends? Abraham Lincoln

"I'll leave this quote on the board," said Mrs. Cunningham. "That way, we can all keep pondering it."

Right that minute, it felt like Dennis was my enemy, and I didn't have one ounce of interest in making him my friend. As far as I was concerned, there wasn't much to like about him.

And Thomas. I guessed he thought of *me* as his enemy, although I never saw myself that way.

I watched for him every morning when my bus rolled by his house. As always, his back was turned to all of us on that bus. And he seemed to be trying hard not to let me get a glimpse of that knot on the side of his head.

Then on Thursday he wasn't out there with his brother and sisters. That got me worrying. Maybe something was wrong. I'd heard of people getting hit in the head and not keeling over until a few days later.

At school, Mr. Nolley came for the 4-H Club meeting. We met in the library, as usual, and he asked us to talk about our fair experiences. Wayne had brought his blue ribbon, and other people had ribbons too. When Mr. Nolley called on me I told them all about following Beth Lutz into the ring and how she beat me and everybody else.

"What did you learn from the experience?" asked Mr. Nolley.

"Don't compete against the Lutzes," I said. Truth was, with so much else on my mind, the cow show didn't seem so important anymore. But I wasn't about to tell any of that stuff about me and Thomas to the 4-H group. So I said whatever came to my mind. "Next year I'll raise a pig. So I can take the blue ribbon away from Wayne. I always wanted to raise a stinking pig." I laughed—just to show them I was kidding. They laughed too, even Wayne.

"Yeah, right," he said. He wasn't the least bit worried about me winning—even if I did show a pig which I wouldn't.

I wasn't the only loser, and Mr. Nolley reminded us that not winning wasn't the same as losing. "When we don't do our best or don't exhibit good sportsmanship," he said, "that's when we lose."

Sportsmanship. I knew he was talking about me not congratulating the winners. I hoped he didn't know I'd snubbed that Lutz girl when I bumped into her after the show.

I sat there feeling embarrassed—not just for talking too much during the show but also for the things I didn't say afterward. Or wouldn't say. Like, *Congratulations*. Or *You did a good job*.

I stared at the rack of newspapers over against the windows. The *Hickory Daily Record* hung there in different sections, and I could see the cartoon page.

Those cartoons gave me an idea. I took a blank page from my project book and drew three frames. The first one showed Lucy entering the fairgrounds with stars in her eyes. In the second frame I had her looking sideways at the fancy Lutz cow next to her in the ring. I drew a little bubble over Lucy's head showing her thoughts: *I wonder if I wore the wrong lipstick* . . . In the third frame the Lutz cow wore a blue ribbon, and Lucy swiped at her lips with her hoof. The thought bubble above her said, *Yeah, I wore the wrong lipstick.*

For some reason, drawing that silly cartoon made me feel a little better. Still, it was missing something—and I knew what that was. Sportsmanship. If I had it to do over again, I wouldn't show a pig like I'd told the group. I'd shake that girl's hand. And congratulate the other winners. That's what 4-H taught us.

I knew Mr. Nolley would be going to Startown School tomorrow. Maybe he could take a message. I tore a page out of a composition book and drew the cartoon all over again. But this time I added a fourth frame. In this one, Lucy was shaking hooves with the Lutz cow. In the speech bubble coming from Lucy's mouth I wrote, CONGRAT-MOO-LATIONS!

When I showed it to Mr. Nolley, he laughed right out loud.

"Can you give it to Beth Lutz when you go to Startown?" I asked.

Mr. Nolley looked me steady in the eye, and I think I saw pride in his face. "I sure will, Jackie."

By the time I got on the bus that afternoon I was feeling better about myself. I was still worried about

Thomas, though. And then, just before my bus turned onto his road, it hit me that I could go check on him.

So when the bus stopped at the house on the corner of Thomas's road. I stood up too. "I'm going to a friend's house today," I told the driver.

10

SEPTEMBER 1959

It was less than a quarter of a mile to Thomas's house, but I was nervous the whole way. The minute I turned into his lane, two dogs started barking. They ran toward me, yapping their fool heads off. The closer they came, the slower I walked. I almost turned around, but then Thomas's mother came out on the porch.

I reckon she decided I was harmless—she hollered for the dogs to leave me alone. First one of them backed off and then the other, but they kept on barking. Thomas's momma came off that porch and made those dogs sit and be quiet, and then she met me in the lane.

"Howdy," I said. "My name's Jackie Honeycutt. I'm sorry to barge in on you, but I'm kind of worried about Thomas."

She tilted her head just enough to let me know she didn't understand my meaning.

"Is he okay? I know he took a blow to the head on Sunday at the river. This morning he didn't get on the bus, so I've been worried."

"Oh," she said, "you can quit worrying. That bump on his head is going down." She laughed. "Thomas wouldn't get out of bed this morning. I had to call him three times till I decided the best way for him to learn a lesson was to go ahead and miss that bus. He could just walk to school." She laughed and shook her head. "He won't be lazing in bed tomorrow morning, I guarantee you. No, he's just fine. Nice of you to worry, though."

"Well, I couldn't help it, after hearing that bottle smack him in the head."

Her little girl was on the porch now, calling for her momma, and Mrs. Freeman started toward the house. But all of a sudden she pulled herself back around to face me. "Bottle?"

"Uh . . . I figured he told you someone threw a bottle at him. Some old drunk who—"

Mrs. Freeman's hand flew over her mouth. "Law!" she said.

I stopped, because the minute the word "drunk" was out of my mouth, I knew I'd messed up. For some reason Thomas hadn't told his family the truth about that knot on his head. But why? I started backtracking. "Uh, please forget that. I didn't realize you didn't know. It was nothing, really."

That was a lie. It wasn't nothing. It was *something*: a mean old white man hating on Thomas just for being colored. But I didn't want to say that to her. I was trying to make her feel better. Stop her from worrying. I was hoping to fix what my big mouth had just messed up.

Mrs. Freeman reached her hand toward the little girl on the porch. "Come here, baby," she said. She gave me a little wave then. "You go on now. Thomas will be home soon. And this time he'll tell me the truth."

"Yes, ma'am," I said. I didn't know what else to do but hurry up the driveway, scurrying to leave before that school bus brought Thomas home. But I didn't make it. The bus reached the end of their lane at the same time I did. Thomas was the first one off.

"Hey, Thomas." I threw up my hand in a wave and started down the road.

"Jackie Honeycutt," he said. "What you doing here?"

I stopped and turned and we waited while that bus drove past, blowing hot exhaust in our faces. I could feel the stares of all those colored kids, who were most likely wondering the same thing—*What are you doing here?*

"I was worried about you, Thomas. When you didn't get on the bus this morning I thought maybe your head injury was worse. Sometimes that happens. It's my fault you got hit, and I just needed to be sure."

"My head is fine," said Thomas. He shifted his schoolbooks from one arm to the other. "You talk to my momma?"

"She said you're okay. Just late for school was all."

"I *know* you didn't tell her about that bottle."

"Uh . . . Thomas, I'm sorry. I didn't realize she didn't know."

"You *told* her?" Thomas threw his hands in the air and his schoolbooks went flying. His sisters took a step backwards. His older brother moved closer and put his hands on Thomas's shoulders, but Thomas shrugged them off. "Don't worry, Johnny," he said. "I'm not going to hurt him."

It sure looked like Thomas wanted to grab ahold of me, but instead, he stuffed his hands in his pockets. I saw through the fabric how his fists were clenching. His teeth were clenched too. "I told you to keep your mouth shut."

"But Thomas, I thought you didn't want me to tell *my* family. And I didn't. Not a single soul. Not until just now. And, well, I didn't exactly tell your momma everything. I'm sorry. Honest, I am."

Thomas's sisters were scurrying around, picking up his books. The younger one said, "Thomas? You keeping a secret?"

Thomas whirled around then. "Don't you dare say nothing to Daddy about this," he told his sisters. "Momma either. I'll take care of her."

By this time his mother was halfway up the lane. I reckoned she'd seen the whole thing.

"You should go on now," said Johnny. He gave his

head a little jerk to send me on my way. "Don't worry. Thomas'll be all right. We'll take care of this."

I wasn't about to argue. "Okay," I said. "I'm leaving." I hugged my schoolbooks to my chest and headed for home.

11

SEPTEMBER 1959

I walked fast, my brain asking questions the whole way. What kind of story had Thomas made up? And why? If an old drunk had hit me with a bottle, Daddy would be the first person I'd tell. But it sounded like if Thomas had his way, his daddy would never find out.

None of it made sense. But worst of all was knowing that every bit of this was my fault. I was the one who smart-mouthed the drunk in the first place. Now, after giving Thomas my word that I wouldn't tell a soul, I'd let the cat out the bag. And made a big old mess of things.

Maybe I just didn't understand colored people. Maybe their families were different from mine. I had to sort this out with somebody, and as much as I loved Lucy, talking to her wasn't going to solve anything. So I headed straight to Ann Fay's house.

I went around back, and there she was, taking clothes off the wash line. Bunkie was playing with a wooden truck that Daddy had made for him, driving it through

71

the dirt. He jumped up and hugged my legs. "Hey, Jackie. Will you play with me?"

I gave him a quick hug and peeled him off me. "Some other time, Bunkie. Maybe Gerianne can play with you."

"Gerianne's taking a nap."

"Oh. Well, sorry, but I need to talk to your mommy."

"What's up, Jackie?" Ann Fay picked up the basket of laundry and handed it to me to carry to the porch. We sat down on the top step with that laundry basket between us. She folded her children's clothes while I thought about how to explain without really explaining. Because even though I'd already messed up and told Thomas's mother about that drunk, I was determined not to make things even worse.

"Ann Fay, do you understand colored people?"

My sister dropped the shirt she was folding, letting it fall into the basket. "I declare, Jackie! Of all the things I thought you were fixing to say, that wasn't one of them."

I told Ann Fay that I'd done something stupid—something that got Thomas hurt—and that when I tried to do the right thing afterward, I made even more of a mess. But of course I couldn't come out and tell her exactly what I was talking about. So none of it made much sense. Finally I asked, "Didn't you have a Negro friend in the polio hospital? Did you understand each other?"

"Jackie, there was a lot I didn't understand about Imogene," Ann Fay said. "But we were stuck in those hospital beds and couldn't escape if we tried. There's something about being in the same predicament that ties you together. Know what I mean?"

Her voice kind of faded away then, and I had the feeling she was seeing right back into that hospital. "Imogene got polio first," she said. "Then they brought me in, and I was suffering real bad. I was *alone,* Jackie. Daddy was off in the war, and even if he hadn't been, they wouldn't have let him in to hold me. Momma couldn't be in the contagious ward either."

Ann Fay picked up one of Gerianne's cotton dresses and used her hands to smooth out the wrinkles. "But right there, in the bed beside mine, was Imogene Wilfong. She talked me through the pain, Jackie. My muscles were cramping, and the hot wraps they put on me burned something fierce. They hurt Imogene too. But still, she talked me through them. *It mostly hurts at first,* she told me. *After a while it starts to feel better.*"

Ann Fay's voice wobbled, and when I looked at her I saw a tear slip from her eye.

Oh, no! Now I'd made my sister cry. I wanted to change the subject, quick. But before I could think of a way, she went right on talking. "Her voice, Jackie—it was like a momma's song saying that line over and over. Everything was hurting so bad—not just my body but my mind too. Bobby was dead and I was sure it was my fault. And there I was, feeling so sick I thought I might be the next to die. But Imogene kept saying, *After a while it starts to feel better.*"

Ann Fay buried her face in Gerianne's dress. That didn't stop the tears, because next thing I knew she was sobbing. Rocking back and forth like she was trying to comfort herself.

I never knew what to do when my sisters cried. Momma always took care of that or else they cried on each other's shoulders. Now, seeing Ann Fay, who was usually so strong, crying her heart out like that—well, it made my throat ache. And my chest hurt.

"It's okay," I said. But I wasn't so sure about that. I hadn't felt okay when I got there, and things had just gone from bad to worse.

Ann Fay lifted her head. "Now I have my own children. How can I keep them safe? This world is a scary place, Jackie. You know what I mean?"

I thought I did know. She wouldn't say it in front of Bunkie, but besides remembering polio and her baby brother dying she was most likely feeling anxious about Russia. And their bombs.

Bunkie dropped his toy truck and came running to his momma. He wiggled up against her, and she pulled him between her knees and held him tight and cried into his hair.

He patted her shoulder with his grubby little hand, and something about that made me feel better. I set the laundry basket up on the porch floor and moved closer to Ann Fay and Bunkie. I started patting her back, then rubbing it like I'd seen Junior do sometimes.

After a while her crying slowed down, and soon I realized she was humming. It was just a sad sound at first, and then it turned into a tune. But I didn't recognize it.

"What's that song?"

Ann Fay lifted her head and swiped at her nose with the back of her hand, which reminded me that I had a handkerchief in my pocket. I pulled it out.

"Here," I said.

She took it and blew her nose. "It's okay, Bunkie," she said. "Mommy just needed a good cry. I'm better now." She gave him a little nudge, but Bunkie didn't go back to playing. He sat on the step below us and leaned against her leg.

"That song—'Nobody Knows the Trouble I've Seen.' They sing it over there sometimes." Ann Fay jerked her head a little in the direction of the colored church on the other side of the cedar trees at the edge of the yard. "I know I can't see Imogene again, but just living so close to that church, listening to the people sing on Wednesday nights—well, it's the next best thing. It keeps her close, you know?" Ann Fay tapped her hand on her heart. She still looked kind of mournful, but then she threw back her shoulders and said, "Who knows? Maybe it wouldn't have lasted. Friendships change over the years."

"Is it too late to find out?"

"Jackie, I've looked high and low for the one letter she wrote, and honest to goodness I can't find it any-where. I thought for sure I'd find it when I married

Junior and moved all my things up here to him and Bessie's. But I didn't. So I've got no address to go on. By now, Imogene's probably married. New name. Living in a new place."

Ann Fay stood up then and paced the ground in front of me, and for some reason I noticed her limp. Normally I don't think about it. It's just a part of her and has been for as long as I've lived. Polio left its mark on her body.

But now I knew. It left a hurting on the inside too.

"Know what Imogene said to me in the hospital?" asked Ann Fay. She stopped and looked me in the eye. "*I hope you know there's a muddy wide river between your people and mine.* That's what she told me."

Ann Fay lowered her voice then, and it was almost like she was thinking out loud. "Maybe she's right, Jackie. Because I went to see Imogene after we were out of the hospital. Junior took me. There we were—two white strangers in a Negro neighborhood. And . . . well, it was awkward, with people up and down her street relaxing on their front porches on a Sunday afternoon and watching what was going on at the Wilfong house. Imogene was polite, of course. But she had a friend there, and it felt like she didn't need me anymore. I guess I was the one who needed her. But after I came home that day. I just let her go. Or tried to, anyway."

Ann Fay could've been behind the pulpit in that church right now—because I declare she took to preaching. "You and me don't understand how wide that river is, Jackie. But someone's got to try crossing it—like Ellie working for civil rights. And like those brave Negroes going into white schools. I don't know much about Thomas, and from what little you told me, I sure don't know what you did to ruin things. But the least you can do is go back to the river looking for him. Say you're sorry and ask to start over."

I sat there thinking about what that meant. It wasn't like Thomas was actually my friend. He was suspicious of me from the day I met him. Now I knew why, although I still couldn't sort it all out. Why did he think I was guilty when anybody on that bus could have thrown something at him?

I knew I could never admit what I'd done, and I sure didn't mention it to Ann Fay. Because if I told anyone that would make it matter. So I pushed it to the back of my mind and listened to what my sister was saying.

Ann Fay sat back down beside me, leaned over, and gave my shoulder a little bump with hers. "You should go back," she said. "But Jackie, if you've done something to make Thomas mad, then you might want to give him a few days to cool off."

12

SEPTEMBER 1959

On Sunday afternoon I headed for the river, in case Thomas had cooled off and decided to take his chances on bumping into me. I wondered if that drunk would show up. Considering the hate he had for Thomas, he might come back and stir up trouble. And this time I'd keep my mouth shut.

But Thomas wasn't there, and to be honest I wasn't surprised. I waited an hour before I decided to go on home. My bucket didn't have a single fish in it because, like I said before, I'm not much of a fisherman.

I hadn't gone more than a few steps when I spotted some glass in the undergrowth. That stupid liquor bottle! I picked it up and turned it over in my hand, and a whole lot of things were turning in my mind too— about how, just when it seemed like Thomas was trying to be my friend, that bottle had changed everything between us. Just the sight of it made me mad. I didn't want to see it again. And I especially didn't want Thomas to come across it. I tossed it in my bucket to take home and throw in the trash.

But partway home I started thinking about going to Thomas's house instead.

I kept hearing Ann Fay's voice—low and sad, saying how she wished she'd tried harder to keep up with Imogene. Between her voice in my head and that bottle clanking around in my bucket—and maybe the guilt I was trying not to think about—I felt like someone was talking straight to me. Telling me to get brave. Go find Thomas. Try again.

When I came to the Freemans' lane, I set the bucket in some brambles not far from their mailbox. No use carrying *that* with me.

Their dogs started barking the minute I turned in at their mailbox. When someone hollered for them to hush, they calmed down and came slinking toward me. Since I figured they recognized me this time, I let them sniff my hands, and after that, they led me down the dirt lane to the house. But still, my legs felt wobbly and my insides did too.

It looked as if the whole family was sitting on the front porch, almost like they were waiting for me— which of course they weren't. Parents and grandparents sat on an old car seat and some rocking chairs. Thomas's sisters, the ones who got off the bus with him the other day, were on the steps playing Penny Penny with some other kids—cousins, maybe? His brother, Johnny, was riding the porch swing with a pretty girl leaning against his shoulder and his baby sister sleeping on his lap. He gave me a nod.

But no sign of Thomas—anywhere.

I couldn't help but think of Ann Fay going to visit her colored friend. Maybe this was how she felt—almost like she was in a foreign country, even though it was practically right around the corner from home.

"Good afternoon," I said. And it was like a church choir the way they all said good afternoon back to me at the same time.

"Uh, I'm Jackie Honeycutt. I'm looking for Thomas."

Thomas's momma was sitting there with her husband, and when he started to stand she patted his knee like she was saying to let her handle this. She didn't let on like she knew me, though. "Thomas is out back," she said. "You go find him." Maybe she was afraid I'd say something she didn't want her husband to know about.

But I'd already learned *that* lesson.

"Thank you, ma'am," I said, and I headed around the house. First thing I saw was their Jersey milk cow in the pasture out beside the barn.

Thomas was sitting on a stump working on a project. He glanced up when he heard me, but he kept right on with what he was doing. Giving me the cold shoulder, I reckoned. I stepped closer till I could see he was building a birdhouse. Tying sticks together with baling twine until it looked like a little log cabin.

"Where'd you learn to do that?"

Thomas grunted and I figured he wasn't going to answer me. Then he said, "I got a daddy too."

"Yeah, I just saw him. But don't worry, I kept my mouth shut."

"Good." Thomas reached for a short twig from the pile he'd made on the stump beside him. He poked it through a loop in the twine and wound it tight. I could see he was intending to keep his mind on that birdhouse. I looked around the yard and saw more birdhouses. Maybe eight or ten of them scattered about—nailed onto trees and sheds and the clothesline posts. Seemed like every one of them was different, made from scraps of wood and metal and empty thread spools, even. I gave a little whistle. "You make all those houses?"

"Most of 'em."

"They're real nifty. I guess that's how you got so many birds in your record book."

Thomas didn't say anything, just kept on working. Maybe he wanted me to go away. But he didn't come out and say that, so I figured I could take my chances. Try putting my toe in that muddy wide river Ann Fay talked about.

I decided to plop myself onto the ground and see what happened next. Nothing, as far as Thomas was concerned. He kept right on adding sticks and winding twine.

So of course I opened my big mouth. "I hope I didn't start more trouble by talking to your momma," I said. "I didn't mean to and I'm really sorry."

Thomas glanced at me, and for a second there I thought he might be about to forgive me. But he just tied a knot in the twine, then reached for a knife laying on the stump and cut the end off.

"I don't understand," I said. "Did you keep it all to yourself? What *did* you tell your parents?"

"Fell on a slippery rock. Hit my head."

"Oh."

"I told Johnny the truth because he thought maybe *you* did it." Thomas looked straight at me when he said that. Like he was trying to see into me. Maybe get me to admit some guilt.

I felt heat rising into my face. And it seemed like my heart went a little haywire. But I tried my best not to let on. "And he was okay with you not telling your parents?" I asked. "Not reporting it to the sheriff?"

Thomas laughed then, but it wasn't a happy laugh. More like he was mocking me. I knew there was something I wasn't getting. "And just what color do you think that sheriff is going to be?" he asked.

"Uh. White."

"When was the last time you heard of a white sheriff taking the word of a colored man? Tell me an incident you know about when the law protected a Negro. Ever read one in the newspaper?"

Thomas had me there. I mean, I couldn't argue his point one way or the other. But I didn't need to because now he was talking again.

"See that house standing right there?"

"Yeah."

"It ain't much, is it? Needs paint, but the landlord's not paying for that. Hard to heat in the winter. Hot as blazes in the summer. But at least the roof don't leak. I don't know what you think when you ride by that house on your school bus five days a week, but at least it's standing there. I'd hate for you to glance over one day and see it burned to the ground."

"Huh?" I asked. "What you talking about a house burning for?"

Thomas stopped winding twine and looked at me. Long. Hard. "I reckon if your daddy decided to put somebody in their place for hurting you, he might just get by with it."

That's all Thomas said. He stared at me like he was expecting an answer. I shrugged. "I guess so."

"You *guess* so. Well, I *guess* you don't know what might happen if my daddy goes after some drunk who throws a bottle at me. I don't have to *guess* anything— except exactly which form the revenge might take. If my daddy goes after that old man, a burned-down house is just one of the things that could go wrong."

13

SEPTEMBER 1959

I didn't throw that bottle away after all. Instead, I rinsed it out, peeled off the label, and set it on my bureau—right in front of the mirror, so it looked like there were *two* bottles sitting there. One for Thomas. One for me.

Of course that bottle hadn't hit *me* in the head, but it sure felt like something had. I went to his house with all kinds of questions and came home with a bucketful of truth.

The *truth* was, if anyone tried to hurt me I could tell Daddy and he'd do something about it. The *truth* was, a Negro man couldn't respond to a white man's anger. Sometimes, according to Thomas, the best way for a man to protect his family was to let some bad things slide. Because bad could always turn to worse.

So *that* was why he lied to his parents. And it was why Johnny went along with the lie. Those two brothers were protecting their family. I realized something else, too. If, somehow, Thomas and Johnny knew I threw that apple, they could've beat me up. But they didn't. Because they thought worse things could happen to them.

Looking at that bottle still made me mad. But it also made me want to cry. Because all that truth was too much to know. And what could I do about it? I couldn't even take back the awful thing I did.

Ellie would know what I could do. Maybe. At least *she* was doing something—working for that civil rights lawyer. Learning about passive resistance—which, best as I remembered, was about changing unfair laws.

But I didn't figure Ellie would be much help. She was so caught up in schoolwork and her integration activities that she barely found time to send us letters. Sometimes she'd call us long-distance, but when she did, Momma usually tried to avoid talking about civil rights.

I likely wouldn't see Ellie until Thanksgiving.

The things Thomas said to me about how Negroes were treated got me reading last week's newspapers. I'd always leafed through the *Hickory Daily Record,* and maybe if there was a story about a bad car wreck I'd actually read it. But mostly I read the sports page for baseball news or to keep up with Ned Jarrett and other NASCAR drivers. And I always read the cartoons.

Now, I started paying attention to smaller articles—looking to see if Thomas was right about Negroes not being defended by the law. I found stories about Negroes trying to get into white schools and some about coloreds robbing stores or fighting or getting in trouble with the law in one way or another.

And then, after searching a few papers, something hit me about those crime articles. If a colored person was in trouble, I'd see the word "Negro" or "colored" in the title. But there were other crime stories that didn't mention race. And I started realizing those criminals were white. But nobody put *that* in the headline.

And I got to thinking about how that made Negroes look real bad. No wonder white people were afraid of them. Even *me,* if I was to admit the truth of it.

14

SEPTEMBER 1959

The day after I went to Thomas's house, Russia landed a rocket on the moon. Like Miss Pauline had said, Russia was winning the space race. And one day after the rocket's landing, Nikita Khrushchev came to America.

That night there was one whole hour of television news just about his arrival. We saw him, his wife, and President Eisenhower going down the streets in an open car while Americans stood on the sidewalks glaring at them. Some people held up signs. One said, YOU CAN REACH FOR THE MOON BUT YOU CAN'T GET AMERICA!

Then there was a ceremony where Khrushchev gave Eisenhower some kind of metal ball with Russian writing on it. Apparently, the Russians had left one like it on the moon. He was rubbing it in, reminding America who got to the moon first. What an insult! But President Eisenhower accepted the gift—if you can call that a gift. He smiled for the cameras, then looked annoyed, and then went back to smiling again.

To make things extra dramatic the television news

announcer stood in front of an advertisement for a family fallout shelter. He just had to remind us that Russia could drop a bomb at any minute and we'd need a place to hide until the radiation settled.

I wished the TV people wouldn't do that. Our house wasn't all that strong, and I knew for sure that if we got bombed it would blow to pieces. The best we could do was hide in the root cellar underneath. When the house blew apart, we'd be left in a heap with the sweet potatoes and Momma's canned vegetables.

A few days after Khrushchev arrived, I got off the school bus and there was Miss Dinah standing in her yard. She had her garden gloves on and stalks of hollyhocks in her hands. "Jackie," she said, "you never stop by anymore. Come inside and I'll find you a Cheerwine."

"Yes, ma'am," I said.

So I followed her to the back porch, past their little sign that said BACK DOOR FRIENDS ARE BEST, and waited while she put the flowers in a vase. She pulled me a Cheerwine out of the refrigerator. Momma was there working on supper for the sisters. Miss Pauline was pulled up to the kitchen table in her wheelchair, playing a game of Scrabble.

"Who are you playing against?" I asked. "Yourself?"

I was only joking, but she was serious. "Yes indeed. Your mother has played two games today and she's tired of it. Dinah never plays with me anymore."

Miss Pauline put a word on the board and added

up her score. Then she wheeled her chair to the other side of the table, drew some letters from the bag, and put them on the tray in front of her. "When is Ellie coming for a visit?" she asked. "She's my favorite Scrabble opponent."

"Thanksgiving, I guess."

"Oh, that's too far away. Jackie, *you* could play with me. Stop in every day. I believe your spelling grades would go up. How are you doing in school?"

"I'm doing okay," I said. I didn't tell her my spelling was atrocious, because she might insist on Scrabble games. "We're talking a lot about Khrushchev's visit. Mrs. Cunningham had us make a bulletin board with a map of the Soviet Union, and now we're learning about all those countries Russia controls."

Miss Pauline gave a little shudder. "Oh," she said. "They'd like to control us too. I don't know why our president let Nikita Khrushchev into this country. Do you realize they're flying his communist flag over the president's guesthouse in Washington? Such a disgrace!"

I guess Miss Pauline forgot she was supposed to be beating herself in Scrabble, because she started gathering the pieces and putting them back in the bag. She seemed real agitated all of a sudden. "I don't trust that man. I do wish President Eisenhower would send him home!"

But Khrushchev stayed for twelve days. And every day we watched or read about his visit. Somewhere along the way he visited a farmer in Iowa, and he tried to visit Disneyland in California. But the security guards wouldn't let him because it was too crowded and they couldn't promise to keep him safe. He got real mad about that.

All this talk of Khrushchev was making me a little nervous, so, just to help me feel better, I drew a cartoon of him knocking on the gate at Disneyland. Mickey and Minnie Mouse stood inside, wagging their fingers at him like he was a bad little boy.

If you asked most any American, they'd say that's exactly what he was. Bad. Very bad.

Before Khrushchev flew back to Russia he met with President Eisenhower again. They didn't come up with a plan to get rid of all their bombs, but at least they agreed that disarmament was important. And they started making plans for Eisenhower to visit Russia. Maybe next summer. Maybe.

15

OCTOBER 1959

"I think Miss Pauline's mind is going," said Momma. "She's sure Khrushchev is so mad about not going to Disneyland that he'll send a bomb our way. I told her if the Russians bomb any place it'll be New York or Washington, DC. But then she argued that *that* would set off World War III. So what can I . . ."

Daddy was listening to every word—whittling at a piece of wood and frowning the whole time.

Momma stopped talking. I guess she'd suddenly remembered that Daddy didn't like being reminded of war. She reached for his hand. "I'm sorry, Leroy. Don't let Miss Pauline's worries get to you. She's old and her mind is wearing out. Khrushchev wasn't so bad after all, now was he?"

Momma didn't sound too sure. But I knew she didn't want Daddy upset about bombs and war. He hadn't had one of his nightmares in a long time, and she wanted to keep it that way.

I kept thinking about that Abraham Lincoln quote

Mrs. Cunningham put on the board. It was still there for us to read every day. *Do I not destroy my enemies when I make them my friends?*

Was Nikita Khrushchev becoming our friend? He seemed like a spoiled brat who would get along with you until you made him mad or didn't give him what he wanted. Then he'd shake his finger at you and pitch a temper tantrum.

But surely he wouldn't start a nuclear war over missing out on Disneyland. Momma was probably right about Miss Pauline's mind going bad.

As if Miss Pauline wasn't enough for her to worry about, Momma came back from the Home Demonstration Club one evening fretting about me fishing with Thomas.

"What?" I said. "We haven't fished together since right after the fair."

"Well, evidently, sometime along the way, somebody saw the two of you together. Blanche wouldn't tell me who it was. Do other people fish down there?"

Oh, uppity Blanche Shuford—president of the Home Demonstration Club.

"Of course other people fish down there," I said. "But I haven't seen them."

"Well, somebody saw you. Who could that be?"

"Beats me."

I knew that old drunk had seen us, but I wasn't allowed to mention him. I had opened my mouth too much already. Besides, it had to be somebody else, because why would prissy Blanche Shuford be talking to an old sot like that?

"Maybe somebody was watching from the woods," I said. But it gave me the creeps just thinking about *that*. Was someone spying on me and Thomas?

"Maybe it doesn't matter *who* saw you," said Momma. "Maybe it matters that you're fishing with a colored boy. Some people around here don't like that."

"Yeah, like snooty old Blanche Shuford. I know she's the president of your club, but you didn't elect her to run your lives. Did you? What business is it of hers *who* I fish with?"

Momma set her sewing basket on the table. "Do not get sassy with me, Jackie," she said. "Maybe there's a thing or two you don't understand. It matters who you keep company with and it matters what people think of you. Someone like Blanche Shuford can turn other people against you—if she takes a notion to."

I guess Daddy decided it was time to step in and defend me. "Myrtle, honey," he said. "Is Blanche Shuford's opinion really that important to you? Maybe you're letting her influence you too much."

"Leroy, I'm not the only one she influences. The other women listen to her too. *And* they listen to Reverend Carl McIntire on the radio. He says talk of racial brotherhood is communist propaganda." Momma shrugged. "I don't know. Maybe it's not true. But Leroy, it's what people believe. In this day and age, with

93

everyone skittish about communism, I don't want people accusing *us* of being communists. For goodness' sake, your own *daughter*, with all her liberal ideas, could be one."

"Myrtle," said Daddy. "Get ahold of yourself!"

"Equality for all," said Momma, mimicking Ellie's voice. "But Leroy, isn't equality for all exactly what communism promises? Ask the Russian people how that's working out."

Daddy shook his head. "Communism is about the government *forcing* equality on you and controlling every part of your life. Ellie has never once hinted at believing in such things."

"The Supreme Court is forcing school integration," said Momma. "Blanche says it's the same thing."

I could see that Daddy was as tired as I was of hearing Blanche's opinions. "Is that what you talk about at your meetings?" he asked. "I thought you did sewing and gardening and collecting food for the needy."

"We do," said Momma. "But we also talk about things that concern the safety of our world and our community. Even if race mixing isn't communistic, it's sure to bring violence. You don't want that for our Jackie, do you?"

16

OCTOBER 1959

I walked Lucy up to Junior's barn. "It's going to be cold tonight," I told her. "But feel how warm it is in here? This'll be your home for the winter. I'm putting you next door to Junior's milk cow so the two of you can gossip day and night. How's that, Lucy girl?" I led her into the stall and helped myself to some of Junior's oats. "Daddy'll bring your barrel of feed up here later. And I'll drop by and feed you twice a day, just like always."

To tell the truth, I was wishing for spring already. I didn't like Lucy being so far from me. She could get sick and I wouldn't be close enough to know or help her. But I didn't mention any of that because I wanted her to feel safe.

That night after supper I studied my spelling words while Daddy read the *Hickory Daily Record*. He was still reading the front-page news when I finished, so I asked for the middle section. I flipped through, looking for interesting stories, and I ran into an article about Jackie Robinson.

Since he'd retired from baseball we didn't hear much about Jackie Robinson. But this story wasn't about baseball. It was about him making a speech in Greenville, South Carolina, to the National Association for the Advancement of Colored People. It was about him saying that 1963 was his target date for complete freedom for the Negro.

1963?

And here it was practically 1960 already. If Jackie Robinson was right, I could be going to the same school as Thomas before we graduated. Honestly, it seemed impossible. I mean with people like Blanche Shuford and that radio preacher keeping the women stirred up, I didn't see how such a thing would happen. Too many people would fight it.

I kept reading. "Whoa! Daddy," I said, "did you see this?"

"What's that, son?" Daddy didn't bother to look up.

He wasn't actually listening, so I slid the page across the table and tapped my finger on the article. "Jackie Robinson," I said. "He used the 'Whites Only' waiting room at the airport. *And* when a policeman tried to remove him, he refused to leave."

Daddy pushed his paper aside and picked up my page. I waited while he glanced over the article. "Robinson's trying to prove a point. And I'm willing to bet we haven't heard the end of it."

"Good!" I said. "I always want to hear more from Jackie Robinson."

"Hmm," said Daddy. He went back to whatever he was reading on the front page. I gave up on him and went to my room.

I pulled out my baseball cards and stared at Jackie Robinson's face for a long time. Instead of putting his cards back with the others, I slipped them in the frame of my mirror where I'd see them every day.

Then I took out my comic book about him and reread every page—about his sensational catches, his home runs, his stolen bases, and all the games he won for the Brooklyn Dodgers. He was the greatest! If you asked me, that policeman in Greenville missed his chance. If I was him, I'd have begged Jackie Robinson for his autograph!

One picture showed Jackie gripping his bat in a way that let you know he was a determined ballplayer. My sketchbook was right there on my dresser, so I opened it and started drawing his picture. I even copied a line from the book—*a symbol of the fighting spirit of the American boy*.

I tore that page out of my sketchbook and hung it on the wall. But I slid the comic book into my binder to take to school. And I put the newspaper article about Jackie in there too.

17

OCTOBER 1959

When Mrs. Cunningham asked if anyone had brought in a current-event item, I raised my hand.

"I found an article about Jackie Robinson in the newspaper," I said. "If you need to be reminded who he is, here's what this comic book says about him." I read the part about him being the marvel of the baseball diamond and the most heroic all-star athlete of all time. I also read the story from the newspaper.

And then I told the class what I thought. "Jackie Robinson, the most heroic athlete of all time, can't even sit with white people at the airport," I said. "He put up with lots of bad treatment when he played ball. Now that he's retired, maybe he should get some respect. Don't you think he's earned it?"

Mrs. Cunningham didn't have to look for someone with opinions on the topic. A bunch of people started talking at once. When she got them settled, she called on Wayne.

"When he was playing ball, Jackie Robinson tried

to use the same waiting rooms and restaurants as the rest of his team," said Wayne. "It didn't work. I bet he didn't have much choice about making a scene because it would cause problems for the team manager. Now that he's retired, he probably figures he can speak up more."

The words weren't even out of Wayne's mouth before the class was in an uproar again.

Mrs. Cunningham made everyone get quiet. She walked to her desk, opened a drawer, and pulled out a ruler. "Since this is a controversial topic," she said, "I want you to measure your words."

Dennis snorted.

"Dennis," said Mrs. Cunningham. "Is there a joke you'd like to share with the class?"

"No, ma'am."

Mrs. Cunningham explained that measuring our words meant choosing them carefully. It meant not getting carried away and dominating the discussion. And it required thinking about how our words affected others. Then she asked who had a response to the article. "Raise your hand."

A bunch of hands went up, and she gave the ruler to Robert. "When you're done speaking you may pass the ruler to someone else. But no one speaks unless they have the ruler in hand."

Robert giggled, and for a minute I thought he forgot what he was going to say. But then he said that everybody was used to "Whites Only" waiting rooms, and

"Colored" waiting rooms, and there was bound to be trouble if we started switching things up. "So maybe we should each stick with our own kind," he said.

He handed the ruler to Sally right behind him. She said, "I think colored people *like* the way things are now. Why would they want to sit in a room with a bunch of white people staring at them?"

The ruler went down the aisle and around the room. Some people passed it right on without saying a word. Every now and then someone snickered or booed, and Mrs. Cunningham refused to let the person with the ruler speak until the room got silent. But we heard a lot of opinions. I could see that people were just plain scared of integration because they said things like "We don't know what could happen. Give 'em an inch and they'll take a mile. They might take over this whole country."

Tony asked for the ruler. "My parents listen to this radio preacher, and he says race mixing is communism. I bet you're a communist, aren't you, Jackie?"

I didn't have to answer that because Pamela raised her hand real fast. "It's not right to accuse Jackie of being communist. I don't think we should listen to preachers who say such things. They're just teaching hate and shouldn't be preachers at all."

Even though I'd gone to school with Pamela all my life, I couldn't say I knew her all that well. But I was starting to think she might understand me better than anyone else in the class. Having her stick up for me like that put a warm feeling all over me.

One person said, "Didn't that article say he wants the Negro to have complete freedom? What does that mean anyway? Nobody knows."

Dennis finally got ahold of the ruler. "My grandmother knows. She says they'll want to *marry* us. She says they're already doing that up North, and we're not having any such thing around here. Think about *that*, Jackie Honeycutt. It started with baseball—and next thing you know, Jackie Robinson'll be saying they can marry white girls. Is that what you want? Do *you* want to marry one of *them*?" He got up and brought the ruler across the room and smacked it against my comic book. "Whatcha got to say about that?"

If you asked me, Dennis wasn't just trying to hurt my comic book, he was smacking Jackie Robinson in the face. And that made me real mad. I gripped that ruler so tight I could feel its thin metal edge cutting into my hand.

"What I've got to say is this. Jackie Robinson should be respected for his great baseball career and all he had to put up with. Did I hear somebody say that colored people like things the way they are? How would you *know* such a thing? Did you ask them? Evidently Jackie Robinson doesn't like being sent to a colored waiting room. If he did, this story wouldn't be in the paper. How would you like to be humiliated every time you went out in public? Huh?"

I was just getting started. Maybe Mrs. Cunningham

could tell I was winding up for a big speech because she headed toward me. I saw her reaching for the ruler, but I got in one last statement. "It's downright ignorant," I said, "treating Jackie Robinson or anybody else mean— all on account of skin color."

"Thank you, Jackie," said Mrs. Cunningham. She turned and went to the front of the room. "Thanks to all of you for expressing your opinion. Remember, when our country disagrees, everyone gets to speak. We've done that today. Now, as you think about what has been said, I want you to also think about what Americans believe about everyone's rights."

She pointed to a poster on the wall. It had a statement from the Declaration of Independence.

We hold these truths to be self-evident, that all men are created equal, that they are endowed by their Creator with certain unalienable Rights, that among these are Life, Liberty and the pursuit of Happiness.

Mrs. Cunningham didn't preach about Jackie Robinson having those rights. Maybe she figured I'd already done enough preaching. She just let us read the poster and sit there and think about it for a minute or two. She put the ruler in her desk drawer, and just like that our current-events discussion was over. We moved on to language arts.

If you asked me, Mrs. Cunningham had just put Dennis Aiken in his place.

But that didn't mean he was done giving his opinion on the subject. Because he caught me in the boys' room after phys ed. If I'd known he was in there, believe me, I would've avoided that place like it was filled with communists.

I was standing in front of the sink when he came out from one of the toilet stalls. I could see him in the mirror, and I didn't like what I saw—the face of pure meanness. "Oh, look who's here," he jeered. "The little communist who's pushing for race mixing. I really ought to show you what I think of that."

From the sound of his voice, which was low and hateful, I had a feeling I was about to be in some deep dookie.

"Hey, Tony," Dennis hollered. He banged on a stall door. "Wanna help me stick Jackie's head in the toilet? I need you out here. Don't bother to flush."

I wasn't about to stick around for Tony to come out of that bathroom stall. I turned and gave Dennis a hard shove, then ran for all I was worth. I heard a bang and a holler and some cussing, and none of that made me want to slow down.

Our teacher was standing at the classroom door, and of course she wanted to know what my hurry was. I didn't have to explain because Dennis was on my heels. He had blood on his hand from where he'd been holding

103

a gash on the back of his head.

Mrs. Cunningham took hold of my arm. "What can you tell me about this, Jackie?"

"I wasn't trying to hurt him. Honest, I wasn't. I just wanted to get away. What would you do if someone threatened to put your head in dookie?"

"I was just *joking*," said Dennis. "I wasn't actually going to do it."

"You boys come with me." Mrs. Cunningham put one arm across my shoulder and the other one on Dennis's and steered us down the hall to the teachers' lounge.

18

OCTOBER 1959

After she tended to the cut on Dennis's head, Mrs. Cunningham sat us down and listened to us each tell our side of the story. If one of us interrupted the other, she gave us a look that stopped us in our tracks.

When Dennis finished talking she looked him straight in the eye. "Dennis, that toilet trick is one of the oldest in the book. If you did such a thing, you'd be expelled from school. Do you understand?"

Dennis nodded. "Yes, ma'am."

Personally, I wouldn't mind one bit if Dennis got kicked out and never came back. But I think I saw fear in his eyes when she said that. Mrs. Cunningham turned to me. "Now, Jackie, I want you to think about something. *You* know the abuse Jackie Robinson endured. What do you think *he* would do in this situation?"

"Uh . . . uh," I stuttered.

"Keep pondering that question." Mrs. Cunningham leaned in and put one hand on my arm and the other on

Dennis's. "Listen. You're my boys." She looked us right in the eye when she said that—first me and then Dennis. "And I need my boys to get along. I need you to set a good example for the younger children in this school. So I'm giving you a chance to act like the gentlemen I know you are. I want you to go to the front steps and talk this out. I feel certain you can resolve it without me getting your parents involved."

Dennis spoke up real fast. That's when I realized why he looked scared about being expelled from school. "Please don't do that. My old man'll have my hide."

Mrs. Cunningham stood and started for the door. "I have faith in the two of you to work this out on your own. Remember that quote by Abraham Lincoln I wrote on the board? Jackie, what's the best way to destroy your enemy?"

I knew what she wanted me to say. "Turn him into a friend," I said.

"Good." Mrs. Cunningham grinned and opened the door for us. She held it while we went through. "It'll be chilly outside, so get your jackets."

I reckon it being cold helped us to agree quicker than we might have otherwise. Plus Mrs. Cunningham was counting on us, and there was something about her that made me want to do the right thing—even if I didn't exactly want Dennis to be my friend.

We sat—Dennis on one wall and me on the other—

with the wide steps between us, staring at the trees in front of the school and at the cars that went down the road every now and again.

Dennis wasn't talking, so I figured it was up to me to get things going. "Want to shake hands?" I asked. "Forgive and forget? I'll forgive you for threatening me and you can forgive me for shoving you."

He shivered and pulled his coat sleeves over his hands. He hunched his head inside his collar.

"Look," I said. "It's cold out here. She wants us to be friends. The sooner we agree to get along, the quicker we can go back inside."

Dennis stood and headed for the door. "All right," he said. "We'll get along, then. I won't tell my old man you put a gash in the back of my head. Hard telling what he might do to you."

If you asked me, he wasn't planning to tell his daddy in the first place. He'd probably lie about how he got hurt—same as Thomas did—but for different reasons. Thomas didn't want his father trying to defend him. Dennis might pretend his mean old daddy would protect him, but I had a feeling Dennis was the one who'd take a licking.

I stuck my hand out, thinking Dennis might actually shake it. But he looked at it like it was covered in dookie and walked on past.

Oh, well. I hoped Mrs. Cunningham knew that I tried

being a gentleman. But as far as Dennis being my friend went—that didn't seem too likely.

19

NOVEMBER 1959

After I fed Lucy I headed for home, but I had no more than reached Junior's mailbox when I thought I heard singing. I stopped. The sound of it was coming from the other side of the Bledsoes' property. That church—Thomas's church. That's where it was coming from.

Ann Fay just might be sitting on her back porch taking it all in. I thought about joining her and I was heading that way when I changed my mind. After all, I hadn't seen Thomas since that Sunday afternoon in his backyard—the day he told me he could get his house burned down if his daddy tried to get revenge on that drunk.

He'd quit showing up at the river. Honestly, fishing season was over, so why wouldn't he stop coming? That's what I told myself but, deep down inside, I knew he was avoiding me.

Still, I could sneak through the shadows around that church building and see if he was there.

At first I stayed in the shelter of the cedar trees

between the churchyard and Ann Fay's house. But when I spotted Thomas I sneaked in closer—to where I could see him clear and easy, along with the rest of his family. The whole congregation was on its feet, swaying and clapping to their song. Thomas's little sister, who looked to be about four years old, was standing on the pew. She reached for him and he picked her up and went right back to singing, jostling her to the beat of the music while she bobbed her head and giggled. They'd get to a certain place in that song and he'd tug on one of her braids—one, two, three—in time to the music, and she'd giggle even harder.

It hit me how I really didn't know Thomas. Sure, I knew he liked Jackie Robinson and birds and fishing. I'd been to his house and got a glimpse of his whole family, but I hadn't heard his sister giggle or tasted his momma's cooking or even been this close to his church when a service was going on.

This church made Thomas smile. In fact, that little building was so full of smiles and *Amen*s and *Hallelujah*s it's a wonder they didn't come oozing out the windows. Or maybe they did—I realized that even I was smiling.

The music ended and the preacher went to the front. He said something which I didn't quite hear, and just like that, the whole congregation called something back to him.

The preacher cupped his hand around his ear like

he hadn't heard them. The next time he called out, the congregation spoke up louder.

He did that a few more times, and each time they looked at each other and laughed and nodded and shouted louder until I reckon he was satisfied.

And then he went to preaching, which was every bit as noisy and just as happy as the rest of the service. Thomas's father got up and added wood to the potbelly stove in the middle of the room. While he did that, the preacher pulled out a white handkerchief and dabbed at his upper lip and wiped his sweaty forehead.

I couldn't hear much, just bits and pieces, but sometime along the way he said how God's eye was on the sparrow and Thomas called out a loud *Amen*. People turned and grinned at him. I guess they all knew he was real fond of birds.

The smell of the wood smoke and the sight of all those happy people sure put a cozy feeling on the inside of me. But on the outside, I was downright chilled. I headed for home and our woodstove.

The whole way there I saw Thomas clear as a picture show inside my head. Rocking his baby sister in time to the music. Singing and shouting—free and easy. And grinning like he'd just landed a big fish.

20

NOVEMBER–DECEMBER 1959

Ellie didn't even come home for Thanksgiving vacation. Instead, she went to her friend Maribelle's house. Apparently they were busy with some civil rights concern that just couldn't wait.

After Thanksgiving break Mrs. Cunningham had us working on a program for the whole school. She put Christmas songs on the record player and we sang along. Some people got skits to act out, and she chose Wayne to say the opening prayer. I didn't have anything special to do—just sing along with the group songs. Too bad, because I wouldn't have minded being in one of those skits.

I helped Wayne memorize his prayer. I'm pretty sure Mrs. Cunningham had made it up, because it was written in her longhand. It talked about peace on earth and all of us practicing peace toward each other.

For current events we kept up with President Eisenhower, who was on a peacekeeping tour to a whole bunch of countries. People in India welcomed him with a banner calling him the prince of peace. An article in the newspaper said his personality was helping our relationship with Khrushchev because he didn't call him names or try to pick fights with him. And he was still thinking about visiting Russia next summer.

The Abraham Lincoln quote was still on the board—the one about turning enemies into friends. But I still wasn't convinced such a thing was possible. Not with some people, anyway.

After our little talk on the school steps, Dennis and I had mostly ignored each other. I guessed our truce—if that's what you could call it—was working out.

But at least I managed to make one new friend. When Mr. Nolley came for 4-H club he brought me a Christmas card. The card was homemade on a piece of red construction paper. On the outside were two cows with Christmas wreaths hanging around their necks. The message inside said, *Merry Christmas from my barn to yours. Your friend, Beth Lutz.* And I guess she'd liked my cartoon because she drew one of her own. It was a picture of her and me with our cows at the fair. Her cow was telling Lucy how nervous she was.

That really surprised me because all along I thought she was so sure of herself. Now I realized that maybe the Lutzes weren't so different from me after all.

I took that card home, and the next morning before school I put it on my mirror. While I was doing that, a spider ran across my bureau and down into the top drawer. Some days I might let a spider go, but this was a big one. So I pulled everything out of the drawer, shook it all out, and still couldn't find the spider anywhere. I figured it ran in behind the drawer, so I pulled the whole drawer out. There it was—in that boxed-in space that holds the drawer—with its legs sticking out from under an envelope that had fallen back there. As I reached for the crumpled envelope, the spider darted out the front and around the side of the dresser. I started to go after it, but something else caught my eye—the name on the return address of that envelope.

Imogene Wilfong.

I couldn't believe my eyeballs. I'd just found Ann Fay's long-lost letter from Imogene!

I ran to the kitchen to tell Momma. "Look what I found! An old letter from Ann Fay's friend."

Momma was busy stirring oatmeal, but I held out the letter for her to see. "Oh, keep that away from the food," she said. "It's dusty. Cobwebby, too. Where'd you find that? It must be time to clean your room."

I wiped the letter off with my hands and then against my pant leg. "Yeah, it's kind of dirty. But Momma, Ann Fay is gonna be so excited. She wanted to get in touch with Imogene, but she lost her address. This is it, Momma!"

"Maybe," said Momma. "But Imogene has probably moved by now."

"Well, it's worth a try. I'm going to call Ann Fay right this minute. It'll make her day."

As I headed toward the phone I heard Momma say, "Jackie, has it ever occurred to you to just let bygones be bygones?"

I stopped in my tracks and turned to look at her. "You don't want Ann Fay to get in touch with Imogene? But Momma, you know how Ann Fay feels about her. Don't you? When she was in the hospital hurting and missing *you*, Imogene was the one who comforted her."

Momma's stirring slowed down when I said that. And her face went a little sad. Like she was remembering when Ann Fay got sick.

"Yes, Jackie. You're right, of course." Momma dished me a bowl of oatmeal and set it on the table. "But now you need to eat or you'll be late for your bus. You can call Ann Fay later—maybe after school."

I didn't want to wait, but I stuck that letter in my shirt pocket and sat down to eat. If I hurried, I could drop it off to Ann Fay when I stopped to feed Lucy on the way to the bus stop. But feeding Lucy came first, and while I was pouring water into her bucket I told her about my exciting discovery. And right in the middle of doing *that* I got a brilliant idea. "Lucy!" I said. "I can save it for Christmas. I'll wrap it up and it'll be Ann Fay's best Christmas present ever. Think what a surprise that will be!"

I worried all day that Momma might go ahead and tell Ann Fay. So I stopped in at the Hinkle sisters' after school to talk to her. She was folding laundry at their kitchen table. "Momma," I said. "Did you tell Ann Fay about the letter I found?"

Momma shook her head. "I haven't talked to your sister all day," she said.

"Please don't tell her, Momma. I decided to surprise her at Christmas. Won't that be nifty?"

Mamma pulled a towel from the laundry basket and folded it. She was making a nice neat pile of towels and another one of washcloths there on the table. "Don't worry," she said. "I won't tell Ann Fay. You can have your Christmas surprise."

"Thanks, Momma. She's going to love it. I bet she'll write to Imogene first thing."

Momma nodded, but from the sigh she let out I knew she really just wanted everything to stay the same as it had always been. Even with her knowing how important Imogene was to Ann Fay, she felt safest with segregation. Evidently, that was one thing the women at the Home Demonstration Club seemed to agree on.

I heard the television in the living room, so I went in to say hi to the sisters. Miss Pauline had nodded off to sleep in an armchair. Miss Dinah was watching television, but she asked me to turn it off.

"Let's talk, Jackie," she said. She patted the couch cushion beside her.

"Yes, ma'am," I said. I sat—but probably not as close as she would've liked. I didn't exactly want to snuggle up to her the way I did when I was little. "Is Miss Pauline okay?"

"Oh, she's fine," said Miss Dinah. "We were watching *Beat the Clock,* and now *she's* beat." She giggled. But then she lowered her voice. "Really, Jackie, I don't know if my sister is fine. She worries all the time. During the day she listens to that radio preacher who won't stop talking about communism, and in the evening the television news makes her fret." Miss Dinah lowered her voice. "She's been downright snappish with your mother today. Myrtle took extra long at the clothesline, and I could see why." Miss Dinah shook her head. "Even *I* put on my coat and scarf and picked up sticks in the yard, just to get away from my sister."

I felt like I should say something to make Miss Dinah feel better. "Ellie's coming home from college in a few weeks," I said. "She loves playing Scrabble with Miss Pauline. Maybe that will cheer her up."

"Oh, I hope so," said Miss Dinah. "We could use a big helping of cheer around here."

21

DECEMBER 1959

On the last morning before my Christmas vacation, Miss Dinah was waiting for me at the bus stop. She had a paper sack with a red ribbon taped to it. "Here you go, Jackie," she said. "I made molasses cookies for your class. I even made Pauline help me. She used to love to bake, you know. Oh, are you wearing a green necktie under your jacket? Looks like someone's celebrating."

"It's my 4-H tie. Today is party day and my class is doing a program for the whole school."

"Wonderful! And what part are you playing?"

"Nothing, really. Just singing with the rest of the class. I guess there's not enough special parts for everyone."

"I'm sure that's true," said Miss Dinah. "But I think *you* should have one." She turned to go. "I hope your classmates like the cookies."

When I got to school, Wayne's bus was parked ahead of ours, so I waited for him. His little sister Clara got off and handed me a folded piece of paper. "Here's a note from Momma. Give it to your teacher for me, okay? Wayne's sick."

"Uh-oh! He's supposed to be in the program."

I held the school door for Clara and headed to my classroom. The auditorium doors were open and I saw Mrs. Cunningham in there, adjusting props on the stage. I figured she'd probably want to know about Wayne right away, so I went in.

"Wayne's sick," I said.

Mrs. Cunningham unfolded the note, read it, and tucked it in the pocket of her skirt. "It looks like I'll have to find a good reader," she said. "Can you help me move this table, Jackie?"

"Sure!" I ran onto the stage and grabbed the other end of the table. "I'll do the prayer for you, Mrs. Cunningham. I helped Wayne practice it, so I know it by heart."

"Do you really?"

"Want to hear it?" I went to the microphone in the middle of the stage, stopped, and thought about the words for a minute. And then I said the whole thing—straight through.

I heard Mrs. Cunningham clapping almost before I said the *Amen*. "Perfect," she said. "Jackie, you've made my day."

When the time came for the program, I was more nervous than I thought I'd be—especially when the whole school started filing into the auditorium. Our class waited in the rooms off to the side of the stage until we heard the piano playing.

The auditorium got quiet, and we lined up and walked onto the stage singing, "Let there be peace on earth." I went to the microphone, looked at all those students, and almost forgot the prayer. But then I remembered it was a lot like the song because it talked about how peace starts with each of us. I asked everyone to bow their heads and I said that prayer straight through. Loud and clear. Not too fast. Not too slow. Maybe even better than Wayne would have.

The rest of the program was full of silly skits and fun songs that the whole school could sing along to. When it was over, we had our party, including Miss Dinah's molasses cookies.

Afterward, Mrs. Cunningham gave me some leftover candy canes. "You saved the day, Jackie," she said. "The gift of gab comes in handy sometimes, doesn't it?" She winked. Then, she put her hand on my shoulder and looked me in the eye. "You do have a talent for public speaking," she told me.

I could feel myself blushing. I glanced away from her steady blue eyes, focusing on the wreath hanging on the classroom door. "Thank you, Mrs. Cunningham."

When I got off the bus. I stopped in at the Hinkle sisters' to tell Momma and Miss Dinah all about my day. Miss Pauline too, of course, but she wasn't much interested. All three of them were at the kitchen table boxing fruitcakes to give as Christmas presents. Miss Pauline was busy instructing Momma on how to wrap them.

Evidently Momma didn't do it perfectly because Miss Pauline said, "Oh for goodness' sake! Just let me do it!" She reached for the box, and Momma let her take it.

Miss Dinah leaned forward and patted Momma's hand. "Don't worry, Myrtle. You were doing just fine."

The next day Ellie came home for her Christmas break. After she settled in, I told her about Miss Pauline. "Momma's not complaining," I said. "At least not most of the time. But Miss Pauline is getting difficult. Maybe you should go play Scrabble with her every day."

"Of course," said Ellie.

And she did. Some days she even sent Momma home for a few hours to rest. But Ellie complained about Miss Pauline too. "I can't abide that preacher she listens to. He cloaks his hateful ideas in religious talk and I just want to shake her for believing him. Miss Pauline used to be so open-minded. But I hardly recognize her anymore."

"I bet you get into some good arguments then, don't you?" I asked.

Ellie sighed. "No. I tried reasoning with her, but she snapped at me. I'd rather keep the peace. She won't be around forever, and I don't want anything to spoil our friendship."

I think we were all glad to have Ellie home again, helping out wherever she could. Ida came to visit more often now, and she and Ellie went shopping and made presents together. One day they decided to meet at Ann Fay's house so they could help Gerianne and Bunkie make Christmas cookies.

I had to feed Lucy, so I walked Ellie up to Ann Fay's. And right there by the Bledsoes' mailbox I broke my promise to Thomas. "Ellie, this is a deep secret. You can't breathe a word of it to anybody." I told her about that horrible old drunk hurting Thomas, me talking to his momma, and Thomas sitting in his backyard saying his house could get burned down if his daddy tried to straighten that drunk out.

Ellie stood there shivering, but she wasn't in a hurry to go inside. She folded her hands together and warmed them with her breath. "Of course I won't tell anyone. And Jackie, you've got to trust Thomas on this. He knows things you and I can never understand. His daddy would want to defend his son. Do you think he did? You haven't heard about any incidents, have you?"

"Nah. But I haven't talked to Thomas in a few months. I think he's still miffed. And honestly, Ellie, he never did trust me." That half-eaten apple crossed my mind, but I pushed it away and kept talking. "It's like Imogene Wilfong told Ann Fay—there's a big muddy river between them and us. Sometimes I wonder if that river's just too wide to cross."

"No!" said Ellie. "That kind of thinking is just wrongheaded. It holds us back. Not just you and

Thomas but the whole country. We've got to talk. And spend time together. That's why I spent Thanksgiving with Maribelle's family. Sure, I *wanted* to come home and be here with y'all, but there was a passive resistance workshop in Winston. It was too important to miss."

"So Maribelle *is* colored? That lawyer you're working for is colored? Has Momma figured that out?"

"Not yet," said Ellie. "But I'll tell her. I'm just waiting for the right time. She tends to worry, you know."

"Yeah, I know. But what exactly is a passive resistance workshop?"

Ellie thought about that for a second and then she said, "Passive resistance is that mailbox standing there."

"Huh?"

"Try to push it over. Go ahead. Beat on it. Kick it. Tell it to move."

"Ellie, are you out of your mind?"

My sister laughed. "The mailbox isn't going anywhere. But it's not fighting back, either. It doesn't have to. It's firmly grounded. That's what passive resistance is, Jackie—knowing where you stand and staying right there. And if someone comes along and insults you or hits you even, you stay right where you are and don't fight back."

"Now I *know* you're crazy!"

"It seems insane, doesn't it? And it's really hard, Jackie. Why do you think I'm taking classes?" Ellie laughed and stamped her feet. "It takes practice.

But let's get going. I'm about to freeze into an ice statue out here and your cow is bawling her head off."

That conversation with Ellie had me thinking. I couldn't imagine standing there taking insults or punches from Dennis Aiken. I wasn't going around looking for a fight, but I knew that if Dennis hit me I'd be swinging back at him.

Ellie could *have* those fancy ideas of hers.

22

DECEMBER 1959

I kept thinking about the things Ellie said—especially how I should keep trying with Thomas. But honestly, what was the point? And what excuse would I give for showing up at his house again?

Then about a week before Christmas, when Daddy bought a sack of oats for Lucy, he came home from the feed mill with a 1960 calendar. He gave it to Momma, but she was busy ironing clothes and didn't pay it any mind. I noticed it had birds on the front, so I picked it up and turned the pages. Every single page had a painting of a different bird. Thomas would love it!

"Can I have this?" I asked.

Momma pressed her iron into the corner of a sleeve on the shirt she was ironing. "Can you have what?"

"This." I waved the bird calendar in front of her.

"Why do you need your very own calendar, Jackie?"

"Not for me. It's for Thomas."

"Thomas?"

"Yeah, Thomas Freeman. My fishing buddy." That

buddy part wasn't exactly true, but I figured at least she'd know who I was talking about. "He loves birds," I said.

"I think I'll keep it," said Momma.

That's when Ellie piped up. She was at the sewing machine, working on a cute little dress to give Gerianne for Christmas. "Why don't you let him have it?" she said. "I'll get you another calendar, Momma. One with flowers, if you want. All the stores are handing them out this time of year."

Momma just shook her head and hung the shirt on a hanger. She handed it to me. "Here, Jackie. Take this to your room. And yes, you can have the calendar."

"Yippee! Thanks, Momma. Thanks, Ellie." I took the shirt to my room and hung it up, and I put the calendar on my bureau. I'd have to figure out when to take it to Thomas. Maybe on Christmas Day.

I also had that letter from Imogene wrapped and ready to give Ann Fay on Christmas.

We all met at the Hinkle sisters' for a big dinner. The sisters gave each family a fruitcake, and some people brought out presents for them. But I saved my surprise for Ann Fay until it was about time to go home. "Ann Fay, I got a present for you," I said, taking the letter out of my pocket.

My sister was in the middle of pulling on her coat, but when she got her hand through the sleeve she reached for the gift.

"Be careful not to tear it."

"You drew me a picture, didn't you?" Ann Fay slipped the envelope out of the wrapping paper. "Or maybe not." She turned it over, and when she saw the return address, I thought her eyes would pop out of her head. She squealed, "Imogene?" Her voice got quieter. "Imogene Wilfong?" She looked at me, and now she was whispering. "*This* is my long-lost letter." She opened the flap on the envelope and pulled the pages from inside. "Oh, I can't wait to read it. Where did you find it, Jackie? I thought it was gone forever."

So I told her about hunting down the spider and finding this instead. "I forgot all about that ugly old spider. It's probably still running around in my room."

Ann Fay laughed. "But this, right here, *this* is beautiful!" Her voice broke then, and she sank into one of the Hinkle sisters' chairs. She stared at that letter and a tear wobbled down her cheek. She bit her lip—tough old Ann Fay didn't want any of us to see her crying. But it was too late because another tear was on its way already.

She pulled the letter close to her heart. "Imogene was my lifeline when I was in that hospital," she said. "I wanted to hang on to her after I came home." Ann Fay dabbed at her eyes with her coat sleeve. "I tried. But it just didn't work out. *Now*, maybe I can try again."

"Attagirl," said Junior. "And I'll help you. Even if we have to ride over to that address in Greensboro." We all cheered, and Junior took Ann Fay by the hand and helped her out of that chair. "I'm gonna take my wife home now. She's got some reading to do."

"And writing too," said Ann Fay. "I won't sleep a wink until I answer this letter."

23

DECEMBER 1959

I still hadn't taken that calendar to Thomas, but once Christmas was over, I dug out used wrapping paper and the fancy bow off the fruitcake the Hinkle sisters had given us. I wrapped the calendar and put it back on my bureau—right beside the liquor bottle. Jackie Robinson was there on my mirror, and that made me feel like he was watching to see what I would do.

But the truth was, I didn't do anything. Honestly, I was too chicken. I didn't feel like facing Thomas's dogs, or his whole family staring, or even Thomas—if you want to know the truth of it. I was afraid he didn't want to see me.

On New Year's Eve, I heard Ellie on the phone with Maribelle, making a plan of some kind. "Will Jackie Robinson be there?" she asked.

I could barely wait until she hung up that phone. "Are you gonna meet Jackie Robinson?" I asked. "Because if you are, you can at least let me tag along."

"No," said Ellie. "And why are you eavesdropping on my conversation?"

"I *live* here," I said. "And you weren't exactly whispering. What are you up to?"

"Don't worry about it, Jackie. You wouldn't be interested."

"Yes, I *am* interested, because it has something to do with Jackie Robinson. Doesn't it?"

"Look," said Ellie. "Can you keep a secret?"

"Of course I can. I didn't tell anybody about Thomas getting hit with that bottle. At least not until you came home for Christmas break. And that happened way back in September."

"Hmm," said Ellie. "Okay, then. In October, Jackie Robinson was in Greenville, South Carolina, and an officer from the airport tried to kick him out of the waiting room."

"Oh, I saw that in the paper! He tried to use the white waiting room."

"No," said Ellie. "Maybe that's what the paper said. But that waiting room is no longer just for white people. Do you realize it's now against the law to force Negroes to use a separate waiting room in a federally funded facility? Well, Jackie Robinson knew. And he refused to move. You can believe his friends and supporters were appalled by the way he was treated."

"Oh. But what's that got to do with you?"

"Tomorrow there's going to be a quiet protest in

Jackie Robinson's honor. A whole bunch of us will march from a church to the airport. Most of us will stay outside, but some Negro spokesmen will go into the waiting room and read a proclamation against segregation."

"Oh, Ellie. Momma's not going to like this."

"Right—and you're not going to tell her." Ellie gave me a real fierce look.

"I won't. I promise. But Ellie, aren't you scared? What if people start throwing bricks at you?" I thought about Thomas. "Or glass bottles?"

"Jackie, I'm white. I'll be the last person to get hurt. But anyway, it's going to be a peaceful demonstration. We're not expecting any trouble."

"Yeah," I said. "But if there *is* trouble, then what? Are you going to stand there like a mailbox and let them hurt you?"

"I'll try, Jackie. We've been practicing, and I'm getting better at it."

"Practicing?"

"Well, the first time my friend blew cigarette smoke in my face I almost hit him."

"Your friend? You mean you practice this with your friends?" It was starting to sink in what Ellie had been talking about. She wasn't just going to classes to *hear* about passive resistance. She was actually trying it out. Evidently she thought she might need it someday. Maybe even tomorrow.

While I was letting that sink in, Momma came

home from the Hinkle sisters'. Of course Ellie changed the subject real fast. "Hey, Momma. I'm just getting ready to fix supper. How was Miss Pauline today?"

Momma pulled off her coat and handed it to me. "Jackie, will you hang this up? I don't have the strength to pick up a spoon. I need me a cup of chamomile tea."

"Sit down, Momma," said Ellie. "I'll make you tea."

While I took Momma's coat to the closet, I heard her asking Ellie if she wanted a full-time job looking after Miss Pauline.

"Ha!" said Ellie. "For some reason she *is* more patient with me. But that might not last if I'm there every day. She's already snapped at me a time or two. Lucky for me, I'm going back to school. And by the way, Momma, there's been a change of plans."

I hurried back into the kitchen because I had an idea what Ellie was fixing to say next. Momma rubbed the back of her neck with her fingertips like she was working on some worry knots that had built up there. "Plans?" she asked.

"You and Daddy won't have to take me back to Winston on Sunday," Ellie said.

Momma stopped massaging her neck. "You're not going back to school?"

"Of course I am. It's just that my friend is coming to pick me up. Maribelle—you know, the girl I spent Thanksgiving with. Her father is the attorney I work for. We're going to South Carolina for Saturday and

Sunday. They'll be stopping by for me in a few hours."

"What do you mean by *they*?" asked Momma. "In a few hours? South Carolina?" Now Momma was out of that chair. Evidently she forgot she was too tired to lift a spoon.

"Maribelle's family," said Ellie. "They have kin people in Greenville. We're going to pay them a visit."

"Couldn't you have told us about this sooner?"

"Plans didn't come together until this morning. We *were* expecting to drive down early tomorrow. But they decided to go today because it might be snowing in the morning. They won't stop in for long, Momma. Just enough to say hello." Ellie waited, and I could see that she knew Momma wasn't going to like what she said next. But finally she spit it out. "It would be nice if you let them use the bathroom. The Green Book doesn't list any places for them to stop along the way."

"You want her parents to come inside?" Momma's voice cracked. "Oh, dear." She glanced around the kitchen. "This house must be a shack compared to what a lawyer's family lives in. Ellie, why do you *do* this to me?" She grabbed a can of cleanser from under the kitchen sink. "I've got to clean the bath—" Momma stopped in the middle of the word. "What's this got to do with a book?"

"*The Negro Motorist Green Book*," said Ellie. "A directory that indicates restaurants and hotels or service stations that welcome Negroes. And Momma, it's only about *this* thick." Ellie held her thumb and forefinger to show how skinny the book was. "It's more like a pamphlet. So, you know there aren't many places where they can refresh. And it doesn't matter if they're doctors or lawyers or ordinary people like us."

"Negroes?" asked Momma. "That attorney is a Negro? Ellie, is there some reason you can't tell the truth up front instead of springing surprises on us like this? *Now* what are we supposed to do?"

"Let them use your bathroom, Momma. They're good people. And like I said, there aren't many places for them to refresh when they travel. I was hoping my family could at least be friendly."

Momma let out a long breath. "Of *course* we'll be friendly," she said. "But if Blanche Shuford finds out about this, I'll be thrown out of the Home Demonstration Club." Momma's voice shook, and I couldn't tell if it was from anger or if she was trying not to cry. She reached for the broom and handed it to me. "Jackie, go. Sweep the front porch, including the steps. Ellie, don't just stand there. Straighten up the living room. And put a nice tablecloth on the kitchen table. Call Ida. She'll fancy this place up."

"Momma!" said Ellie, loud and bossy—like she was the mother, instead of the other way around.

Momma stopped in her tracks.

"I promise they won't be judging your home,

134

Momma. Only your heart." Ellie tapped her chest.

"Oh." Momma sounded kind of shocked. And she looked as guilty as Bunkie getting caught in a lie. Her lip trembled.

"By the way, I already cleaned the bathroom," said Ellie. "But if you could put on a pot of coffee, that would be nice. I'll set out the china cups."

Momma nodded and turned away. "But first I'm checking that bathroom," she said. "And putting my best rug on the floor."

24

DECEMBER 1959

Ellie tried to talk Momma into resting while she made a light supper. "Don't worry," she said. "Maribelle's family won't need to eat. They're coming later."

But Momma told Ellie not to bother cooking. "The rest of us can eat *after* they leave. That will keep the kitchen clean until they get here."

Daddy just shook his head and patted Momma's shoulder. "Myrtle," he said. "They'll come and then they'll go. And that will be the end of it. I'm sure they've seen poorer places. You've got nothing to be ashamed of."

Personally, I couldn't see what was wrong with our house. Daddy had painted the outside a few years ago and even put on green shutters. And the linoleum on the kitchen floor was practically brand-new. Most days Momma was perfectly happy with her kitchen and the colorful dishes on shelves and cabinets.

When Maribelle's family arrived, *her* mother liked it too. "So pretty!" she said. "I love your cozy house."

Momma squinted like she suspected Mrs. Bradley was lying. And when she got a good look at how fine Mrs. Bradley was, she realized she'd been so worried about the house she hadn't prettied *herself* up. "Oh," she said, all flustered, "I still have my apron on." She untied it and pulled it off; then she combed her fingers through her hair.

"Not to worry," said Mrs. Bradley. "We're a little travel-worn ourselves." She smoothed her skirt with her hands.

Why did women worry about such things anyway?

"Would you care to use the restroom?" asked Ellie. "And after that, Momma has coffee and pecan pie for you." Actually, Bessie Bledsoe had made the pie because Momma was too busy cleaning, but Ellie didn't bother to explain this.

Ellie introduced me to Maribelle, who was sparkly eyed and full of smiles. "Hi, Jackie. Why, you're not nearly as bad-looking as Ellie told me." She laughed. "I'm just kidding, Jackie. Ellie never said that. Come meet *my* little brothers."

She squeezed the shoulder of the taller boy. "This is Luther," she said. He gave me the slightest nod and the tips of his fingers for a handshake. I couldn't tell if he was shy or just too good for the likes of me. "And this little rascal"—Maribelle pulled the short one into a side-wise hug—"is Colt. Luther and Colt, meet Jackie."

Colt shook my hand and grinned real big.

We sat around the table and had pie and coffee. At first it was mostly Maribelle and Ellie doing the talking—catching up on Christmas news and discussing college life. Daddy asked about the trip to South Carolina. "I hear you're outrunning the weather tonight. Aren't you worried the girls will get snowed in at Greenville? They could miss school on Monday."

Mr. Bradley laughed and shook his head. "Oh, no. I grew up in Greenville." He chuckled. "Where it snows in the morning and melts in the afternoon."

"I guess you're going to visit family, then?"

"Well, yes. And to support some friends."

He didn't say they were going to be part of a march against segregation. But I knew what he meant. And I knew *why* they were doing it. "Friends?" I asked. "Are you friends with Jackie Robinson?" I blurted it out. I wasn't planning to. And I'd promised Ellie I wouldn't say a word. But when Mr. Bradley said *friends*, it hit me all of a sudden that maybe he knew him.

Mr. Bradley turned to me. "I don't know Jackie Robinson personally. But I have family and friends in Greenville. They're the ones who planned the march."

Ellie spoke up real fast then. "Mr. Bradley, sir, I haven't mentioned that to my parents. I didn't want them to worry."

"Worry?" asked Momma. "*Should* we worry?"

"No, Momma, it's nothing. I promise. We're just making a statement."

"We?" asked Momma.

"Us," said Ellie. "All of us." She looked around at the Bradleys. "Right?"

"Not me," said Luther. "I'm playing Monopoly with my cousins."

It got real quiet then—like nobody wanted to be talking about this. Ellie never intended to bring it up, and I guess the Bradleys didn't know if they should be explaining it either.

But I knew what was planned, so, like usual, I opened my big mouth. "Don't worry, Momma," I said. "They're just planning a nice quiet walk from the church to the airport. And some people will go inside and read a statement. But not Ellie. She'll be just fine."

Mr. Bradley spoke up then. "Would you like us to curtail Ellie's involvement?"

"No!" said Ellie. "That's not fair. I'm an adult. I can decide what's best for me. Momma and Daddy, listen! It's important for white people to participate in the movement. If you knew what this was about, you would care."

"What *is* this about?" asked Daddy. "School integration?"

"Daddy," I said, "remember when we saw in the paper about them trying to run Jackie Robinson out of the airport waiting room? That's what this is about. Right, Mr. Bradley?"

"Oh, Jackie," said Ellie, and in her voice I could hear how she was furious with me. "I thought you were going to keep your mouth shut. But you just keep blabbing away."

"Well, somebody's got to explain something. We can't just sit here and—"

Daddy held his hands up like a referee calling for time out. "That's enough, Jackie. If Ellie wants to tell us, she can."

Maribelle spoke up. "Ellie, I think you better explain."

"Daddy, Momma," Ellie said. "I didn't tell you because I didn't want you to worry. And obviously I should've never told Jackie either."

I heard Luther snicker.

"But yes," said Ellie. "I'm participating in a march tomorrow. It's a response to the way Jackie Robinson was treated. Really, it'll be perfectly safe." She stopped and looked around the table.

It seemed like everyone was staring at their pie. Except Colt and Luther. Colt's pie was all gone, and he was watching Luther, who had his eyes closed like he was pretending to be somewhere else altogether.

Now that Ellie had gotten dragged into telling the truth, she just kept going. "Daddy," she said, "Mr. Bradley fought in the war just like you did."

"And he almost died," said Colt.

"He went over there to save the Jews," said Ellie. "And look what he came home to—Negroes being treated horribly too." Ellie was on her feet now, pacing

140

the floor like she was Perry Mason arguing a case in court. "Don't tell me we're better than Germany because we don't have concentration camps. Plenty of Negroes are dying without a fair trial. All because some white person accuses them of looking sideways at their sister. Or because they fight back when someone attacks them."

"Daddy still has nightmares," said Colt. "He dreams about the war all the time."

Mr. Bradley let his fork fall onto his plate. He dropped his forehead into his hands and looked like *he* wanted to be somewhere else too.

Mrs. Bradley reached for Colt's hand. "Hush," she said.

Daddy spoke up then. "I know all about war dreams."

I couldn't believe he actually said that to a perfect stranger. Mrs. Bradley glanced at Momma, and Momma nodded just the least bit, letting Mrs. Bradley know she understood about having a husband haunted by the war.

Mr. Bradley looked up and cleared his throat. "But the war is over," he said. "I'm fighting for Negroes now." His voice sounded fierce. Like he was trying extra hard to be strong.

Nobody said a word then. It appeared that everybody except me and Colt were counting the flowers on Momma's best tablecloth. Momma poured cream in her coffee even though she always drank it black. She stared into the cup like she was trying to decide if she could drink it mixed like that.

Daddy reached into his shirt pocket and pulled out a stick he'd started whittling on. From the way he stared at that stick and rubbed his thumb against its smooth surface I figured he was probably thinking about soldiering. And about how Mr. Bradley wasn't so different from him.

Maribelle glanced at her wristwatch. "We should be leaving. Ellie, want me to help you carry your things to the car?"

"Let *me*," said Daddy. "While Myrtle fetches your coats."

Everybody got up from that table in a hurry then. It was like they couldn't wait to get out of the conversation. I ran ahead of them to open the door, and when I did, I couldn't believe my eyes.

While we'd been eating pie and talking, bad weather had slipped up on us. As I stood in that doorway I felt the cold dampness on my face. The ground was turning white.

25

DECEMBER 1959

"Snow!" said Colt. "Yippee! Daddy, Momma, it's snowing!"

That brought the adults to the porch in a hurry.

"You'll have to spend the night," I said.

Of course that was just me running my mouth without thinking. The second those words came flying out of my mouth, the room went dead silent.

Finally Momma said, "Uh . . ."

"Of course not," said Mrs. Bradley. "We'll go home."

"No, Virginia," said Mr. Bradley. "It'll only be worse going that direction. We're heading south. If we leave now I'm sure we'll drive out of it."

Next thing I knew, I was standing on the porch with Momma and Daddy, waving goodbye.

"Reckon it's safe out there?" asked Momma. "I couldn't forgive myself if there was an accident."

Daddy stood behind Momma and pulled her up against him. "Like Mr. Bradley said, they'll drive out of it. Probably before they hit Shelby. Now, can we go find something to eat?"

Momma pulled out some leftover biscuits, but she was distracted and had trouble deciding what else to serve. So Daddy asked me to crack some eggs and scramble them in a bowl while he fried some livermush. We ate the eggs in biscuits with slabs of livermush and mayonnaise on the side.

We had just cleaned up all the dishes when headlights flashed through the window. I jumped up to see who was coming down the lane, but Momma was closest to the door. She opened it and peered outside. "Oh, help!" she whispered. "They're back."

Momma was right. Next thing I saw was Ellie coming up on the porch. "Momma, it's not safe out there. South of here the snow turned to freezing rain. Jackie was right. The Bradleys need to stay here tonight. But they don't want to impose. They insisted on staying in the car while I asked."

Ellie stood on the step half-turned, like she couldn't wait to get back to her friends. The snow settled on her shoulders while she waited for Momma to agree.

Momma was trying to stutter out an answer, but Ellie was answering for her. "Where else could they possibly go, Momma? They don't know anyone around here, and it's not safe to be out. The car was slipping all over the road just getting here." Ellie grabbed Momma's hand. "It's scary out there." She sounded desperate, and I knew she was thinking about the car accident she'd been in a long time ago.

I could tell Momma was thinking about that too. "Of course they can come in," she said. Her words came out slow and tired-sounding.

Daddy stepped up behind her. "Myrtle, I'll help carry their luggage while you and Jackie make up the beds."

I followed Momma into the house and straight back to her bedroom. She shut the door and leaned against it for a second with her eyes closed. "Jackie, strip that bed. We'll put clean sheets on for Mr. and Mrs. Bradley." She glanced around the room, which was kind of a mess since we'd carried in clutter from the other rooms. "Oh, my dear," said Momma. "We didn't clean *this* room. Get the broom and dustpan. Quick."

So I swept the floor while Momma made the bed up fresh. She stuffed the dirty sheets into the hamper under the window, but then she pulled one of the pillowcases back out and used it as a dust rag on the nightstands. She glanced at the bureau and shook her head. There was a jumble of deodorants, combs, a pile of mending, a couple of pocketknives, and even some bolts that Daddy had pulled out of his pockets.

She scooped everything except the toiletries into the bottom drawer of the bureau. "I don't even *know* these people," she muttered. "And now they'll be sleeping in my bed. Dear Lord in heaven, what are you trying to tell me?"

I didn't know these people either, and that Luther fellow wasn't very friendly. Was the Lord really trying to tell us something? Is that why we were stuck in this house with them in the middle of a snowstorm?

I could hear that everyone was in the living room by now. Daddy was stoking up the woodstove and Ellie was taking coats and hats and telling the Bradleys to have a seat while she heated up some milk for hot cocoa. "I'm sure Momma is making up beds," I heard her say.

"We better go," said Momma. "We've got more beds to get ready. Don't forget to take the broom and dustpan out of here." She glanced around the room. "I guess it's presentable." But she let out a long sigh, which told me she wasn't convinced.

By the time she made it to the living room the frown lines were smoothed out and she was smiling like she actually meant it. "I'm sorry I wasn't here to greet you," she told Mrs. Bradley. "We changed the sheets in our room. You may stay there tonight."

"Oh, no," said Mrs. Bradley. "We're not going to put you out. If we could just sleep right here on the floor that would be wonderful."

"Of course not," said Momma. "It's all settled and the room is waiting. Just as soon as Leroy and I take a few of our clothing items out."

"Momma," said Ellie, "Maribelle and I will make the rest of the beds. If you and Daddy take the spare room, the rest of us can sleep in the big one. We'll take one

146

bed and Colt and Luther can have the other. Jackie can have the floor. It'll be like a pajama party—with little brothers."

"And no knock-knock jokes allowed," said Maribelle. She elbowed Colt and shook a finger in his face. But she was smiling, so I had a feeling she was only teasing him.

After we went to bed—which, for me, was a pile of blankets on the floor—I found out that Colt had a head full of jokes. We were barely settled when he spoke up. "Knock, knock."

"Who's there?" I asked.

"Mustache."

"Mustache who?"

"Mustache you a question but I'll shave it for later."

"Ha-ha!" I said. "Very funny." But really, it *was* pretty funny, so I stuck it in the back of my mind to pull out someday when I needed it.

Colt had more where that came from. "Knock, knock."

"Who's there?" asked Maribelle.

"Howl."

"Howl who?"

"Howl you know unless you open the door?"

Of course we howled about that one.

"Jackie, it's your turn," said Maribelle.

"Okay. Knock, knock."

"Who's there?" asked Colt.

"Cows say."

"Cows say who?"

"No, silly, cows say moo."

"Of course," said Ellie. "You *would* have a cow joke. Luther, got a riddle?"

"Nah," said Luther. "I don't know any."

"Now that's a joke right there," said Maribelle. "Come on. It's your turn."

But Luther was a stick-in-the-mud who refused to have a good time with us. So Colt told every joke he'd ever heard and howled at them like they were the funniest thing since the last episode of *I Love Lucy*. He didn't just howl, he snorted. And the rest of us almost died laughing at how funny Colt sounded.

Even Luther snorted over his brother's silliness. Maribelle knew exactly what she was doing when she told her brothers no knock-knock jokes. She was trying to break the ice between us.

We stayed awake until midnight because, after all, it *was* New Year's Eve. And exactly at twelve o'clock Ellie said, "Happy New Year, everybody!" Then she and Maribelle started singing "Auld Lang Syne."

Colt thought of another joke he wanted to tell, but the girls told him it was time to be quiet and settle down. I guess he told it to himself because he wouldn't stop giggling. I'm pretty sure he was still snickering when I dropped off to sleep.

26

JANUARY 1960

I heard voices in the kitchen and smelled coffee and bacon. Momma was up early making breakfast. I grabbed my clothes and hurried to the bathroom to get dressed. But she stopped me. "The bathroom is being used right now. Get dressed in your room," she said.

"Momma, there's girls in my room."

"Then use the spare room. Colt and Luther can dress in there too."

I hurried toward the spare room and almost bumped into Mr. Bradley coming out of Momma and Daddy's bedroom. This house sure was crowded!

"When you're dressed come back and help me put breakfast on," called Momma.

I pulled plates out of the cupboard, but Mrs. Bradley came along and reached for them. "Show me where the silverware is," she said. She was just a little bit bossy in a friendly way that made you want to cooperate.

We all sat down to breakfast and talked about the weather and how Daddy and Mr. Bradley had seen on the TV that it was sleeting in Greenville, South Carolina, right that minute. Nobody mentioned the demonstration, but I was sure we were all wondering if it got snowed out. I could see from the look on Ellie's face she was disappointed not to be there.

Breakfast could have been awkward if it wasn't for Colt and me telling stupid jokes about school.

Why did the boy eat his homework? *Because his teacher said it was a piece of cake.*

What'd you learn at school today? *Apparently nothing. I have to go back tomorrow.*

Why are some fish at the bottom of the ocean? *Because they dropped out of school.*

Where do pencils go on vacation? *To Pennsylvania.*

We made up tall tales about how awful school was. Our parents laughed and commented on how silly we were until we started in on the mean-teacher jokes. And then we had to hush.

After breakfast Mrs. Bradley insisted on helping with the dishes while Momma put leftovers in the refrigerator.

When I put on my coat and boots to go feed Lucy, Colt wanted to go along. Maribelle said she'd go too. "Coming, Luther?"

Luther turned up his nose. "Cows stink," he said. "I've got a book to read."

Outside was so white and dazzling that at first it hurt my eyes. Colt horsed around in the snow, which wasn't that deep. There hadn't been much more during the night.

We heard Lucy bawling before we were halfway to the barn. "She knows I'm late," I explained.

After we were inside, I brought Lucy out of her stall to where Colt and Maribelle could get a good look. "Isn't she a beauty? And she's real friendly." I scratched Lucy's head.

Colt reached out and touched her face.

"I named her after Lucille Ball, you know. Because she's a show cow." I noticed Maribelle didn't even try to touch Lucy. "Sorry, she's a little dirty. But I promise, when I took her to the fair she was spick-and-span and beauty-parlor perfect. Now that it's winter, she misses her baths."

"You give your cow a bath?" asked Colt. "In a bathtub?"

"Ha-ha! No. I use the garden hose. But sure, I give her baths. When she's in the show ring the judges watch for all sorts of things. Is she clean? Does she have a good shape? Are her hooves as shiny as Fred Astaire's dancing shoes?"

"So it's like Miss America for cows?" Maribelle giggled, and I couldn't help but laugh too.

"Yeah. Kind of like that. Want to pet her?"

"That's okay," said Maribelle. She even backed away a little.

"Are you scared of her?"

"I guess I'm just a city girl."

"She won't hurt you, you know. Ellie says you're

practicing passive resistance. Now *that* sounds scary. This is just a nice cow."

Maribelle laughed. "I'm sure that does seem strange. Maybe I'm just a fraidy cat." She lowered her voice. "Want to know a secret? I'm halfway relieved we didn't have to march in Greenville today. Because, even though it's just a quiet demonstration, well, you never know what might happen. And I'm really not all that brave."

That surprised me. "But why would you do it?" I asked. "I mean, if you're scared, can't you just stay safe and play Monopoly with Luther and your cousins?"

"No," said Maribelle. And she threw back her shoulders. "I can't. This is too important, Jackie. I can't let fear hold me back." She reached out her hand then and even rubbed the side of Lucy's face with her knuckles. When she did that, I realized something. You could be scared and brave at the same time. At least that's how Maribelle seemed to me.

Before we left, I gave Colt a fistful of oats and showed him how to let Lucy lick them out of his hand. Most of the oats went on the ground, but he worked up his courage to let her lick his hand clean. He giggled the whole time, and when we got back to the house he wanted to make a snow cow.

Of course Luther stayed inside and read a book. He hadn't said two friendly words to me after that first handshake. I didn't know what his problem was, except evidently I was annoying—maybe because I told jokes and people laughed and he didn't have a funny bone in his body.

But sometime along the way, Maribelle went to their car and brought in a Monopoly game. "You didn't get to play this with your Greenville cousins," she told Luther. "So we're going to have ourselves a game right here."

Her daddy warned her not to get started because the snow was starting to melt. "We'll be leaving soon as the roads clear," he said.

But Maribelle gave him a look and jerked her head a little in Luther's direction, letting her father know she was determined to make her brother be friendly. "Are you good at this game, Jackie?" she asked.

"I don't know. Never played it."

Just that quick, Luther showed his face from behind that book he was reading. "You *never* played Monopoly? Where've you been—in the barn?" He laughed.

"Oh," I said. "So you *can* make a joke?"

"Na-ah-ah!" said Maribelle. "No fighting, no biting. Luther, behave yourself. You can explain the rules."

Luther was happy to oblige. He spread that Monopoly board on the kitchen table, organized the money in the rack, and promptly announced he was the banker. "Now which token do you want?" he asked.

The tokens were little metal pieces for moving around on the board. "The Scottie dog," I said. "Because we had one, you know. Mr. Shoes. But he died last year."

"Aww," said Maribelle. "That's sad."

Colt wanted to know what color our dog was and why we named him Mr. Shoes and why he died. But Luther didn't care two cents about my dog. "I thought we were playing Monopoly," he said.

"He died of old age," I told Colt. Then I made my voice real gruff, just to make fun of Luther. "Now let's get serious about playing this game." I was starting to wonder if Luther even belonged in the Bradley family. I mean, he looked just like his father, but if you asked me, when God was handing out nice bones in that family he skipped right over Luther.

While we played, Ellie brought out a sewing project. Next thing I knew, she and Momma and Mrs. Bradley were getting all excited about fancy stitches and appliqués. I could hear Daddy and Mr. Bradley in the living room talking about the war—something Daddy usually tried to avoid. I wondered if Mr. Bradley avoided it too. It seemed like a miracle that the two of them could talk to each other.

Even though I'd never played Monopoly, I caught on. Pretty soon I was collecting rent on four railroads and some properties. Luther didn't exactly like paying money to me, but at least I showed him I wasn't stupid. And since he owned Park Place and Boardwalk he collected plenty of rent from me too. He even laughed at a few of my jokes. As far as I could tell, he tried not to, but they were funny, so what choice did he have?

While we played, the snow slid off the roof and the

adults made plans for the Bradleys to return to Greensboro. Momma and Mrs. Bradley made sandwiches for them to eat along the way and filled thermos bottles with hot cocoa and coffee. But probably none of that was necessary because, by the time they left, the ice everywhere was melting.

27

JANUARY 1960

Their car slipped and slid through a few muddy patches in the road, but next thing we knew, the Bradleys and Ellie were out of sight. And just like that, the house felt empty. None of us really said much about the Bradleys. Maybe we needed time to let it all sink in. Or maybe it was because what had just happened was kind of a big deal, and talking about it would make it smaller somehow.

That night we read in the newspaper about the demonstration they'd missed out on. Fifteen Negroes had stood in the waiting room of the Greenville airport while a preacher read a resolution about how they would no longer be satisfied with the crumbs of citizenship. While that was going on, about two hundred and fifty others stood outside in the sleet and snow. There was a rally at a church where the main speaker said that integration was coming real soon.

When we went back to school on Monday I took

that newspaper article as a current event to share with the class. After all, I'd already told them about Jackie being disrespected at the airport. I figured I'd let everybody know that people decided to speak up about it.

I had the article right there in my pocket, so I raised my hand, and once I started telling the story I just followed wherever my mind took me. I sure wasn't expecting to tell the whole class that a colored family had slept at my house because of a snowstorm. But I did.

Mrs. Cunningham clamped down real fast on all the smart-aleck remarks that started flying around the room. She pulled out her ruler and made us wait to speak until it was in our hands. But just because she held down trouble in the classroom didn't mean there wouldn't be any.

Sure enough, at lunchtime Dennis followed me through the cafeteria line, making a big deal about keeping his distance as if, all of a sudden, I was infected with polio. And after Wayne and I found a table, he was real loud—reminding everybody of who I'd been eating with at my house and how they really ought to stay away from me.

I pretended not to hear him, but still, he was making me mad. "That hoodlum's itching for a fight," I told Wayne.

"Don't give him the satisfaction," said Wayne.

So far, it was only me and Wayne at our table. But for

some reason Pamela showed up. She always sat with her friends, but there she was, standing right across from me. "Is this seat taken?"

I threw my hand out. "Be our guest."

Her friend Betty sat down too.

"What brings y'all here?" I asked. "Didn't you hear? I've got cooties."

Pamela shrugged. "I think what your family did was really nice."

"But tell us," said Betty. "What were they like? Didn't it feel *strange*?"

"Strange? Uh, I don't know. Yeah, I guess so."

"Were they nice?" asked Betty.

"Not all of them," I said. "Luther had a chip on his shoulder the size of our gymnasium. He's a ninth grader—too smart and way too good for the likes of me. Oh, and I forgot to tell you—they have money because the dad is a lawyer."

"A colored lawyer?" asked Betty. The way she said it made it sound like she didn't think such a thing was possible. "So what did y'all *do* the whole time? I mean, where did they sleep? Did you eat together?"

"Of *course* we ate together," I said. "What do you think we are? Downright rude?"

If Dennis had been sitting nearby I might not have started bragging, but he was three tables away and Betty seemed so impressed by my story that I decided to make the most of it.

Pamela sat there listening, and I had a feeling from the way she nodded and half smiled that she was proud of me and my family. But Betty wanted to know how my father and Mr. Bradley got along and what did the adults talk about and weren't we just relieved when they finally left?

I told her practically everything, including a few knock-knock jokes. Lunch went really fast because I talked the whole half hour.

Wayne interrupted me a couple of times. Or tried to. Evidently he felt the need to rescue me from my own story.

"Man!" he said on the way back to class. "How does it taste?"

"Huh?"

"Your foot. Because you just put it in your mouth and chewed on it for a half hour. I hope you're ready for trouble."

28

JANUARY 1960

Wayne was right about me sticking my foot in my mouth. The very next night, when Momma came back from the Home Demonstration Club, I knew the minute she walked in the door that something bad had happened. Daddy and I were sitting there watching *The Real McCoys*, but she marched over to the television and turned it off.

"Momma!"

"Hush," she said, turning to look me in the eye. "I *cannot* believe it. You actually went to school and told your whole class about the Bradleys staying at our house? Jackie, do you have any idea what you've done?"

"Uh . . . uh," I stuttered. "Momma, I wasn't actually planning to tell all that. I was just sharing a current-event story about that demonstration in South Carolina. But I guess I got carried away. And Momma, I thought maybe you changed your mind about coloreds. Didn't you like Mrs. Bradley? She was nice, wasn't she?"

"Her being nice is not the point. The point is that

Blanche was more than happy to remind me—in front of the other women—about the dangers of race mixing."

"Even in an emergency?" I said. "Would Blanche Shuford just let them freeze to death? Or have an accident on the highway? Did you ask those women what they would do if a Negro family was standing on their porch in the middle of a snowstorm?"

"Of course not. It wouldn't happen to *them*, Jackie. *Their* children don't spring surprises on them the way Ellie does. *Their* children aren't working for civil rights. And *their* children don't go to school and tell everything that happens at home. For goodness' sake, Jackie. Do you ever think before you speak?"

Momma took off her coat and dropped it on the couch beside me. It landed with a thump, and a wave of cold air washed over me.

Daddy, who'd been sitting there listening, got up and started putting wood into the stove. Smoke billowed out into the room. Momma frowned and stepped away. But she didn't take her eyes off of me. I knew she was waiting for an explanation.

"I know, Momma. I talk too much. I'm sorry. But somebody else does too. Who told Blanche Shuford? I suppose she has spies stationed in our school?"

"She has a grandchild in your class, Jackie. And she's worried about him. She wants to protect him and all our children. And she's right. You've seen the news. If President Eisenhower hadn't sent troops into Little

Rock, Arkansas, to guard those Negroes, they could have been hurt. But it's not just coloreds in danger. In Clinton, Tennessee, they beat up a white minister for escorting Negro children to a white school. You could get hurt just for talking about this, Jackie."

"Grandchild? Who, Momma? Who in my class is Blanche Shuford's grandchild?"

Momma threw her hands into the air. "I don't know. His name is Dennis. And according to him you bragged to every last one of your classmates that we had a colored family in our house. Over*night* even! That's exactly how Blanche said it. Over*night* even!"

"Dennis Aiken is Blanche's grandson? Are you sure, Momma?"

"I don't know his last name, Jackie. Do you have another Dennis in your class? But really, it's not Dennis I'm concerned with. It's you. Why can't you keep yourself out of trouble?"

Daddy gave the logs in the woodstove one last poke, and sparks crackled upward. He closed the door and said, "Myrtle, leave the boy alone. Come in the kitchen with me and see if you can cool off a little." He looked at me then. "Jackie, it's time you got ready for bed."

Some people might think that him sending me to my room was a punishment, but I knew better. He saw how fired up Momma was, and this was his way of protecting me. And right that minute I was more than happy to let him handle Momma.

29

JANUARY 1960

I dressed for bed, but I sure wasn't ready for sleep. I sat in my room and drew cartoons of spaceships—and missiles carrying bombs that dropped on Dennis's house down below. I didn't even know where he lived, but in my pictures he lived right next door to Blanche Shuford and there was a path going from one backdoor to the other. In my little story, both of their houses were on fire.

You would think with me putting all my anger onto those pictures that I could go to bed and sleep, but I didn't. I stayed awake for a long time. When I did sleep, I had stupid dreams—the same ones all night. The next morning I couldn't even remember what they were. I could hardly wait to get up, but when I did, my head hurt and my brain felt like smashed potatoes.

All the way to school I kept thinking about that talk I had with Dennis on the front steps of the school. I knew Mrs. Cunningham had sent us out there to make peace. I tried, but Dennis obviously hated my guts. I thought then that it would be easiest just to avoid him.

But after last night I was done avoiding. Before the bell rang, I cornered Dennis in the back of the room. I might have kept my mouth shut if Mrs. Cunningham had been in the room, but she wasn't.

"You're in trouble," I said.

"Whatchu talking about?"

"You know exactly what I'm talking about. Why'd you go running to your precious grandmother, telling her my family's business? If you're trying to get my family in trouble, it's not gonna work."

Of course that part wasn't true. As far as I could tell, it *was* working. But I wasn't about to give him the satisfaction of knowing it.

"We'll see about that," said Dennis. "My family knows what your family is up to and we'll make sure you don't get by with it."

"Oh, yeah? Well, guess what. Your precious grandmother might be president of the Home Demonstration Club, but she's not in charge of the world. And she's sure not in charge of my family. We Honeycutts have a mind of our own, and we're going to do whatever we think is right. So don't try to stop us."

I was bluffing. Honestly, my family didn't exactly agree on what was right. And no wonder—because nobody else did either. If they did, we wouldn't be seeing all those stories about integration and violence in the news.

Dennis just smirked. That was all it took for me to

lay into him. I should've thought about how it would get me in trouble, but mostly I thought about how mad my momma was when she came home last night. It was all Dennis's fault. His and Blanche Shuford's. They were my enemies, and I sure didn't want to be friends with either one of them—no matter what Abraham Lincoln or Mrs. Cunningham had to say about it.

I smacked my fist into his ear. It felt so good I went after him again. But his fists were flying too. Next thing I knew we were both on the floor. I almost had him pinned when I felt someone pulling me off him.

Uh-oh. It was Mrs. Cunningham. "Boys! What is the problem?"

"He—he—he started it," said Dennis. He was still on the floor shaking his head like he was trying to get his senses back—not that he ever had any. "I was—I was minding my own business and here comes Jackie and starts smart-mouthing me. Then he hits me. For no reason at all."

"Liar," I said. "I had plenty of reason."

"Jackie!" said Mrs. Cunningham. "Be quiet! And go wait for me in the hall. Dennis, pull yourself together and go to your seat."

"Wait a minute," I said. "*He's* getting off scot-free?"

"Jackie." The sound in Mrs. Cunningham's voice shut me right up.

"Yes, ma'am," I said. I walked past my classmates, or

maybe I stumbled—at least that's what it felt like. Every last one of them was staring at me.

I hurried into the hall and stood there leaning against the wall—taking deep breaths and holding my aching head. A little kid went by, probably delivering some papers to the principal's office. She looked at me like I was an alien from outer space. "What're you staring at?" I growled.

She ducked her head and hurried away, but I saw how her face puckered up when I said that.

I felt like a creep for acting like a big bully. That's not who I was. I was just grumpy, that was all. And tired from not getting sleep. And mad because me and my family didn't do anything to deserve what Dennis's family was doing to us.

Mrs. Cunningham came out. After she asked the teacher across the hall to keep an eye on her class, she took me to the teachers' lounge.

There was a couch in there and she motioned for me to sit. Then she pulled up a straight-backed chair and sat right in front of me. "Talk to me, Jackie. I saw you hit Dennis. What motivated you to go after him?"

I didn't want to start crying, but I'd been on the verge of tears ever since I scared that little girl. Now, I couldn't hold back. It's hard to talk when you're blubbering like a baby but I told Mrs. Cunningham everything. All about Blanche Shuford fussing at my mother and then Momma coming home and yelling at me. I told her about me confronting Dennis and him threatening my family. I told her he smirked at me so I hit him. "All we did was be nice to somebody in the middle of a snowstorm," I said. "What's wrong with that?"

Mrs. Cunningham reached out and put her hand on my arm, and *that* just made me cry harder.

"Jackie," she said. "Sometimes we do the right thing and it doesn't pay off the way we think it will. It might even bring more trouble on our heads. But that's not a reason for doing the wrong thing. And hitting Dennis was wrong."

She stood up and went into the little bathroom that was in the lounge. When she came back she had a roll of toilet paper. "Here," she said. "Blow your nose and pull yourself together. I'm going to let you work in here for a while. You can't get by with fighting, Jackie. I could tell you to write a sentence one hundred times—maybe something like *I will not start fights*. But what good would that do? Instead I want you to write a paragraph telling me another way you could have responded to the situation with Dennis and his grandmother."

She headed for the door. "I'll send someone up here with notebook paper and a pencil. They'll slide it under the door and leave again." She opened the door and stepped into the hall, but then she turned back for a second. "And Jackie, the problem between your mother and Dennis's grandmother isn't something *you* can fix. *I'll* handle Dennis. Understand?"

"Yes, ma'am," I said. What else could I say? She was the teacher, and I sure hoped she'd set Dennis straight. But I didn't see how she could straighten Blanche Shuford out.

At least she hadn't sent me to the principal's office for a licking. I wasn't too thrilled about her writing idea, though. It would be easier to fill a page with the same stupid sentence one hundred times.

Soon I heard footsteps heading toward that door and then the paper and pencil poked beneath it. I waited for the footsteps to go away again, but instead someone tapped on the door. I opened it, expecting to see Wayne standing there. But it was Pamela.

"Sorry about what happened," she said. "But Jackie, I think you and your whole family are really brave."

Pamela didn't wait for me to respond. She just turned and left.

I closed the door and picked up the paper and pencil. There was a page there with a poem in Mrs. Cunningham's handwriting—"If," by Rudyard Kipling. What did she want me to do with that?

Read it, I guessed. It was long and it said a whole bunch of things. But basically, what I took from it was to not let Dennis get to me. Do the right thing even when others didn't.

It sounded so easy. But it wasn't.

I sat at a table against the wall and worried about what to write. What did Mrs. Cunningham expect me to say—that I should have come to school with a gift for Dennis? Give him my favorite comic book? Ha! I wasn't about to let him rip Jackie Robinson all to pieces.

While I sat there, I heard classes going by on their way to the library or outside to recess. Sometimes kids talked and teachers yelled at them to be quiet in the halls. Doors opened and closed and a bell rang for morning break. I heard the clock on the wall tick-ticking. And something about all those ordinary sounds helped to settle my insides. I realized I didn't feel so angry anymore.

I still didn't know how to handle Dennis or Blanche and I didn't know what to do about Momma being upset, but I realized that letting some time pass changed how I felt. So that's what I wrote. I said that I shouldn't have acted so fast when I was upset. I could have kept my big mouth shut and waited to see what happened. I could've taken some time to think through what to say to Dennis. I wrote that maybe if I'd done that, I would have come up with a better solution. Maybe I would even be like Jackie Robinson and not fight back.

I still wasn't sure if that was possible.

30

JANUARY 1960

I reckon Mrs. Cunningham had herself a heart-to-heart with Dennis because he kept his distance after that.

The New Year was moving along pretty fine. Then one day it got really sweet because a package came in our mailbox—from the Bradleys. The box rattled a little when I shook it. Momma opened it up and gave a little squeal. "Chocolates! How sweet!"

I started to rip the cellophane off the box, but Momma grabbed my wrist. "Jackie! Where's your manners? First, we read the note." She opened the envelope that came with the candy, pulled out a card, and read the message aloud.

Dear Mr. and Mrs. Honeycutt,

Words cannot express our gratitude for the generous hospitality you extended to our entire family on New Year's Eve and the following day. We know how unexpected the circumstances

170

were and recognize the considerable risk you
took in welcoming us into your home. It is
evident where Ellie gets her kindness and
concern for justice.

If there is anything we can do to repay you,
please let us know. Next time you're in
Winston-Salem we would love to have you
join us for a meal.

Please accept the chocolates as a small token
of our heartfelt appreciation.

Sincerely,
William & Virginia Bradley

There were other notes in the package. One was from Maribelle saying what a good friend Ellie was and how happy she was to meet our family. She even sent greetings to Lucy!

Colt and Luther had written notes too. "Look at that," said Momma. "Such polite boys."

Luther's note was polite for sure. But he didn't write any more than he had to. Colt's was my favorite.

Dear Jackie,

Thank you for letting me sleep at your
house and make a snow cow with you. Now
here is a riddle.

*What do you call a snowman in summer
time?*
A puddle. Ha-ha-ha!
Here's another one.
What do snow cows like to eat?
Ice Krispies! Mooooo!

Yours truly,
Colt

That cracked me right up. He even drew a picture of
a snow cow!

Daddy took out his pocketknife and made a slit in
the cellophane. He lifted the lid on those chocolates. First
he offered one to Momma, and she took a cherry cordial.
When it was my turn, I picked one with a fudge filling.

"We'll get them out again on Sunday," said Momma.
"And share them with the family."

On Sunday, after we ate our meal and each had a
slice of cake, Momma passed the box around. And when
that was done Ann Fay said she had some good news.
She reached over and pulled an envelope out of Junior's
shirt pocket. "Guess what it is!"

"A letter?" said Ida.

"Bingo!" said Ann Fay. "I heard back from Imogene.
Want to hear what she said?"

She didn't wait for us to agree. Of course we wanted
to hear.

Dear Ann Fay,

*Thank you for getting in touch. After all
these years, I cannot believe you found my letter.
I know I have your letters somewhere because I
don't throw anything away. I still live in
Greensboro but not at the old address. That is
my parents' home.*

*I am married to a good man and we have
three children, ages 8, 6, and 4. They keep me
busy. Maybe we can meet sometime. Wouldn't
that be fun?*

There was more to the letter, details about Imogene's
family and how she was getting along after having had
polio. Ann Fay got choked up reading it. "I can't believe
she wrote me!" she said. "Junior, one of these days you're
gonna have to take me back to Greensboro to find her."

"Of course, my lady," said Junior. "Your wish is my
command."

Maybe it was Ann Fay hearing from Imogene that
finally pushed me out the door with that calendar for
Thomas. The two of them reaching out to each other
gave me the guts to do the same thing. Also, I'd been
thinking about Maribelle working up the nerve to
touch Lucy. And how she planned to go to that march in
Greenville, not knowing if she could end up getting
hurt.

It seemed like taking a calendar to Thomas was the least I could do.

I walked fast, hoping to get rid of my nervousness. For some reason, the idea of talking to Thomas was scarier than standing in front of the whole school and saying that prayer. Mostly because I had a feeling I'd just be bugging him.

His dogs came running out to meet me—barking the whole way. So naturally, that got the family's attention. One of Thomas's sisters opened the door and stared at me. She didn't bother calling off the dogs.

I talked to them in a quiet voice, telling them to take it easy and I wasn't there to do anybody harm. "You know me," I told them. "We met before. Remember?"

Then I heard Thomas. "Hush!" he yelled. "Leave him alone."

The dogs stopped yapping and ran back to the porch. Thomas met me at the bottom of the steps. His little sister, the one he'd bounced around while singing at that church meeting, came out and hung on to his leg. He picked her up and told his other sister to go inside and shut the door.

"Hey, Thomas," I said. "Merry Christmas."

Thomas squinted and even frowned a little. "Christmas is come and gone," he said.

"Yeah. I'm late, but I brought you a present." I held out the gift and his little sister reached for it.

"Uh, thank you." Thomas didn't look too excited. Or even interested, if you asked me.

"Aren't you going to open it?" asked his sister.

"You open it, Lettie," said Thomas. He turned it over and told her to be careful. "Momma will want to reuse that wrapping paper," he said. He pulled off the bow and stuck it in Lettie's hair.

Thomas liked the calendar. I could see it from the way his face went kind of soft when he saw the birds on the front. He almost smiled but he was trying not to let on how he felt. I could see that too. "Nice of you to think of me," he said.

He put Lettie on the porch floor. "You're shivering," he told her. "Take that bow and paper to Momma." Then he sat on a step and leafed through the calendar.

"It's got birds on every page. I thought you might like it."

"It's real nice. Thank you." Then he stood up. "I didn't get you anything."

"That's okay. I wasn't expecting you to. Only reason I have that calendar is, Daddy brought it home from the feed mill."

Thomas stood and I could tell he was ready to go inside again. I didn't blame him. It was cold out there and I hadn't exactly told him I was coming. Still, would it hurt him so much to show a little gratitude for the effort?

"I'm gonna head for home," I told him. "Maybe I'll see you at the river come warm weather."

"I don't know," he said.

And that was the end of that. I headed out the road. Sometimes I wondered why I even bothered with Thomas Freeman. He never did trust me, and a few bird pictures on a feed store calendar wasn't going to change that.

31

FEBRUARY 1960

When I stopped by the Hinkle sisters' after school, Miss Pauline was sitting in her wheelchair by the basement door. It was wide open and the stairway light was on.

"Hey, Miss Pauline," I said. "Do you need me to get you something from downstairs?"

"No. I'm just waiting for the flash. When it comes, we're going to the basement. You too, Jackie. Duck and cover."

"Yes, ma'am," I said. I wasn't about to argue with Miss Pauline even if her mind was mixed up. But was she really planning to sit and wait for Russia to drop a bomb on us? She might as well just move on down there.

Momma carried the Scrabble game into the kitchen. "Miss Pauline, let's play a game. Maybe Jackie will join us."

I shook my head, but Momma didn't let that stop her. "Sit down, Jackie. Draw some letters from the pile. Miss Pauline will help you."

"I will not play that game," said Miss Pauline. "And I

won't help the boy play it. How can you be so frivolous at a time like this? I'm ashamed of you, Myrtle." She reached to the shelf beside her and turned up the volume on the radio. "No talking," she said. "I'm listening for important announcements."

Momma just looked at me and gave her head a shake. According to her, Miss Pauline seemed perfectly normal some days and then, at other times, she was completely unreasonable. I could see which kind of day this was.

Miss Pauline stayed right by the stairs, twisting her handkerchief and shuffling her feet like she was practicing to use them. Every so often she adjusted the radio dial, changing from one station to another as if the last one wasn't telling her what she wanted to hear.

Finally she tuned in Carl McIntire. It must have been on some faraway station because mostly I heard static. But I did hear him say that communists in America were trying to inspire hate between the races.

If you asked me, that didn't make any sense. Because civil rights meant all people should be treated equally.

So there I was—stuck listening to that man and playing a spelling game with my mother. And I knew that after all the times she'd played with Miss Pauline, Momma was tired of Scrabble. So after we each put three words on the board, I told her I was done.

"May as well be," said Momma. We poured our letters back into the bag and I went to the living room.

Miss Dinah was working on a jigsaw puzzle at the

table by the window, so I sat down to put some pieces in. "I'm sorry about my sister," she said. "Your momma and I both explained that the Russians won't be bombing us, but she's not listening to reason. Do you realize she had your momma take a thermos of coffee down there? And sandwiches. Just in case we see the flash and need to take cover. Jackie, the mice will get to those sandwiches faster than she can."

I could sure see how Miss Pauline was hard on Momma's nerves. Right now she even had me on edge. But working on that puzzle helped to calm me. I stayed until Bessie came to take her shift. Then Momma and I walked home together. When we left, Miss Pauline was still by the basement door.

"I declare," said Momma. "I don't envy Bessie, trying to get that woman into her bed tonight."

Later, when we were sitting down to supper, Daddy switched on the radio. Momma came right behind him and almost turned it off. I guess she thought better of it because she stopped herself and adjusted the volume instead. But I knew she'd had enough of radio noise for one day.

The man on the radio was saying that over in Greensboro four Negro college students had gone into a Woolworth store and sat down at a lunch counter where seats were reserved for white customers only. The staff refused to sell them coffee and doughnuts, but they just stayed. Finally, when the store manager couldn't convince them to leave, he closed the whole lunch counter. And why? Because Negroes weren't supposed to sit and eat with white people.

"*This* is the start of something," said Momma. "And it could turn ugly in a hurry. I don't think I can bear more news of unrest in this world." Now Momma *did* get up and turn the radio off.

Daddy shrugged and let it go, but after supper he suggested she go lie down and rest. "We men will clean up the kitchen," he said. "Right, Jackie?" After Momma disappeared into her room, he said, "Jackie, your momma is carrying the cares of the world on her shoulders right now. You and me will have to be extra patient with her."

Momma was right about things getting ugly. Three days after that radio announcement, television cameras were at that Woolworth store. And who did we see but Ellie's friend Maribelle, sitting with some other Negroes at the lunch counter and reading a big fat book—like she expected to be there for a long time.

"Look," I said. "It's Maribelle Bradley!"

Some white troublemakers crowded up behind Maribelle and her friends. We couldn't hear what they were saying, but anybody could see they were up to no good. After what she'd told me in the barn, I figured Maribelle was scared, but honestly she wasn't showing it. One of the boys leaned in real close to her and blew cigarette smoke in her face. She kept her eyes on her book and didn't flinch or bat an eyelash.

I jumped up and yelled at the television, "Smack 'em with that big book, Maribelle!"

The camera moved away, so I didn't know what happened next. But Daddy grabbed my hand and pulled me onto the sofa. "If Maribelle fights back, *she'll* be the one getting hurt," he said.

Daddy was right and I knew it, but all the same, it burned me up to see how they treated her. This was exactly what she and Ellie were practicing for at those passive resistance workshops. But still, how could a body learn to take that kind of meanness without fighting back?

I thought about Thomas standing by his mailbox, working his fists in his pockets. I could feel again how mad he was at me for telling his mother that old drunk had hit him with a bottle. He could have socked me good. But he'd kept his anger pushed down.

I didn't think I could do that. But I guessed I'd never had to. Not the way colored people did. Because like Thomas told me when I went to his house that Sunday afternoon, Negroes couldn't respond to a white man's anger. If they did, things would just get worse.

Thank goodness, Dennis had left me alone ever since our fight. But at school the next day, he slipped up behind me at the water fountain. "I bet you think it's right what they're doing in Greensboro, don't you?

Because I heard you *love* eating with them."

I wanted to stick my fingers in the fountain and aim the water at his face. But instead I walked away. Maybe I *was* learning some self-control.

Over in Greensboro certain whites were agitated for sure. All week television and newspapers showed some tough guys walking past those lunch counters with chains and Confederate flags. Police kept a strict eye on everybody.

We didn't see Maribelle on television anymore, but it was hard not to worry about her because you could just feel that trouble was building. The Greensboro police said there was a powder keg of racial tension at the demonstrations. If the sit-downs continued, something could explode.

Then, on Saturday, when we were eating supper, the man on the radio said there was a bomb threat in the Woolworth store.

It turned out to be nothing. Just a hoax. But Woolworth closed the whole store for the rest of the day. And the protesters called an end to the sit-downs because the store manager agreed to negotiate with them. I reckoned we all breathed a big old sigh of relief when we heard that. Maybe they would work something out!

At Sunday dinner, the sit-downs were mostly what we talked about. Ann Fay said she hoped they kept up the demonstrations because after all her friend Imogene should not have to eat standing up at a lunch counter.

"And besides," she said, "we're talking about meeting one day. Maybe we could go in there and have lunch together. Now wouldn't that be something!"

"Ann Fay!" said Momma. "Stop talking crazy. It's not the least bit safe for you to get involved in such things. Think of your children. Your place is at home with them."

"Oh, Momma," said Ann Fay. "I'm not talking about demonstrating. I mean later—after those young people get the rules changed. Maybe *then* I can eat there with Imogene."

Momma sagged in her chair. "Oh," she said.

"It's a good thing Ellie's in Winston-Salem," said Ida. "Otherwise she'd be sitting at that lunch counter with Maribelle."

That Sunday was our one day of rest from worrying—because on Monday, some students staged a sit-down protest at Woolworth in Winston-Salem.

32

FEBRUARY 1960

"Ellie's right there with them," said Momma. "I just know it."

But evidently Ellie wasn't in on it, because the newscaster said that all the protesters were students from a Negro college.

"Oh, good. I'm going to call and warn her to stay out of it." Momma headed toward the phone but then stopped. "No, I won't. If it hasn't crossed her mind yet, I sure don't want to put it there."

Of course Ellie didn't need Momma to give her ideas. She had plenty of her own. We saw that for sure a few days later. There she was on television, all bundled up in her coat and scarf, carrying a sign that said EQUALITY FOR ALL. There were protesters marching behind her. Coloreds and whites both. Holding up signs with opposite messages.

Momma gasped when she saw her. "Oh, Ellie," she moaned. "Please be careful."

That night Daddy had nightmares again. I heard him

hollering through the walls, and then I heard Momma's voice. "Leroy, wake up. It was just a dream."

"Huh? Where am I?"

"Home, Leroy. You're at home. The war is over. Hush now." Their voices settled into a low hum that went on for a long time. Part of me wanted to wrap my comforter around me and go curl up on the foot of their bed. When I was little, if I had a bad dream, I could crawl right between them and go back to sleep. But now, I had to be scared all by myself.

I wondered what they were talking about in there. War with Russia? Atom bombs? Did Momma have to make promises to Daddy like she did to Miss Pauline, reminding him that Russia wouldn't be interested in attacking little old us?

When I stopped to think about it, Daddy was right. Momma did have a lot on her shoulders. Helping Daddy through war dreams. Worrying over Ellie and if she should be involved in civil rights. And trying to figure out whether to believe Blanche Shuford when she said race mixing was part of a communist plot. My mind went to all sorts of places—from fear of Ellie getting herself hurt, to the bad things that could happen to all of us. Russia *could* bomb us. Communism *could* take over our country and we'd lose our freedom altogether. What if that radio preacher Miss Pauline listened to was right? It was hard to know who was telling the truth anymore.

I pulled my blankets up around my shoulders to

block the cold air and hoped that tomorrow would be sunny and cheerful.

But Saturday was gray as a tin roof and the weatherman predicted snow before the day was out. "Surely Ellie won't be out demonstrating in this weather," said Momma.

I wouldn't have put it past her, but I kept that to myself. The snow started before noon and went on into the night. Church was canceled on Sunday, and Momma said that was a gift straight from heaven because there was bound to be a fuss from somebody over Ellie being on TV.

Schools were closed on Monday, but by Tuesday I had to face the music. The minute I stepped onto the bus, I heard Charlie, who was near the back, yell out. "Was your sister on television? My momma said she was."

Good grief! I gave him a confused look, trying to throw him off.

At school, Dennis was slouching by the side door and I had a feeling he was on the lookout for me. Why else would he be standing there shivering in the cold? Sure enough, the moment I reached the top step, he went inside and let the door slam in my face.

"Dennis, you're a stinking coward," I yelled. He didn't want to get in trouble at school because it could lead to a licking at home, but that wouldn't stop him from finding ways to aggravate me.

When I got on the bus that afternoon, a little girl

handed me a slip of paper. "Some boy told me to give this to you," she said.

After I sat down, I unfolded the note. In Dennis's handwriting, it said, *Guess what! Your favorite teacher can't protect you all the time. And you ain't heard the last of me.*

I crumpled the paper. What did he think he could do to me?

Evidently, the sit-down protests were making him real nervous. Lots of people were worked up because they were spreading to other cities. Not just in North Carolina. But all across the South—from Virginia to Texas and Tennessee and Florida.

I wondered what Thomas was thinking about all this. Would he ever go into the Hickory Woolworth store and sit at the lunch counter? No one around here had even tried it. If they had, we'd have read about it in the newspaper or heard it on the radio.

I imagined the two of us going there together. Me ordering a sandwich and sliding it over to Thomas. It was just a wild idea. He'd never go there with me, and I'd be shaking in my boots if we did. I hadn't practiced passive resistance the way Ellie and Maribelle had. I wanted Thomas and Jackie Robinson and other Negroes to be treated right, but I'd never have the courage to do more than run my mouth at school. I wasn't likely to take a chance on being beat up or going to jail over it!

Police in Raleigh had arrested protesters. And I read

in the paper that Dr. Martin Luther King was telling Negroes they should be willing to fill the jails to gain their rights.

Then, one evening in late February, the news showed a picture of police in Winston-Salem handcuffing a group of protesters. We didn't see who all they loaded into their paddy wagon. But some of them were white, and the reporter said they were students from Wake Forest College!

33

FEBRUARY 1960

Momma was on her feet and reaching for her coat on the hook by the door. "We've got to go! What if they hurt her?"

"We're not going anywhere," said Daddy. "We don't even know if she was arrested."

"Leroy Honeycutt, this is Ellie we're talking about. If students from Wake Forest were part of the demonstration, we both know she was one of them."

"But what if she wasn't?" asked Daddy. "Winston is a long way to go on a wild-goose chase. We'll call her dormitory. Go ahead. Call."

"Now?" asked Momma. "It's only seven o'clock. It'll be expensive."

"Driving to Winston is expensive," said Daddy. "And besides, it'll be worth a long-distance call to put your mind at ease."

Momma nodded and headed for the phone. But she stopped and turned. "What if she *is* in jail? Maybe I don't want to know."

"Go *on*!" said Daddy. He was losing patience with her. Or maybe it was fear making him yell. It seemed like we were all on edge nowadays.

We waited while Momma called the operator and someone in Ellie's dormitory answered the phone. But I could tell from Momma's side of the conversation that my sister wasn't around.

My mother was right—Ellie was probably in jail.

Momma slumped onto a kitchen chair. I reckoned she had run out of steam by now, because she didn't insist on going to Winston-Salem. "What will you do, Leroy? Bail her out?"

"I'm gonna sleep on it," said Daddy. "Maybe this is for the best. Spending the night in jail might convince Ellie just how serious this is. But Myrtle, if she's dead set on participating in the movement, you and I both know we can't stop her."

"Oh, Leroy, you make it sound so easy," said Momma. "But people will find out and there could be no end of trouble. Blanche is already turning my friends against me."

Whatever Blanche knew, Dennis would hear for sure. He'd already promised I hadn't heard the last of him. But what could he actually do, since the only time I saw him was at school? Mrs. Cunningham had her eye on him and me both. I could feel it. *See* it.

Daddy reheated some leftover coffee and poured a cup for himself and one for Momma.

I sat at the table and tried to answer questions about North Carolina soldiers in the Civil War. But there was so much swirling around in my mind that didn't have a thing to do with North Carolina history. I mostly doodled on the edge of my paper—not thinking much about what I was drawing until I realized I'd made a picture of Ellie behind bars.

The phone rang and Momma jumped. But Daddy picked it up. "Hello. Yes, we did call. Where are you, Ellie?" Daddy held the receiver so that Momma and I could hear.

"I'm in my dorm now, but I worked late tonight. There was an incident, you know."

"You're not in jail?"

"No. And I'm so frustrated I didn't get arrested."

"What?" Daddy shook his head. "Myrtle, did you hear that?"

Momma let out a big old sigh of relief.

"After Mr. Bradley saw me on television last week, he said I can't protest anymore—not as long as I'm working for him. And Daddy, I know that's out of respect for you and Momma. For heaven's sake, he's not stopping his own daughter from demonstrating. But he has to protect me, the white girl. His logic is that since I want to be a lawyer, I need to practice the legal side of things. Go with him to negotiations. Tomorrow, we meet with city officials and store owners about the sit-downs. I'll be transcribing for him. But at least that's *something* for the cause. Right, Daddy? Is Momma listening?"

"Yes, yes, Ellie, I'm here." Momma's voice shook. She dabbed at her eyes. "I'm so relieved you're not in jail."

"Oh, Momma. Dr. Martin Luther King says there's no shame—just dignity—in going to jail for a good cause. And anyway, if I *had* been arrested tonight I'd be out by tomorrow. Mr. Bradley and some businessmen are posting bail."

Ellie was a bundle of energy—so excited about the whole thing because she really believed they could make a difference. When we hung up the phone Momma said, "I bet that girl doesn't sleep a wink tonight. But, one thing for sure, *I'll* rest easier."

34

MARCH 1960

Staring into the darkness of my bedroom, I couldn't get Thomas off my mind. Would he want to eat hamburgers and a milkshake at a lunch counter with me? Or go to the same school I did?

Whenever I came around he didn't seem much interested in race mixing. But then again, maybe it was just *me* he didn't like. I thought back to that day when I took my Jackie Robinson comic book to the river. He seemed proud that Robinson was working for civil rights, and for about five whole minutes we had a friendly conversation.

But then he turned on me. Accused me of having a guilty conscience. Like he suddenly remembered that he didn't trust me. But still, I was confused. If Thomas was carrying a grudge about me throwing that apple at him, why did he hunt me up after the fair? He even seemed sorry that Lucy didn't win. He talked me into going fishing, and I thought he wanted to be my friend after all. But then that drunk showed up. After that, everything I did was wrong.

I turned onto my belly and pulled the covers over my head. I was done with trying to figure Thomas out. And I sure didn't want to think about throwing that apple. I needed sleep.

When I woke up, the house felt extra quiet. The room was bright like when we had a full moon. I sat up in bed and listened, and then I knew what it was. I ran to the window and pulled back the curtain. Sure enough— the whole backyard was covered in white. The shed, Momma's clothesline, and the sandbox I used to play in.

It looked like there'd be no school today. When day-light came, I had to trudge through blustery snow to feed Lucy. I gave her fresh hay, some oats, and water from the barrel. Then I heard someone hollering my name and clanging on a bucket to get my attention.

"Well, Lucy, I think I hear Bessie calling me now. And you know what that means—a woodstove and some-thing hot to drink." I headed for the Bledsoes' backdoor.

Bessie put a cup of hot cocoa in my hands and set a bowl of warm bread pudding on the small table beside the rocking chair. I drank the cocoa so fast it burned my tongue, but I didn't care.

Ann Fay was feeding Gerianne and Bunkie breakfast, but she wanted to talk about Ellie. "I talked to Momma this morning," she said. "She told me Ellie was mad about not getting arrested."

"Yeah. Can you believe it?"

"I know your momma's relieved," said Bessie. "But

even if Ellie *was* in jail your family should just hold your heads high and not let other people worry you none. Respect yourselves and others will respect you too."

Hmm. Bessie should tell *that* to Dennis Aiken and his grandmother.

"But you know how Blanche Shuford is," I said. "She was rude to Momma at the last club meeting. And Momma thinks Blanche is turning the women against her. I don't know if she'll go back."

Bessie nodded. "Oh, I hope she will. Blanche has her opinions, and she pushes her ideas on others too, but those women are all goodhearted."

"Not Blanche," I said.

Bessie didn't answer. She just sort of bobbed her head from side to side like she was trying to make up her mind if she agreed with me or not.

"Do *you* like her?" I asked.

"I may not like everything Blanche does or says, but let's just say I understand her. Sometimes people are just doing the best they can, Jackie—under *their* circumstances, anyway."

On the way home I kept thinking about Bessie saying she understood Blanche. What did she know about that woman that the rest of us didn't?

What little *I* knew about Blanche I'd heard from Momma. How she had a fine backyard with a goldfish pond and snowball bushes and beds of irises in every color. Each year when her magnolia tree bloomed she held a garden party with punch and fancy sandwiches. And she was downright snippy about race mixing.

From all I could tell, she wasn't one bit like Bessie Bledsoe, who made the best desserts and gave them away. She looked after the Hinkle sisters like they were her own flesh and blood. And I never heard her say a grumbly word about anybody.

That night the phone rang and Momma said it was for me. "It's probably Wayne," I said. "Hello."

"No, I'm *not* Wayne." That voice. I knew exactly who it was.

"Dennis?"

He started right off calling me names I won't repeat. Then he said, "Just because I can't touch you at school don't mean I won't find a way. I know where you *live*, Honeycutt."

I have to say he caught me off guard, so I stood there and stuttered for the longest time. Finally I got my wits about me and said, "You got the wrong number." I hung up the phone.

My hands felt sweaty for no reason, and suddenly I didn't feel so good. But I told myself he was just acting tough. He wouldn't be coming to my house.

With snow on the ground, nobody was going anywhere much. Daddy put chains on his tires and went back to work on Friday, and we went to church on Sunday. But schools didn't open on Monday or Tuesday on account of buses getting stuck on all the muddy roads.

Blanche Shuford decided the Home Demonstration Club should meet on Tuesday night. But Momma said she wasn't going. "I can't take one more lecture from that woman," she said. "But Leroy, if you're going up there to light the fire you can take my sewing machine. I volunteered it because the club is making a quilt to raffle at the fair next fall."

During the winter months Daddy always fired up the woodstove so the clubhouse would be warm when the women came. This time I rode along so I could help unload Momma's sewing machine. But when we got there, smoke was already coming out of the chimney and Blanche Shuford was standing by the stove—warming her hands.

"Thank you, but your services won't be needed," she said. Her voice was cold as all outdoors. "Clarence lit the fire. He brought extra wood in too."

"Yes, ma'am," said Daddy. He looked around. "Didn't see any sign of Clarence when we came in."

Blanche snorted. "Since he doesn't much care for sewing and women's conversations, he found someplace else to go."

"I have Myrtle's sewing machine in the truck," said Daddy. "She won't make it tonight."

Blanche waved him off with the back of her hand. "The other ladies are bringing machines. No use to drag Myrtle's in here." Then she changed the subject. "They say it's going to snow again. Starting at midnight."

"Yes, ma'am," said Daddy. "Have a good evening.'

Back in the truck, he hit the steering wheel with his fist. "She could've called and saved us the trouble. I sure don't mind if Clarence loads the woodstove, but I don't like her snubbing my wife. Of *course* she needed Myrtle's sewing machine. Your momma says there's never enough to go around."

"She's trying to punish us," I said. "On account of us having the Bradleys at our house. And now, Ellie being on television."

I didn't tell Daddy about Dennis threatening me because I didn't want him starting something up with Dennis's daddy. From the little I'd heard about that man, he wasn't somebody you wanted to mess with.

When I woke up in the morning the snow was coming down thick and the weatherman predicted eighteen inches. Or more! A year ago I would have been thrilled. But after two weeks of bad weather I was sick of all this cold dampness and slipping and sliding all the way to the barn.

Junior had asked me to milk for him this morning because a man up the highway needed help with his kerosene heater, so I was outside extra early. The world was gray and blustery, and I couldn't wait to get inside the barn.

Before I reached the door I heard Lucy bawling. At least I *thought* I did—except the sound didn't come from inside. "Must be the wind," I said. "Or my imagination."

I pushed the door open. "I'm here, Lucy." I couldn't see anything at first. I closed my eyes and all I saw was the brightness of the snow behind my eyelids.

Lucy was quiet. I shook my head, trying to get my eyes to adjust. When they did, I saw that her stable door was wide open. But Lucy wasn't there!

35

MARCH 1960

"Whoa!" I hollered. "Lucy!" I dashed around the barn, checking every stall, just in case Junior had moved her for some reason. But she wasn't in any of them. Where could she be?

Oh, no! The doors at the back of the barn were slid partway open. She'd gone out that way. But I was sure I'd shut her stable door last night. I always did.

I shoved the backdoors open and hollered some more. "Here, Lucy."

She was out there, bawling from somewhere near the back gate. What in the world? I ran through the snow. It was coming down thick now, but I saw her brown shape up against the fence. When I reached the gate I knew this was no accident because it was latched—with Lucy on the outside.

Somebody had put her there on purpose!

I flung the gate open and ran to her. Snot hung frozen from her nostrils. Her eyelids were crusted with snow.

"Lucy, who did this to you?"

I guess I forgot about being tired. All I could think of was talking Lucy into the barn. "You can do it, Lucy. Together we'll get there. How long have you been out here? All night, from the looks of it. Who did this?"

I just kept saying it. "Who did this? Who did this?" And I got madder with every step. And every step all I could think of was the one person who hated me for no reason at all. The one person who called me up and threatened me. "Dennis Aiken." He said he knew where I lived. But my cow? How did he know Lucy was in Junior's barn? Had I said something at school?

Probably. Me and my big mouth!

Finally we reached the barn. Inside, I brushed the snow off Lucy. She was trembling—great big shivers. "Oh, Lucy, I'd give anything for a hot summer day right now!"

I didn't have any lessons for what to do in a time like this. If only I could talk to Arnie. Or the Lutzes. They might know. I just did whatever came to my mind. I grabbed an old horse blanket from one of the stable doors and dried her off as best I could. I blew my warm breath onto her eyelashes and used my fingers to brush away the snow.

Her nostrils were half clogged with icy snot, so I cupped my hands around her muzzle and blew on them until they dripped. And then I led her into the stall. "Get down in the straw, Lucy." But I didn't need to tell her. She'd been standing for too long—waiting for me to open that gate. I brought in fresh straw and bunched it all around her.

"Rest now, Lucy. I'm gonna run for blankets."

I ran to the house and barged in. "Ann Fay, someone took Lucy out of the barn. I have to warm her up."

"What?" said Ann Fay.

"I need blankets. And towels and a hot water bottle. Oh, and warm water in a thermos."

I grabbed the phone and called home. "Momma, send Daddy to the barn. Lucy's freezing." I hung up before she could ask any questions, and then I asked Ann Fay to call Arnie for me. But I couldn't wait around to see what he said. I took the towels and blankets and a bottle of warm water and stumbled to the barn.

Lucy's big eyes begged me for help. "It'll be okay, Lucy," I said. "I brought some warm water for you." I put the flat, rubber water bottle against her belly. "There, maybe that'll help. And blankets, Lucy girl." I tucked them around her.

Junior had a bottle he'd used for feeding animals. I found it in a barrel in one of the stalls. I rinsed the bottle and poured the warm water into it. "Here, Lucy. Drink."

"Jackie! Whatever happened?"

Thank goodness, Daddy was there! The minute I heard his voice I starting bawling like a baby— blubbering out the story. "Lucy. Somebody let her out.

On purpose, Daddy. For pure meanness." I could hardly talk for crying. Daddy pulled me up against him and I thought maybe everything would turn out okay, but I still couldn't stop crying.

"There, there," he said. "We'll get her fixed up. What have you done so far? Is she dry?"

"Except her tail." I went to her tail and started working the ice out of it. "I'm trying to get her warmed up. Ann Fay gave me blankets. And a hot water bottle."

"I brought one too." Daddy put the warm bottle between the blanket and Lucy. "This other one's cooling down. Want me to get more hot water from the house? Or do *you* want to?"

I didn't want Daddy to go. He'd just got here. But I couldn't leave Lucy either. "Hurry," I said. "And ask Ann Fay if she called Arnie."

It seemed like forever, but when he came back, he had a two-gallon picnic jug with hot water. "Now we've got ourselves a supply. Look, Jackie. She's perking up. Your sister talked to Arnie. According to him, you're doing all the necessary things. I'm proud of you, son."

Daddy was right. Lucy's eyes were brighter, and she was starting to move around some.

We settled into the hay with her, and sometime along the way, I fell asleep between her and Daddy. I woke up when I heard Junior's voice.

Junior was not above cussing once in a while if he thought the situation demanded it. So that's what woke

203

me up. Of course, I had to tell him the whole story.

"Were there tracks?" he asked.

"I don't know. I didn't see any. But I wasn't thinking straight."

"Too much snow anyhow," said Daddy. "There wouldn't be tracks."

"Somebody's gonna regret this," said Junior. "Any idea who did it?"

While I was trying to figure out if I should tell them about Dennis threatening me, Daddy spoke up. "Best thing is to catch 'em in the act. We'll sleep here tonight for sure. Maybe they'll be back around. Although, with this snow, probably not. We'll take it one day at a time."

36

MARCH 1960

We cleaned out a stall next to Lucy's, and Daddy brought in a small kerosene heater and set it in a safe place away from the hay. I slept in that barn for the next two weeks. Daddy and Junior took turns staying with me.

Even Wayne came over and spent a couple of nights. The two of us built forts in the snow and tunnels in the haymow. I milked Junior's cow whenever he was out plowing other people's driveways and parking lots. Wayne helped me carry wood from the shed to Junior's back porch, and we played with Bunkie. But after a while, making snowmen wasn't fun. I was sick and tired of snow.

In all that time, nobody came back around to bother Lucy, so I started believing that she'd be okay. Finally the weather improved and school opened again, so I moved back home.

My first night back Ellie called to tell us that Wake Forest College had voted against integration. "I'm so upset!" she said. "The whole student body voted and we were about a hundred votes short of what we needed. After all the meetings and pep talks and flyers we put out! What is wrong with people? If a Christian college can't even admit my Negro friends, why would I expect Woolworth to open their lunch counters? Oh, I despise that Reverend Carl McIntire! You should hear the students around here quoting him."

Ellie was sure fired up, but not like normal. Usually she was feisty and determined. Now she was mad and sad. "One fellow has been trying to enroll here for several years," she said. "We actually thought this would be the breakthrough. I'm just devastated for him." Ellie was crying when she hung up the phone.

There was something about that phone call from Ellie that got me upset too. I wandered out to the front porch and huddled on the cold steps and stared at the deep blue shape of Bakers Mountain ahead of me.

I thought I understood why Ellie cared so much. It was on account of those friends she'd made. Maybe Ann Fay hankering after Imogene had something to do with it, also. One thing I was figuring out was—as long as white people didn't know Negroes personally, we could never understand their viewpoint. Thomas had educated me on things I never even thought about before.

Sitting there, staring at Bakers Mountain, I realized I wanted to be more like Ellie. I wanted to speak up and do something important about civil rights.

But how? And where? Anything I said or did would get back to Momma. She had enough troubles on her shoulders already.

At school I kept my eye on Dennis—trying to sort out if he looked guilty. He mostly left me alone, which, if you asked me, was kind of suspicious. But since I didn't have any proof, I couldn't exactly accuse him of trying to hurt my cow.

Still, he was the one who'd called me up, saying he knew where I lived. And that note he sent me said Mrs. Cunningham couldn't protect me all the time—which kind of explained why he would strike in the barn, where she couldn't do anything about it.

Dennis was definitely my number one suspect.

After missing so much school, we had to make up by going on Saturdays. On that first Saturday Junior was waiting for me when I got off the bus. "Miss Pauline has a job for us," he said.

"A job? What is it?"

"Beats me. But she says I'm gonna need your help."

We headed for the Hinkle sisters' backdoor, and Bessie let us in. "Miss Pauline is sure impatient today," she whispered. "And for some reason she's being very secretive."

We went to the living room, where the sisters were sitting. "Junior, we need you to build us something important," said Miss Pauline.

"Would you like a soft drink?" asked Miss Dinah.

"Not now," said Miss Pauline. "We need to talk about the fallout shelter."

But Miss Dinah got up and headed to the refrigerator anyway. Maybe she was done letting her sister boss her around.

Junior had been standing by Miss Pauline's wheelchair, but when he heard what Miss Pauline wanted, he reached for the chair behind him and sat down real fast. "A bomb shelter?"

"Don't act so surprised," said Miss Pauline. "Every household should have a fallout shelter. Junior, you could earn yourself a lot of money building those on the side. We're willing to pay you to practice on us. Then you'll be ready to make one for your little family."

Miss Dinah came back with two opened bottles of Cheerwine and handed one to Junior and one to me.

"The Russians have put a rocket on the moon," said Miss Pauline. "That means they can land a bomb on us. They could blow us all to pieces in a flash. But *not* if we're prepared. I intend to be ready."

"Uh, well, Miss Pauline," said Junior, "I don't know anything about building a bomb shelter."

"Junior, *that* is no excuse. You can make or fix anything you set your mind to. And I have these to help you out." Miss Pauline pointed to a stack of magazines on the coffee table. "*Popular Science* has published multiple examples. Study them and choose the fallout shelter with the best design. Don't worry about the cost. We have an account at Hickman Hardware."

Junior set his Cheerwine on the coffee table. He reached for the magazines and started flipping through the pages.

"Don't take too long figuring it out," said Miss Pauline.

"Uh, yes, ma'am," said Junior. "I will see what I can learn."

"At the bottom of the basement steps would be the best place. That way we can get to it in a hurry."

I sat there wondering how in the world Miss Pauline intended to get downstairs in an emergency. I guess she was reading my mind because she said, "I can go down on my backside."

Miss Dinah spoke up. "Junior, this will put my sister's mind at ease," she said. "We'll have Myrtle buy extra groceries for us and gather containers for collecting water. It'll make Pauline feel prepared for whatever may come."

"You should be preparing too, Junior, " said Miss Pauline. "I hope you're planning ahead for your babies."

"Uh, well, yes," said Junior. "But not quite like you mean. I'm not expecting the Russians to drop bombs on us anytime soon."

"Who knows when they might attack," said Miss

Pauline. "Why do you think Nikita Khrushchev visited the United States? To spy on us, of course. Promise me, Junior, that you'll start right away. I'll pay you. And Jackie, too."

I'd get paid for this? I sure wasn't expecting that. All of a sudden the idea of building a bomb shelter sounded pretty good.

"And Jackie, listen to me," said Miss. Pauline. She looked straight into my eyes. "Don't you breathe a word of this to anybody. Understand? There won't be room in that shelter for the whole neighborhood."

"Yes, ma'am," I said. It would nearly kill me not to tell Wayne or talk about it in current events. But I wouldn't dare disobey Miss Pauline.

On the way home I asked Junior, "Is Miss Pauline losing her mind? Or should we all have bomb shelters?"

Junior shrugged. "Old people can be extra fearful. Paranoid. And Russia *is* unpredictable. Miss Pauline's not the only person building a bomb shelter in this country. And to tell you the truth, I'm surprised she didn't come up with this sooner."

"Are you gonna do it for her?"

"I'm sure I will," said Junior. "When Miss Pauline speaks, I listen."

"I bet you couldn't say no if you wanted to."

"You're right," said Junior. "But there's more to it. Miss Pauline pulled me through a bad spell, you know. When I was about your age my pop died. I was angry and confused. She was my teacher and I wanted her to take it easy on me. Of course she didn't, and now I'm glad of it. If it wasn't for her, I'd be a school dropout. Miss Pauline won't be around forever, and I intend to treat her good while she is."

37

APRIL 1960

We worked on that bomb shelter on Saturday afternoons and some evenings. Junior figured out the design, and I did whatever he asked. Mostly I mixed concrete and helped carry it in buckets through the house and down the stairs. It was the heaviest work I'd ever done and I felt like quitting. Especially when Miss Pauline sat in her wheelchair at the top of the stairs, telling me to hurry. How was I supposed to hurry with a bucket of cement in my hands? Did she want me to fall down the stairs?

"We don't have time for you to dillydally around," she'd say. "The Russians are likely testing their weapons right this minute."

She could make a body downright nervous about bombs. Momma had said it was no use arguing with her, but one day I tried to. "But Miss Pauline, President Eisenhower and Khrushchev are discussing disarmament. They're actually talking about destroying their weapons."

"Don't be foolish, boy. It's all talk. Even if they agreed on such a thing, we'd have no way of knowing if the Russians actually did it. They could easily hide weapons from us. Go on now, Jackie. I'm not paying you to stand here and talk."

"Yes, ma'am." I hurried outside to mix up another bucket of concrete. I could sure see why Miss Dinah liked to escape outdoors once in a while. And I understood why Momma came home looking so worn down.

The sisters' closed-in back porch was filling up with extra canned goods, dried fruit, household supplies, and toilet paper. One day Junior even drove to the hardware store to pick up a special chemical toilet he'd ordered.

We finally finished the shelter. When Miss Pauline gave me that last five-dollar bill she hung on to my hand and I saw that she had tears in her eyes. "You've given me some peace of mind," she said. "I'm inclined to try that bed out the minute your mother makes it up."

We'd built three beds down there—one for each of the sisters and the other one for whoever was caring for them, when and *if* they ever needed the shelter. Now that it was built, Momma and Bessie would make the beds and stock the shelves.

Miss Pauline was bossy and even grumpy and unreasonable at times, but if you did something to please her then you knew you'd really accomplished something. And we had. I didn't know anyone else who had built a bomb shelter. Certainly not anybody in my class at school.

I got to wondering if any other house up or down

the highway had one. After all, Miss Pauline wasn't the only person worrying about Russian bombs. Deep down inside, all of us felt uneasy.

On the Monday after we finished, Momma came home from the Hinkle sisters' shaking her head. "I don't know how much longer I can look after Miss Pauline," she said. "If it wasn't for Bessie taking the weekends I might just lose my mind."

Daddy gave Momma a kiss and helped her remove her coat. He hung it for her on the hook by the door. "Might be time to move Miss Pauline to an old people's home," he said.

"Don't even suggest it." Momma headed for the kitchen to start on supper, so we followed her. "According to her, those places smell of urine and pine oil disinfectant. And besides that, how many of them have fallout shelters? No, sirree, Miss Pauline is not going anywhere. She sits by the basement door, worrying that the fire department whistle will announce an attack any minute. She's all set to crawl down those steps."

"I can't see how she's going to do that," I said.

"She's practicing. We went down and back twice today. She had to double-check everything in the shelter. Food supplies, toiletries, blankets, heater."

Momma pulled a pot with leftover soup out of the refrigerator and set it on the stove. "We went over the list at least three times," she said. "Please God, when I get old, don't let me be like that woman."

Daddy pulled Momma into his arms. "You don't have to do this, Myrtle. Someone else can care for the ladies."

"No," she said. "I have to. They've got no family."

"Miss Pauline can afford to hire someone."

"Leroy, who *else* is going to care about the sisters the way Bessie and I do?" Momma slipped out of Daddy's hug and started setting the table. "She may drive me to distraction, but I will not abandon her. Or Miss Dinah either. They're family—even if we aren't blood kin. It's like a marriage, Leroy—till death do us part."

Daddy took the drinking glasses out of Momma's hands and put them at our places on the table. "Just don't let it be the death of *you*, Myrtle."

38

APRIL 1960

Back at the beginning of April the lunch counter protests had started up in Greensboro again, because more than a month of negotiations hadn't done the Negroes a speck of good. They agreed that this time they wouldn't sit down and ask for service. Instead, just a few people at a time would march in front of the stores with their signs.

As far as I could tell, the stores were getting the better end of that deal. It seemed like the movement for Negroes eating with whites was losing steam. But Ellie didn't think so. She called one night and declared they were making great progress—especially in Winston-Salem, where she was working with Mr. Bradley. "If the stores in Winston open their lunch counters—and they will—then the ones in Greensboro will have to also," she said. "And just look at all the cities the movement has spread to. The Greensboro protests might be quiet, but in other places things are definitely heating up."

She was right about the movement spreading. I read about it in the paper every day and even started clipping and saving the articles. Now I had a new collection. Of course the stories were on the television too, along with news about Eisenhower and Khrushchev planning peace talks. I was pulling for both of them—peace talks and the lunch counters to open.

At school Mrs. Cunningham was getting us ready for our eighth-grade graduation program. She introduced us to music from *The King and I*, a movie about an English woman who went to the country of Siam to teach the king's children.

One of the songs was "Getting to Know You," about the teacher getting acquainted with her new students. If that song wasn't perfect for Mrs. Cunningham I didn't know what was. She sang along, and after we'd heard the chorus a time or two she motioned for us to sing with her.

Then she played "I Whistle a Happy Tune"—about whistling when you're scared so others won't know how you feel. When you do that you fool yourself into being brave. Mrs. Cunningham figured out real fast that Dennis Aiken could actually whistle a tune. She crooked her finger at him. "Come here, Dennis."

He shuffled to the front of the room. Mrs. Cunningham put her hands on his shoulders and looked him in the eye. "What a fine whistle you have there," she said. "Could you to do that for all of us?"

Red color crept up the back of Dennis's neck. He shrugged. "I guess so."

"Good. Now, let's turn around and face the class. Betty, play that song again."

Mrs. Cunningham stood behind Dennis with her hands on his shoulders, and when it got to the whistling part, he did it loud and clear while she stood there smiling and tapping along with her fingers. You could just tell from her big grin how happy she felt when one of her students could shine like that. Even Dennis Aiken!

The whole class broke out clapping and Dennis turned even redder. "I think you've got yourself a solo for graduation," said Mrs. Cunningham. She picked Gloria and Norma to sing "The School Song" from the movie.

She handed out a prayer and some poetry to be used in the program, and she asked Wayne to lead the audience in the Pledge of Allegiance.

Dennis was downright obnoxious about being chosen for a solo. Now he went around whistling that song just to show off. Except, if I was nearby, he whistled the *I Love Lucy* theme song.

"Ignore him," said Wayne. "He's just trying to get your goat."

"Yeah. And it's working. You know he threatened me and my family. And I still think he had something to do with locking Lucy out in that snowstorm."

39

APRIL 1960

Sometime early in the morning I heard Lucy mooing outside my window. I stayed real still, trying to figure out if she was in our yard or just in my dream. Then I heard her again, and this time I jumped out of bed and ran to the backdoor. Daddy was right behind me. I flung the door open. There in the dark, getting ready to open our screen door, was Junior.

"I brought Lucy home," he said. "I think she'll be safer here from now on."

"What happened?" I pushed past Junior and rushed to Lucy. "Did someone let her out again?"

"Worse." Junior sank onto the top step.

Daddy stood behind him, his light blue pajamas shining in the darkness. "What happened?" he asked. "It's too early for you to be milking. How did you know something was going on?"

"Happened last night," said Junior. "Ann Fay and the kids were at the Hinkle sisters' while Momma went to Home Demonstration. So I headed out to the barn to do some cleanup, and someone was in there. But whoever it was heard *me* before I heard *him*. By the time I was inside he'd run out the back, leaving the door open. Only sign of him was a few footprints in the mud. Lucy's stable door was open and she had backed into the corner. I had my flashlight with me, and here's what I found in her stall." Junior pulled an evergreen branch out of his pocket. "Yew," he said. "Don't take much to kill a cow."

"Someone tried to *poison* her?" I felt light-headed. And sick to my stomach. I buried my face in Lucy's hide and wrapped my arms around her neck, breathing in her sharp sweet scent.

"Look," said Junior. "She's fine. Whoever it was dropped the yew just inside her stall and ran. But thank heaven I came when I did or she'd be dead by now."

Junior went on with his story, telling how he'd moved his cow and Lucy into an unused stall with fresh hay and slept right there with them. "Brought Lucy home before daylight so's nobody would see me," he said. He shook his finger at me. "Don't breathe a word of this. Not even to your friend Wayne. Nobody knows Lucy is here now. Got that?"

"Yeah, of course." Junior wasn't getting any argument from me.

"We'll catch the rattlesnake that's behind this if I have to sit out there every night with my shotgun."

"Hold it right there, son." Daddy sat down beside Junior. "I won't have you doing anything rash."

220

"I'm not gonna hurt anybody," said Junior. "But Leroy, you better believe that the sound of my gun going off will send a message. Loud and clear."

"We should call the sheriff," said Daddy.

"Yes, sir," said Junior, "we should. But what's he gonna do? It's been a month since the last incident. Sheriff sure don't want to sleep in my barn every night."

By now, Momma was standing at the screen door, listening. "I've got coffee on," she said. "You can talk inside."

But Junior said he wanted to help me settle Lucy in the lean-to and then he'd best be getting home to his family. "Gotta get to work."

He walked with me and Lucy out to the pasture and opened the gate for us. "Got any ideas who might be after your cow, Jackie? Anything you're not telling us?"

"Only idea I got is Dennis Aiken," I said. "He hates me on account of us being sympathetic to coloreds. Says we're communists."

"Hmm," said Junior. "Dennis Aiken. I'm gonna ponder that one."

"He's Blanche Shuford's grandson."

"Yup," said Junior.

"She wouldn't put him up to something like that, would she, Junior? Bessie says Blanche is a good woman even if she is snooty about some people. She said she understands Blanche."

Junior nodded. "I expect my momma probably does.

But Jackie, I know who Dennis is. Short little fellow. Right? Those weren't his footprints. There's a full-grown man behind this treachery."

A full-grown man? Who in the world? I just couldn't imagine what man would be after my cow. And for what reason?

When I went to school my mind was in that lean-to with Lucy. Mrs. Cunningham had us singing those graduation songs, but hearing Dennis whistle just grated on my nerves.

Later, when the other students took a morning break, Mrs. Cunningham asked me to stay behind. "Is everything okay, Jackie? You didn't sing along today."

"Uh, yes," I said. "Everything's fine. I just didn't feel like singing."

"You aren't having trouble with Dennis again, are you?"

"No," I said. "We ignore each other."

I knew from the way she tilted her head and squinted that she didn't believe me. "I'll take your word for it," she said. "But if you need to talk, let me know. And Jackie, I have a request."

"A request?"

"How would you like to make a speech at graduation?"

"A speech? At graduation? Me?"

"You, Jackie."

"Really?"

Mrs. Cunningham sat there nodding and smiling. "Jackie, you're a natural. Look how well you did with that prayer at our Christmas program—and with no time to practice even. You enunciate clearly and use your voice to hold attention. And I've noticed in class that you can get quite passionate about certain subjects." She winked.

Her words sure gave me a warm feeling. But a graduation speech with all the parents and grandparents listening? I didn't know what to think. It felt important, and Mrs. Cunningham asking made *me* feel important. Still, right now, with Lucy on my mind, I didn't know if I could focus on getting a speech ready. "What would I talk about?"

Mrs. Cunningham was still smiling at me. "If you get stuck, maybe I can help. But give it some thought first. You've spoken up about some important topics this year. Think about what you've learned and how you can apply that to the future. Be optimistic. Give your classmates some hope for what's ahead. Challenge them to help you make the world a better place."

I hoped she wasn't expecting me to talk about integration. Sure, I thought it was terrible how people treated Jackie Robinson and the Bradleys and Thomas's family too. I'd even talked about it in class. But I couldn't stand up and say *that* to a few hundred people who'd most likely disagree with me.

Ellie would do it. I knew she would. But Ellie didn't

have a cow that someone tried to kill. Besides, she was off in another city and didn't even see what Blanche Shuford was doing to Momma.

Later that night, after I was in bed, I thought back over what I'd learned this year. For one thing, I'd learned a lot about current events and how much they affected our lives. Mrs. Cunningham had tried teaching me to measure my words and not react too quickly when I was upset. She also wanted us to learn that we could turn enemies into friends.

But I was failing that lesson—with Thomas and Dennis both.

I guess I dropped off to sleep thinking about that speech, and sometime in my dreams I heard a knocking sound and a voice calling for Daddy.

I shook myself awake and realized that the pounding I heard was at our backdoor. Junior was out there calling Daddy's name. I jumped out of bed and headed for the door, but Junior had let himself in already, and Daddy was there.

"Leroy, I need you," said Junior. His voice was hoarse and shaky. "It's Miss Pauline. I think she's—" Junior stopped, like he couldn't make himself say the words. He grabbed his head with both hands and pressed his palms against it. "I—I think she's dead."

40

APRIL 1960

We guessed it was the bomb shelter that killed Miss Pauline. She couldn't stop fretting over it, worrying about how to get down there at a moment's notice. Sometime in the night she must have decided to practice on her own.

Bessie said she heard a thumping sound and got up to check. "I went straight to her room, but she wasn't in bed. She never leaves her bed without ringing her bell." Bessie had that little china bell in her hand now, and it made soft tinkling sounds because her hands were trembling so much. "She didn't answer when I called, so I started searching the house. The door to the basement was open. I flipped the switch and that's when I saw . . ." Bessie's mouth quivered, and a big old sob pushed the words aside.

She swiped at the tears that started to come, and then she gave up on that and covered her face with both hands. The bell crashed to the shiny wood floor and broke into pieces, but nobody seemed to care about that. Tears poured through her fingers and dripped into the

225

sleeves of her housecoat. Her soft, round body shook. "Have mercy!" she called out. "I never expected she'd try such a thing. I should have been listening for it."

Momma took her elbow and pulled her away from the broken glass. She wrapped her arms around Bessie and patted her head like she was a child. "No, no," she said. "Don't think that way. You were *always* listening for her bell. I imagine she wanted to do this on her own."

"But why didn't she turn on the light?" wailed Miss Dinah. "I don't understand that." Miss Dinah was slumped onto the sofa, hugging her housecoat around her and trembling all over. Her hair was a mess and her glasses were lopsided. She looked so tiny—like a broken doll thrown against the sofa cushions. "Oh, Pauline," she wailed. "What will I ever do without you?"

Momma stood there looking from Miss Dinah to Bessie. I knew she couldn't comfort both of them at the same time, so I went and sat beside Miss Dinah. I didn't know how I could help, but I thought of all the meals we'd shared, the puzzle making, and how we both loved Cheerwine. When I was little, we'd sit together on the sofa watching Lucille Ball. She liked to hold my hand, and when they showed scary information about what we should do in case of atom bombs, I always wanted to hold hers, too. But then I got too big and started pulling away, so she quit trying.

Now, I reached for her hand. It was cold and felt

so thin I thought it might break. But she gripped my fingers until I started worrying she might crush them. She slumped against me and moaned. But she didn't stay there for long because now Daddy and Junior were going down the stairs to fetch Miss Pauline.

"I don't want to be here," said Miss Dinah, and her voice was real agitated. She put her hand on my knee and pushed herself up off the sofa. "I have to get out of this house."

"Jackie, the keys are in my truck," said Junior. "Take her to Ann Fay. She's awake— waiting to hear how things are."

Miss Dinah almost walked out of the house in her nightclothes. She was already shivering. "Wait," I said. "Let me get your coat."

I went to the hall closet, and I guess I grabbed Miss Pauline's coat because it hung nearly to Miss Dinah's ankles. But she hugged it close and wouldn't let go. "It smells like her," she said. She buried her face in the fur collar.

It didn't take a minute to get to Junior's house. Ann Fay was at the door before we were out of the truck—a dark shape against the light in her kitchen. "Junior?"

I hopped out of the truck. "It's Jackie. Junior told me to bring Miss Dinah to you. She doesn't want to be in that house."

"Huh?" said Ann Fay. She hurried down the steps to

where I was opening the door for Miss Dinah. "How is Miss Pauline?"

It dawned on me that Ann Fay hadn't heard yet. "Miss Pauline is, uh—Ann Fay—Miss Pauline is dead." I whispered the word *dead* so Miss Dinah wouldn't hear it.

"Dead?" Ann Fay gasped and then she reached for the truck door and hung on. "What in the world? Oh, poor Miss Dinah."

Between us, we got Miss Dinah into the house and settled on a rocking chair.

"Poor thing. She's shivering." Ann Fay put water on the stove for making hot tea and cocoa, but Miss Dinah wasn't interested in either one.

I knew Ann Fay wanted to know the whole story, but she wouldn't ask me right then. She stood behind the rocking chair and ran her fingers through Miss Dinah's hair until it was nice and smooth. Finally she started singing. "*Nobody knows the trouble I've seen. Nobody knows my sorrow.*"

Tears ran down Miss Dinah's cheeks.

"That's not very cheerful," I said. "Can't you sing something else?"

"There's a time to laugh," said Ann Fay, "and a time to cry. This is a time for crying." Her lip started quivering, and the next thing I knew both of them were sobbing. A sharp pain stabbed at my throat.

I asked myself if this was really happening. Had

Junior got me awake out of a deep sleep or was I still dreaming? I put my elbows on the table and banged my head into my hands like that could wake me up and this would all be over.

But nothing changed. I was still there. My head was groggy, and there was a miserable burning inside my belly. Miss Pauline had died. In a bomb shelter that I helped build.

It was like someone had knocked a leg out from under a chair I was sitting on. For all my life it had always been us three families—the Honeycutts, the Bledsoes, and the Hinkle sisters. That sign at the Hinkle sisters' back porch—BACK DOOR FRIENDS ARE BEST—said just how we were. Like family, we used each other's backdoors, and if the kitchen was a mess, that was okay. We didn't have to put on airs. We celebrated good times and propped each other up when things went bad.

Now one of our props was gone.

The clock above the stove said three forty-five. Too early even for Junior's rooster to start waking people up.

I stared around the room—at Junior's hats on a hook at the backdoor and the colored bottles on the window-sill. This house looked just like it always did. But *nothing* felt the same.

After a while, I heard Ann Fay telling Miss Dinah how Imogene, in the polio hospital, said God collects our tears in His bottle. "That's why I have those bottles on my windowsill, Miss Dinah. They remind me that God sees our sorrows. And He *feels* them too. You know that, don't you?"

I thought about that empty liquor bottle on my dresser and I imagined it full of tears. I couldn't see Thomas crying, though. He seemed so tough—mostly calm and steady. And what feelings he did show were angry ones he wouldn't talk about. But he was a high schooler. So of course he wouldn't be crying. Not in front of me, anyway.

Still, Thomas hadn't always been as big and tough-skinned as he was now. I tried not to think about when he was younger and I threw that apple at him. But it wasn't easy. Not with Ann Fay over there singing again.

"*Nobody knows the trouble I've seen. Nobody knows my sorrow.*"

But somebody did know about Thomas's sorrow, and that somebody was me. Maybe I didn't know all that much. But I knew about one terrible day back when he was in sixth grade.

I put my head down and squeezed my eyes tight as I could. But I couldn't stop the tears from leaking out. My throat felt like a knife was stabbing me, so I got up and ran outside and let the crying come. I couldn't push away the thing I did to Thomas or what had just happened to Miss Pauline. And I sure couldn't change the awful mess our world was in either.

So I just let the crying come.

41

APRIL 1960

When Ellie came home for Miss Pauline's funeral she pulled Miss Dinah into her arms and held her like she was a motherless child. The two of them cried like babies. And that got the rest of us going all over again.

We weren't used to seeing Ellie like this, all broken apart and crying her eyes out. "Miss Pauline was a lot like me," she said. "A simple country girl who went off to college and made something of herself. If it wasn't for her I wouldn't be where I am today."

Miss Dinah hadn't been back to her house since that terrible night, and even after Miss Pauline's funeral she refused to go. Momma had brought her to our house, and there she was—settled in the spare room.

Momma called a meeting. We ate pie that Bessie had made and drank tea and coffee and talked about what could be done. Miss Dinah told Ann Fay and Junior to move into her house. "I'll sign it over to you," she said. "It has a fallout shelter, so you'll be safe there."

"But what about you?" asked Ann Fay.

"That fallout shelter was my sister's idea, and I went along with it for her peace of mind. But look how it turned out. For all I care, the Russians can just blow me right up."

"Have mercy!" said Bessie. She reached for Miss Dinah and hugged her as best she could there at the table. "Want to know what *I* think? You and me should live in Junior's house. It's not really *his* house anyway. It's mine. I won't have to move back and forth anymore."

So, just like that, it was decided. Ann Fay sat there with her hand over her mouth trying to argue, but then she stopped. "Are you sure? You might change your mind, Miss Dinah. You're in shock right now. Next week you'll feel different."

But Miss Dinah shook her head. "I know what I'm saying. That house is too big for me. And Junior's already keeping it up. He might as well live in it."

That's how my sister and Junior ended up owning the Hinkle sisters' fine brick house out by the highway. Ida and Arnie and everybody pitched in to swap things from one house to another. Miss Dinah couldn't figure out what to do with all her and Miss Pauline's stuff, so finally she said, "Just bring my bed and my color television. Ann Fay and Junior can have the rest."

Ellie stayed home an extra day to help with the move, and Miss Dinah gave her first choice of anything of Miss Pauline's that she wanted. "Even her sewing machine?" asked Ellie. "That's all I need." But in the end she took boxes of books, some photographs, and the Scrabble game. She hugged it to herself. "I can't believe we've played our last game together."

Every bit of this was hard to believe. I wanted Miss Pauline back, fussing and bossing us around. But she was gone. All on account of Russia and bombs. All on account of fear.

42

APRIL 1960

There was something so awful and unexpected about the way Miss Pauline died that it put a sadness over all of us. And of course it happened right after I promised Mrs. Cunningham I'd make a speech at graduation.

Now my mind wouldn't settle. If graduation speeches should have hope, where was I supposed to find that? I told Mrs. Cunningham someone else could make that speech. "Like Wayne," I said. "He'd be good. I'm not much in the mood for talking about hope."

But Mrs. Cunningham told me not to make a fast decision. "Hard times come to all of us, Jackie. But in those times we need hope the most. When you leave the safety of Mountain View you'll face unknowns. What can you say that will inspire you and your classmates to face the future with courage?"

I could see Mrs. Cunningham wasn't going to let me back out.

Easter Sunday came. If it wasn't for Miss Pauline being gone, it would have felt like all the others. Ann

Fay sang in the cantata at church. The women had new dresses and hats with ribbons and feathers on them. Little girls wore white shoes and frilly dresses.

Ellie didn't come home because she was in Raleigh at a meeting. Dr. Martin Luther King would be speaking there.

Bessie and Miss Dinah joined us for Sunday dinner. Bunkie said the blessing, and he finished up with "All together now."

"Amen!" We all said it.

"Good!" said Bunkie. "Please pass the jelly."

"Biscuit first," said Ann Fay. She cut open a biscuit and handed it to him. Then she said, "Jackie, how would you like to go to Greensboro this week?"

Before I could say yes or ask what for, Momma said. "Not to Woolworth, I hope. One protester in the family is all I can handle."

"Don't worry, Momma," said Ann Fay. "According to the news, it's been calm in Greensboro lately. And anyway, the reason we're going is, I'm finally gonna see Imogene Wilfong!"

"Woo-hoo!" I think most of us gave a big shout-out to that.

"Why take Jackie?" asked Daddy.

"Because I *want* to go," I said. "I never get to go anywhere."

"And Imogene wants to meet you," said Ann Fay. "After all, you helped reconnect us. Don't worry,

235

Momma. Imogene knows a safe place for us to meet for a picnic."

I could see Momma was trying her best not to interfere with Ann Fay's plans. Not that it would do any good, because Ann Fay generally got what she wanted. "Gerianne and Bunkie can stay with me and Leroy," said Momma.

"No, they're going with us. Children help break the ice, and Imogene is bringing hers. There'll be a creek for them to play in." Ann Fay had her plans all made and there wasn't any use arguing, so Momma didn't try.

Daddy was busy removing extra jelly from Bunkie's biscuit. "You got enough for you and me both," he told Bunkie. He looked at me. "Well, I'd feel better if Jackie stayed home. But if Ann Fay is taking my grandchildren, then surely it'll be safe. You going too, Junior?"

"Yes, sir. Looks like I'm the chauffeur. Don't worry, Leroy. I promise to keep everybody outta harm's way."

43

APRIL 1960

We left for Greensboro before noon on Thursday because that was the day that suited Imogene. I was out of school for Easter break, and Junior decided to take a vacation day. Ellie was done with her meeting in Raleigh and wanted to go along. Junior would pick her up at her dormitory in Winston-Salem.

Ann Fay was just plain nervous about seeing Imogene. One minute she'd be leaning forward and rocking in her seat like somehow that would get us to Greensboro faster. She told Junior that a traffic light had turned green even before it did. Then she slumped back in her seat, worrying over whether she and Imogene would find anything to talk about.

"Don't worry," Junior told her. "Imogene will love you."

"I don't know," said Ann Fay. "It's been a long time. What if we've both changed?"

"Well, I don't know about Imogene," said Junior. "But *you* get better every day."

That was Junior—so in love with my sister, even when she was falling apart.

We picked Ellie up, and I declare that girl could not stop talking about that meeting she'd gone to. "There were hundreds of students all fired up about protesting," she said. "And so many great speakers. I wish you could have felt the excitement."

Ellie had Gerianne on her lap, bouncing her up and down the whole time she talked. I guess she had to do something with all that energy. "Dr. Martin Luther King was the main speaker. And he just made you want to be part of it. Like he said, the movement isn't just about sitting at lunch counters. It's a demand for respect. He even encouraged us to be willing to go to jail and not accept bail."

"Are you going to jail?" asked Bunkie. "And what's a bail?"

"Bail means someone can pay to get me out of jail," said Ellie. "But don't worry, Bunkie. I'm not going to jail because Mr. Bradley won't let me join the protests. I'm learning a lot about negotiating with city managers, though, and I promise there's going to be a breakthrough soon. You watch!"

Ellie talked the rest of the way to Greensboro, and something about her excitement was catching. She made me wish I could be part of something big and important like the protest movement. And I think it helped

Ann Fay to be ready for that visit with Imogene, because when we got to the park, she was opening the car door almost before Junior had the car stopped.

Imogene and her family were there waiting with a picnic all spread out on a blanket.

Ann Fay and Imogene headed straight for each other—both limping just a little from when they'd had polio. When they got close they stopped and looked at each other—like they were trying to figure out if this was the right person. Then Imogene broke into a big old smile and stuck out a bouquet of flowers.

I couldn't see my sister's face, but I heard her say, "Yellow roses. Oh, Imogene, you remembered." Her voice choked up then and she buried her face in the flowers.

"I could never forget," said Imogene. "I remember you wanted that rose for yourself, but you gave it to me. A dozen roses can't ever repay you. Not even a thousand."

"They're so beautiful."

"But not as good-looking as you, Ann Fay Honeycutt." Imogene held out her arms and Ann Fay fell into them, and from that point on you couldn't get them to stop talking or making over each other's kids like they were cuter and smarter and funnier than any other child ever born on the face of the earth.

Imogene's husband introduced himself to me and

Junior. "Benjamin Riley," he said. We shook hands, and Junior and Benjamin talked about the weather and what a doozy of a winter we'd just come through.

Mostly, though, we listened to Ann Fay and Imogene catch up with each other. Somehow, in the middle of all that talking, I figured out that yellow roses had been purchased in honor of President Franklin Roosevelt when he died. Later, some people gave them to the polio patients. But the colored patients didn't get any, so Ann Fay gave hers to Imogene.

I knew how much Ann Fay admired Roosevelt. Giving up that flower must have been real hard for her. But until now I'd never even heard her mention it.

Imogene's children took Bunkie and Gerianne by the hands and waded into the creek, even though they squealed when their toes hit the cold water. They all ate too many deviled eggs and chocolate cake and barely touched the pimento cheese sandwiches. But the rest of us did that while we listened to Ann Fay and Imogene gossip about life in the Miracle of Hickory polio hospital and what their lives had been like since then.

All of a sudden Ann Fay stopped talking and just stared at the children holding hands, crossing over that creek. "Imogene, remember the muddy wide river?"

"Huh, girl? What are you talking about?"

"We were sitting in those hospital beds, and I told you maybe we could go to the movies after we got out.

You had to remind me that you'd have to use a separate door. We wouldn't even be able to sit together."

"Oh, I do remember. I thought the polio had gone to your head."

"And you said, 'Ann Fay, I hope you know there's a muddy wide river between your people and mine.'"

"Did I say that? I do *not* remember that part." Imogene shook her head. "But that river—it's there. You know that."

Ellie spoke up then. "But the river's not as wide as it used to be. Someday real soon, the two of you will meet in a restaurant and have a cup of coffee. And to *think*, it all started right here in Greensboro."

"At the Woolworth store," I said. I'd seen that store in the news, of course, and I knew it looked exactly the same as our Woolworth in Hickory. But after listening to Ellie's excitement about the protest movement—and now that I'd heard Ann Fay and Imogene's stories—I knew it would never again be just any ordinary store building. Something big was happening there.

I wanted to be part of something big. I still didn't know how I could speak up for civil rights, but maybe I could at least catch a glimpse of others who were doing their part. Maybe that would give me courage. "Can we go see it?" I asked. "Just drive by it at least."

"Yes," said Ann Fay.

"No," said Junior. His voice was gruff. "Your daddy

241

wouldn't want me taking you near the demonstrations."

But Ann Fay grabbed his arm. "Look at me, Junior Bledsoe." He glanced at her for only one second, and that was all it took. I could tell from the way his face just sort of melted when their eyes met that he knew exactly who would win *that* argument.

"What about the kids?" he asked. "I'm not putting them in harm's way."

"Junior," said Ellie. "It's quiet downtown these days. Only a few people have been marching and carrying signs. Today is the first sit-down since negotiations started back in February. Why don't we all jump in the car and go together?"

Junior looked at Benjamin like he was counting on him to help argue his case. But Ellie was the one studying to be a lawyer, and she had plenty of arguments. There was no harm in driving by. Sightseers went there all the time, and the only people who ever got hurt were a couple of disorderly drunks asking for trouble. "Junior," she said. "This is history in the making. Don't you want a glimpse of it?"

Benjamin told us he'd love for Imogene to ride along. "But if I stay here with my babies, the rest of you can squeeze into one car," he said. "I'll meet you back here later."

And quick as that, Junior threw up his hands. "What can I say?" he asked. "I'm just the chauffeur."

44

APRIL 1960

As soon as Junior turned onto Elm Street we saw people carrying signs that said WE ARE HUMAN, END SEGREGATION NOW, and CAN'T SIT? WON'T EAT!

The protesters held their heads high and thrust their signs out in front of them. People stood across the street and stared. But, just like Ellie had predicted, everything was quiet and peaceful.

There was the famous Woolworth store. You couldn't miss the red-and-white-striped awning or the large red sign with gold letters spelling out F. W. WOOLWORTH CO. I could barely see the lunch counter just inside the door. But before I could tell if anyone was protesting in there, we were past it.

It was over too soon. One city block and it was all behind us. "Junior," I said. "Go back."

"What?" said Junior. "No."

"Yeah. We didn't see much of anything. I want to see more."

The truth was, I didn't just want to *see* more.

243

I wanted to be part of it. I wanted to be brave for a change—like Ellie. To speak up where it really mattered. Where Blanche Shuford wasn't minding my business and Momma wouldn't have to hear about it from her. But I was about to miss my chance. So when Junior stopped at the next light, I opened the door and hopped out. "I'll be back," I said. "Just give me ten minutes."

"Jackie, for God's sake, what're you doing?" yelled Junior. "Get back in this car." But a horn honked behind him then because the light had turned green.

I shut the door and Junior didn't have any choice but to take off. I could hear how mad he was from the way he shifted the gears, but he went one way and I went the other—back up the street to the Woolworth store.

When I got closer I saw the sign right out front that said END SEGREGATION NOW. A Negro fellow was carrying it, and he looked real serious, but I went straight to him. I turned around and walked beside him. "Hey," I said. "I'm Jackie. Mind if I walk with you?"

"Uh. I guess it's okay. You alone? Where's your family, Jackie?"

I motioned out ahead. "They went down the street, but they'll come back and get me." I reached over and held on to the cardboard edge of that sign and we kept walking, leading the other demonstrators. I almost couldn't believe I was doing this. It felt kind of like a funeral procession or maybe a graduation ceremony the way the people walked real steady and solemn.

Mostly all I heard was the sound of our feet on the sidewalk. And every step made me feel taller. Stronger. Braver. From across the street somebody was yelling out insults. "Communists! Troublemakers." And a few other things I wouldn't repeat.

The fellow beside me shifted that sign to his left hand and stuck out his other one for a shake. "My name's David. Mind if I ask why you're doing this, Jackie?"

Thomas's face flashed through my mind. Also that half-eaten apple. Maybe that was why I was doing this. Maybe I thought this would clear my conscience. I didn't know for sure, but there I was in Greensboro, North Carolina, where people were trying to change all the badness. Or some of it, anyway. "Because," I said, "it's time for change. And I don't know what else I can do."

David grunted a little. "Want to carry this sign to the end of the street?"

"Sure," I said. I took it and held it high so I could see beneath the poster board while I walked. When I lifted it, I realized how this could make you tired after a while. Maybe David was relieved to let go of it.

Just then, a photographer stepped right in front of us. "Hold it," he said. Of course we had to stop—either that or go out around him. He snapped our picture and stepped back to let us pass. We were past the Woolworth store now and I'd missed my chance to peer inside.

But then a door opened at the Kress store and people poured out—whites and Negroes both. Policemen gripped them by the elbows or prodded them in their backs.

Right there, in the middle of that group, was Maribelle Bradley!

"Hey, Maribelle!" I hollered. She looked around to see who'd called her name. I waved and our eyes met and hers went real wide. She lifted her head and smiled. But she couldn't wave. Her wrists were handcuffed together!

David and I were about six feet away, and I could see most everything. A white boy got up into Maribelle's face and screamed at her. "Girl, you're going to jail, where you can eat sitting down! Bread and water." And just like that, he spit on her.

I saw how Maribelle flinched, but that was all. She didn't say a word.

"Hey! Cut it out! That's my friend." I rushed forward and gave the thug a shove. Before I knew what was happening, his fist was coming at me. When it hit, everything went dark for a second. Maybe longer. Next thing I realized, I was on the sidewalk, staring up at faces, including David's, looking worried. I saw a police officer too.

"You okay?" the officer asked.

"I think so." I tried to sit up, but my head hurt and I felt dizzy.

"Take it easy," the policeman said. "You just got yourself a shiner. Maybe you asked for it. Did you come here to start trouble?"

"No, sir," I said. "I just wanted to march, but then

that creep spit on my friend. Where is he?" I sat up and the policeman helped me to my feet.

"Don't you worry. We'll take care of *him*. You seem pretty young. Where's your family?"

"Uh, down the street, I think. They're coming back for me."

All of a sudden Junior was there. "Jackie Honeycutt! Have mercy. It sure don't take you long to get in trouble."

"He belong to you?" the policeman asked.

"Yes, sir," said Junior. "I'll take him home."

There was still a sharp pain in my eye, and I could tell it was swelling shut because I couldn't see so well. But I did see David standing there with a torn poster. The word *segregation* was split in two. He stuck out his hand again. "It was a pleasure to march with you," he said. "But you need to get home now." He grinned. "And stay out of trouble."

45

APRIL 1960

It was going to be hard staying out of trouble with my face splashed across the television.

Evidently that photographer shared his pictures with the TV station. So there I was on the evening news. It was a still picture of me and David. He was smiling, but I looked pretty dumb—like I was biting my lip. Like that sign was too heavy for me to carry.

Then the picture changed and I saw Maribelle too, getting arrested inside the store.

According to Ellie, we didn't need to worry about Maribelle. Mr. Bradley would pay her bail and she'd be out in no time. "And besides *that*," Ellie had said, "they got themselves arrested to make a point. A little jail time brings attention to the cause."

Even if I didn't need to worry about her being stuck in jail, the thought of that spit sliding down Maribelle's face made my stomach turn.

I was on the sofa, watching all this with one eye. The other one was completely shut by now and Momma made me hold a bag of ice to it. She kept fussing over me. "Jackie, do you need more ginger ale? You didn't eat much. Are you sure you're okay?"

"Yes, Momma. I'm fine." The truth was, I didn't feel all that great and I mostly wanted to sleep, but Momma and Daddy kept waking me up to check my pupils—worried that maybe I had a concussion.

"We should've never let you go," said Daddy.

"It was bad enough worrying about Ellie," said Momma. "Now we've got two of you asking for trouble. What will you get into next?"

"I'm sorry, Momma."

I *was* sorry that I ended up making a scene in public because now Blanche Shuford would hear about it and there would be even more trouble for Momma. Maybe for all of us. But I wasn't sorry for joining that march. It felt right even if I did get hurt.

Momma didn't have to worry about what I'd get into next. I was going to stay out of trouble and hope to be rid of this black eye before graduation. Because now I realized I *didn't* want to back out of that speech. That Greensboro experience had me all fired up. I'd think of something to say.

On Sunday I looked so beat-up that Momma and Daddy let me skip church. When they came home they were quieter than usual. Somebody had probably given them the cold shoulder. "Did they kick you out of the church?" I asked.

"The Reverend was polite," said Daddy. "But I don't think he approved of your actions. Did you have to get yourself on TV?" Daddy's voice had an edge to it.

"I didn't try to," I said. "I just wanted to do something right for a change!"

"And you think that was right?" asked Momma. "Maybe next time you should think before you act."

Apparently my parents were done worrying about me. It appeared that I didn't have a concussion, so now they'd gone from worrying to being just plain mad. Or hurt. Probably someone at church had snubbed them. But if so, they weren't telling me about it.

The rest of the family dribbled in with dishes of food in their hands, shaking their heads when they saw my swollen black eye. Ida said that Ellie must be real proud of me.

"That's quite a shiner you got there," said Arnie. He boxed me on the arm and shook my hand. "Congratulations!"

We relived everything over the dinner table—starting from the minute Imogene got to the park and finishing up with dropping Ellie off at her dormitory.

Momma listened without saying much of anything. Then finally she said, "Remember last Sunday, Ann Fay? You promised it would be safe. Now look what happened. Jackie could've been hurt worse. And who knows what bad things will come of this?"

"I'm really sorry," said Junior. "I never should've

taken them downtown. I knew better, and I did it anyway."

"Because *I* wanted you to," said Ann Fay. "Momma, Daddy, don't be mad at Junior. I'm the one who convinced him to take us."

The truth was, we'd all talked Junior into it, but Ann Fay was the one he couldn't say no to. Still, I knew me getting beat up was actually my own fault: I jumped out of that car. And I wasn't one bit sorry. Because I actually spoke up, and after being there, I was like Ellie— believing those protests would do some good.

After we ate, I dozed off—sitting up in the armchair while Junior and Arnie listened to baseball on the radio and the rest of the family played Parcheesi. I woke up once and heard Ann Fay telling how she and Imogene were already making plans for Imogene's family to visit her and Junior.

They had all gone home by the time Momma woke me later. "Someone's at the backdoor asking for you," she said.

"Who?"

Momma didn't answer. Instead she went to sit with Daddy on the front porch. My head hurt and I really wanted to keep sleeping. But I stumbled through the kitchen to the screen door.

Thomas. What was he doing in my backyard? I hadn't seen him in months. But there he was—waiting at the bottom of the steps with a big paper sack in his hand.

The sweet smell of wisteria blossoms floated in on a breeze. I took a deep breath, pushed the door open, and went outside. "Hey, Thomas."

"I heard what happened."

"You did?"

Thomas set the bag on the ground, so I figured he was tired of holding it.

"Have a seat," I said. I slumped onto the top step, and he picked up that bag and put it on the step beside me.

"Momma sent you some rice pudding. Hers is the best. She says it'll fix what ails you."

"Oh. Okay." That really surprised me—all these months of not talking, and now he showed up with rice pudding? "Thank you," I said. "What made her do that?"

"We don't have a TV, you know. But Momma cleans for a doctor's wife. You were on the evening news at their house. Said she knew you right away." Thomas shook his head. "But oh man, bet she wouldn't recognize you now. Don't that hurt?"

That was a stupid question and I wanted to shoot back a smart-aleck answer, but I figured this wasn't the time for it. If Thomas had come here to be friendly, I didn't want to blow it. "Yep. Sure does," I said.

"What in the world were you doing in Greensboro? And how'd you get ahold of that sign?"

"Thomas, if you sit down, I'll tell you."

Finally he sat on the step just below mine, and I told

252

him how I admired my sister and her friend Maribelle. I wanted to be brave and speak up about segregation the way they did, but I didn't know how. I told him about us going to Greensboro to meet Ann Fay's friend and about me making a split-second decision to jump out of that car and join the march. "It was powerful, Thomas. I could feel it. Those people are making a difference. I hope I helped at least a tiny little bit. At least I spoke up and people actually saw it."

Thomas sat there nodding, and for some reason he seemed different. Not so stiff as usual. Not watching me out of the corner of his eye all the time. He reached for a blade of grass at the bottom of the step and smoothed it between his fingers.

"Momma saw you," he said. "And that sure enough made a difference in *my* family. Usually, over Sunday dinner, we talk about the preacher." Thomas chuckled. "Tell his sermon to each other and argue about the points he made. This time we tried to puzzle out what Jackie Honeycutt was up to. Was he serious about what he did? Could we trust him?"

"Oh," I said. I stared out past the garden to where the blue wisteria was climbing all over the edge of the woods. I couldn't help but wonder—if I'd been a fly buzzing around the Freemans' sugar bowl, what would I have heard?

"Aunt Martha said you can't trust white people and I shouldn't let my guard down. Johnny said yeah, but there was a good chance your family would take heat for what you did. We went back and forth for a while, and finally Lettie—that's my baby sister—realized who we were talking about. She stood on her chair and jabbed her finger and said you were real nice on account of you gave me that bird calendar hanging on the kitchen wall." Thomas laughed. "You ought to have heard her preach it!"

My face hurt when I laughed, but I couldn't help it. I was also smiling because of Thomas telling that story so free and easy. I didn't think I'd ever heard him say that many words in a row. He kept going.

"The long and the short of it is, we decided Jackie Honeycutt is welcome at our house anytime." Thomas stood then. "I need to shove off," he said. "Momma says no hurry on that dish. Bring it back when you feel up to it."

46

APRIL 1960

When I woke up, my stomach felt worse than it had the day before. And according to the mirror I didn't *look* so good either. There was no way I could face my classmates. Whether they'd seen me on television or not, most of them would soon hear what I'd done. I didn't expect anyone to congratulate me for it.

I crawled back in bed, but Momma came into my room and opened the window shade. "Jackie, why aren't you up? At this rate you'll miss your bus."

"Good. I feel bad and I look worse. I need to stay home."

"No sirree!" she said. "It'll take a few weeks for that black eye to clear up, and you can't miss that much school. Time to face the music."

So I got dressed and ate some of that rice pudding for breakfast. Thomas's mother was right about it being good for what ailed me. It was cool and creamy and easy on the stomach. It seemed kind of funny that she was the one giving me comfort right now—instead of my own momma.

I gathered my books and headed for the bus stop, dreading the questions about to come my way. Of course everybody noticed my shiner. I ignored their questions and kept going—heading straight for the classroom.

When Mrs. Cunningham saw me, her eyebrows went up and I think I saw worry in her face. But she didn't ask questions. Students crowded around my desk. Some of them didn't have a television or hadn't seen the news, so they said things like—"Oooh, Jackie! What happened?" and "Were you really on TV?" and "Don't that hurt?"

"It's no big deal," I said. "I ran into a thug, that's all. Now leave me alone." I didn't actually need to explain, because a few people had seen the news and gossip was spreading fast. Most of it was exaggerated.

Dennis came by my desk on the way to the pencil sharpener. I was pretty sure he knew exactly what happened, but he had to put his two cents' worth in anyway. "Did a little girl whoop up on you? *Again?*"

"Dennis," said Mrs. Cunningham. "Do you need help with that pencil?"

"No, ma'am," he said. "I think I can handle it."

Mrs. Cunningham called the roll and then she asked for current events. Dennis was the first to speak up. "According to my grandma, Jackie Honeycutt was on television. I bet he can tell us what's going on in the news."

Maybe he thought he could make a fool of me in front of the class, but I decided right then and there *that* wasn't going to happen. If someone was going to tell this story, it might as well be me. I raised my hand.

"Last week I went to Greensboro and I marched in front of the Woolworth and Kress stores. I carried a sign that said END SEGREGATION NOW. I wasn't planning to, but I saw those people marching and all of a sudden I just knew I *had* to. After all, it's just plain ignorant that colored people have to eat standing up in those stores. Anyway, a photographer took a picture of me carrying the sign—that's what people saw later on the news. Then the police brought some protesters out in handcuffs. One of them was my sister's friend. And this good-for-nothing guy *spit* on her. Right in her face."

I heard a few people gasp, but someone in the back of the room clapped.

"How nasty and hateful can you be?" I said. "Him spitting on her made me so mad I gave him a shove, and just that quick, he socked me good. So now you know why I have a black eye."

Everybody seemed to have an opinion about that and they all started talking at once, which Mrs. Cunningham put a stop to in a hurry. "Raise your hand if you'd like to express how you feel about Jackie's actions." From the corner of my one good eye, I saw lots of hands going up. And I thought I saw a little twinkle in Mrs. Cunningham's eye too. "Great! Take out a sheet of paper."

Judging from the moaning and groaning, a whole lot of people suddenly changed their minds about expressing themselves. But it was too late and I was glad.

"Obviously we have some strong feelings in this room," said Mrs. Cunningham. "You have thirty minutes to express them. Keep it respectful." She turned to me. "Jackie, I want you to write a paragraph defending your decision to march in Greensboro."

I didn't know what more to say than I already had, but then I remembered the poster on the wall—the one with part of the Declaration of Independence on it. I wrote that quote about everyone having the right to life, liberty, and the pursuit of happiness. I said that Negroes couldn't possibly be happy with some of the rules in our society, so I marched to help bring change.

Later, during phys ed, Mrs. Cunningham thought I should sit out of the softball game. "Let's not take any chances on injuring that eye again," she said.

I expected to be on that bench all by my lonesome, but then I saw Pamela headed my way. "Mind if I sit?" she asked.

She didn't wait for an answer, and next thing I knew, she was right there beside me, our arms practically touching.

"I asked Mrs. Cunningham if I could sit out with you," she said. "So we can talk without Betty listening in."

"Ha! I thought you and Betty were good friends."

"We are, but we don't agree on everything. Like integration." Pamela used the toe of her shoe to trace a figure eight in the dirt. "I wanted to tell you what I wrote on that paper, Jackie. I told Mrs. Cunningham that I'm a little jealous of you."

"You are? Why?"

"Because. You have a really good heart. And you're brave. You stood up for integration. I've never done anything like that."

"Actually you did," I said. "Remember when Tony accused me of being a communist? You defended me in front of the whole class. And when Dennis tried to turn everyone against me, you and Betty started eating at my lunch table. See, you're brave too."

"Yeah, I guess so. But you speak up a lot, Jackie. And look what you did last week. You went out there and joined a march. It takes a really good person to do something like that."

Maybe I should've just let her believe I was good, but for some reason I couldn't. "Actually," I said, "I was mean to a colored boy once. Back in fifth grade I hit him in the back of the head with a half-eaten apple."

"On purpose?"

I could see from the way Pamela tilted her head and pulled back a little that she was surprised. But that didn't stop me, because sometimes when I opened my big mouth I just kept going. And there was something about Pamela that made me want to talk.

I told her the whole story. Boy, did I feel embarrassed, admitting I did it for a measly dime. I wouldn't have blamed her if she decided to leave me there and go play ball. But she didn't.

"I was stupid in fifth grade too," she said. "You're not like that now. Even when you started that fight with Dennis, I knew you didn't do it out of meanness. He's the one that's a bully."

"Yeah. He is."

Pamela stood then. "I hope your eye heals up real fast, Jackie, because it sure looks like it hurts. I guess I'll go now. It was nice talking to you." And just like that, Pamela took off.

I watched her run into the outfield and then I glanced down, and right there where she'd been drawing a figure eight in the dirt I noticed something different. It was the shape of a heart!

I thought about that heart all week—wondering what it meant and if she intended to do it. Or was it like those figure eights—something absent-minded to do while she talked? Either way, the thought of it made me happy.

On Thursday I got a letter in the mail. From Imogene Riley, of all people. I opened it and there was a newspaper clipping with a picture of me holding that sign, marching with David. She sent a little note with it.

260

Jackie,

Thank you for helping your sister and me get in touch with each other. It's easy to let friendships slide, but I promise that from now on I will keep writing to Ann Fay and we'll see each other when we can.

I thought you would like to have a copy of this article from the Greensboro paper. Someday you can show your children what a brave thing you did.

I'm proud of you, and guess what? I really believe that muddy wide river is going to dry right up.

Your friend,
Imogene

There was a caption with the picture and an article about some whites marching with Negroes. The article mentioned a scuffle between two troublemakers.

I knew what that made me. A troublemaker. One thing for sure—when it came to passive resistance, I wasn't any good at that stuff!

47

APRIL—MAY 1960

President Eisenhower was going to Russia! Not until June, but at least Nikita Khrushchev had invited him. According to the newspapers, they hoped to discuss disarmament.

But first, they would meet in Paris with the president of France and the prime minister of England. Of course in our class discussion the same old arguments came up about not being friendly with communists because they were infiltrating the United States and stirring up racial trouble.

Now that I'd marched in Greensboro I felt even stronger about speaking up. I didn't really care anymore what Dennis thought of me or what he went home and told his grandmother. They already knew where I stood. So I raised my hand. "Negroes don't need communists to tell them how they want to be treated," I said. "Why do people think that? Colored people have minds of their own, and they're speaking up because they're sick and tired of being treated like trash."

Mrs. Cunningham reminded the class that the reason for the meeting between Eisenhower and Khrushchev was to consider disarmament.

While the class discussed nuclear weapons I looked around and tried to imagine if any of them had a secret bomb shelter in their basement. I doodled on my notebook page, drawing without thinking, and next thing I knew, I was drawing the inside of the bomb shelter I'd helped Junior build. Shelves full of canned goods. Three empty beds. The funny toilet.

My mind went to Miss Pauline crumpled at the bottom of her stairs. Americans shouldn't have to live in fear the way she did. I was glad President Eisenhower was trying to find a way to live peaceably with Russia. What if I made a speech about that? About world peace!

Mrs. Cunningham raised her eyebrows when I mentioned it. But she didn't argue. After all, in one way or another, she'd been talking about peace all year long. "Write down your main points," she said. "Then show them to me. And don't forget to make it personal. Peace starts right here, you know." She tapped on her heart.

I was pretty sure I knew what she was talking about. Turning enemies into friends. Me and Dennis.

But surely she didn't expect me to bring *that* up in public.

She'd love it if I started with that Abraham Lincoln quote. I could talk about how our relationship with Russia was moving from being enemies to trying to be friends. By the time I made that speech at graduation the big meeting in Paris would be over and our president would be packing his bags for Moscow.

But I wasn't sure how to make it personal. I mean, after Thomas coming over on Sunday I was starting to believe that enemies could become friends. At least I hoped it was happening. Still, I couldn't see me talking about Thomas at graduation. Speaking up in class about civil rights was one thing. Talking to an auditorium packed with people was another.

I finally decided to include some of the things Mrs. Cunningham had taught us. About measuring our words and listening to others and how that could encourage good relationships.

I kept checking myself in the mirror. If I was going to stand up there and say anything, I needed my black eye to get better. Over the last week it had turned to purple and then to green. But it still looked rough on Sunday, so Momma let me skip church again.

Thomas had said I was welcome at their house. And even though I felt shy about seeing his whole family again—especially looking so beat-up—I did want to see him. Besides that, his mother's empty pudding dish was sitting on the counter by the backdoor, staring at me.

So, on Sunday afternoon, I put it back in the bag Thomas had brought it in and I headed for the river—just in case I got lucky and found him fishing.

He wasn't there, so I started toward his house.

I decided to take the trail Thomas always used. Just like I figured, it came out on the back end of their property, which meant I wouldn't have to greet the whole family on the front porch. I passed their barn and heard some pigs snuffling around inside. There was a mule in the pasture and a Jersey milk cow too. I stopped to get acquainted with the cow. "Howdy," I said. "You're a big girl. I bet you've had a couple of calves by now." I picked some tall grass for her to eat from my hand.

"Hey!" someone called. I turned, and there was Thomas's brother Johnny hollering from the crest of the hill. "Come on up!"

I waved and ran toward him, but he turned around and went back. There was a softball game going on with his family—all ages. A few adults sat on blankets and watched.

Thomas's littlest sister was at bat and the pitcher rolled the ball to her. She hit it, but it barely went five feet. Still, every single person out there cheered. "Woo-hoo! Go, Lettie! Run them bases!" For all their excitement you'd think she was Jackie Robinson. She ran like him too—brave as could be—with her pigtails flapping and her laughing the whole way. The family could have tagged her out at every base and twice in between. But they let her run it out.

Johnny hollered for Thomas. He jerked his head in my direction and everybody turned and stared at me coming their way.

"Y'all go on and play," Thomas called back to them. He met me behind second base.

"Ouch," he said. "Still hurts to look at you."

"Thanks, Thomas. Playing ball?"

"Nope. I'm fishing. Can't you tell?"

"Ha! Well, I brought your momma's dish back. The rice pudding was good."

He took the bag with the dish. "Wanna play?" He turned to go and motioned for me to join them. "Come on."

I didn't know these people. All of a sudden I felt real shy, but his cousin, or somebody I didn't recognize, hollered at me, "Come on. You be on our team."

They made me bat next. After watching a few wild pitches go by, I reached out and grabbed an outside ball and smacked it into right field. I made it to first base, but the throw was wild, so I took my chances and ran for second. Thomas's family cheered almost as loud for me as they did for Lettie.

I was so caught up in the game I didn't even think about cars going by on the road. But after a while someone tooted their horn. Not once but four times. Long and loud. Like they were mad. Whoever it was drove by real slow in a dark-green pickup truck. Some old man in a slouchy hat. Nobody I recognized.

There was some mumbling among Thomas's family members, but whatever they said, I didn't think they wanted me to hear it.

The next day at school I found out exactly who that was. As I headed up the steps, someone grabbed my elbow. Dennis Aiken. "How come you didn't wave when my granddaddy blew the horn yesterday?" he asked.

"Your granddaddy?"

"We saw you out there playing baseball."

"Softball," I said. "And what's it to you?"

"Maybe I'm taking notes on who's pushing for race mixing. Granddaddy said he even saw you fishing with one of them boys."

Well, I swanee! You could've knocked me over with a chicken feather when he said that. "Wait. That mean old drunk is your grandfather? He threw a bottle at—"

"Hey! Watch your mouth." Dennis gave me a shove, and I landed on my backside half off the steps and half on. And oh, man—my tailbone took a beating.

Dennis didn't stick around for me to pick myself up and let him have it. I had a feeling he regretted saying his granddaddy saw me and Thomas fishing. But it was too late now. The truth was out.

My mind was in a whirl as I walked down that hall. I just couldn't get it through my head that the drunk was Dennis's grandfather. Blanche Shuford's husband? I didn't think so. She was way too snooty for the likes of him.

48

MAY 1960

I was out in the pasture with Lucy, reminding her how to follow me in the show ring. Reminding *myself* how to lead her—because I was most likely going to enter the 4-H dairy contest again. "Lucy," I said. "You're getting big. One of these days Arnie will say you're ready to have a calf."

Lucy's mind wasn't on becoming a momma. She sniffed the air and tossed her head. When I looked around to see what was agitating her, I caught sight of some-one coming out of the woods. "That looks like Thomas. Remember him?" I watched while Thomas climbed through the strands of barbed wire, and then I headed toward him. From the set of his shoulders and the way he stalked across that pasture, I guessed he was upset about something.

"Hey, Thomas. Everything all right?"

"Nope." He looked me in the eye. "My brother saw you hand-feeding our cow the other day. I told him you didn't do it."

"Do what?"

"Someone gave her yew."

"Yew!" I practically shouted it. "Is she okay?"

"She's dead. I told my brother you didn't do it."

I stood there staring at Thomas.

"You *didn't*—did you?"

"Me? Kill your cow? No! Of course not. Why would you think such a thing?"

This was too much. First, finding out that the drunk who threw that bottle at Thomas was Dennis's grandfather. Then him seeing us playing ball together. And *now* someone giving a poisonous plant to both our cows.

That filthy old drunk. Someone needed to hit *him* in the head. If I knew where he lived I'd march myself over there right this minute. But what would I do? What *could* I do?

"Thomas," I said, "you know I love cows." My voice was shaking. If I didn't watch out, I'd be blubbering like a baby. I bit my lip and tried to think how to explain. "I fed her some grass—trying to get her to warm up to me. But listen, Thomas. A few weeks ago someone tried to give yew to Lucy. My brother-in-law found it before Lucy did." I grabbed Thomas's arm. "Let's go. We gotta talk to Junior."

"No," said Thomas, and his voice was so hard it stopped me cold.

"But Junior knows everybody around here. He can help us track down the cow killer. Somebody with the last name of Aiken." I turned to go.

"No!"

"What? Why'd you come here if you don't want help?"

"My family don't need your family's help. I came here to get your word you didn't kill our cow."

"I didn't do it. So now what?"

Thomas shrugged. "That's what we got to figure out. Me and you. And we're keeping our daddies out of it."

"Well, Junior's not my daddy."

"I *said*, me and you. If you don't understand that, then forget it." Thomas turned away, but I grabbed his arm.

"Okay, okay. What's next? Got any ideas?" When I asked that, it hit me that I hadn't told him yet about Dennis Aiken's grandfather. "I know who drove by your house on Sunday when we were playing softball. Remember how he laid on the horn? It was the same old man that hit you with a bottle."

"I know that."

"You do? But how?"

"Just cause I'm colored don't mean I don't know white people. Especially *mean* white people. Those kind make sure we know who they are."

"But when he threw that bottle at you, did you know him then?"

Thomas nodded. "Course I did."

And you didn't tell me? Or your parents? What's

wrong with you, Thomas? That's what I wanted to say. But I didn't. Thomas had already told me. He wasn't looking to get his house burned down. Still, someone killed his cow! Was he fixing to let that slide?

"Thomas, if we don't do something, it could get worse. We gotta stop this guy."

"Yeah, well, we're not gonna act too fast. We got to think it through. And say our prayers."

Thomas turned, and this time he did march off. I stood there and watched him go. But Lucy was beside me now, pushing her muzzle into my hand. Reminding me that Thomas's family had just lost their cow.

And he wanted me to *pray*? But praying wasn't enough. I had to *do* something. So I ran and caught up with him. "Thomas, just tell me what to do and I'll do it. You got a plan?"

Thomas stopped. He didn't turn around on account of I reckon he was trying to figure out if he could trust me. He stood there staring into the trees, and a crow flew overhead. I heard another crow off in the distance. The two of them called back and forth to each other.

"We're going be smart about this," said Thomas. "Put your mind to it for a few days. See if you can sleuth out some clues you hadn't noticed yet. Then we'll meet at the river on Sunday and see what we both came up with. We gotta nab that Clarence Shuford."

"Clarence Shuford? That's who drove by in that truck on Sunday? I thought it was somebody named Aiken."

271

"Nope. I know who killed my cow—now that I have your word it wasn't you. I was just narrowing down the choices."

"What you gonna tell your daddy?"

Thomas shrugged. "I'll tell him somebody tried to kill *your* cow too. Same way. And you and me are gonna figure it out. Good thing he never heard about that bottle. You know what I mean?" Thomas turned to go. "See you on Sunday."

49

MAY 1960

I almost couldn't believe that mean old drunk was Blanche Shuford's husband. It didn't make a lick of sense—not with her being so hoity-toity. But evidently it was true, and the more I thought about it the madder I got. The worst part was, even if I *could* think of some way to get back at him, Thomas's family would get the blame. Things could get ugly for them.

Thing *was*, getting revenge wouldn't bring back his family's milk cow. What they needed was another one. Maybe Arnie would sell them one on credit.

By Sunday, I still hadn't come up with any good ideas, but then, on the way to the river, it hit me that I never even told Thomas about Lucy and the snowstorm. So I filled him in first thing.

"Now *that's* important," said Thomas. "When was this? What day of the week? What time of day?"

"Huh? I don't know. Nighttime. Lucy was out in the snow for hours, but I don't know exactly how long."

"What about the yew? When did he try to poison her?"

"Junior showed up at my house with Lucy early one morning. But he found the yew the night before. I don't know when that was. Oh wait! Maybe I do. He said his momma was at the Home Demonstration meeting that night. So it was a Tuesday."

"And I'm willing to bet there was a Home Demonstration meeting the night before you found Lucy out in the snow."

"Hmm . . . Thomas, you're a genius! It was real cold, and Daddy and I went to the community building to carry in wood and light a fire. Blanche was there early, and Clarence had the stove fired up already. He was gone, though. But the next morning I found Lucy outside the fence. Froze half to death."

"When's the next meeting? 'Cause he'll be back, and we've got to be ready for him." Thomas was rubbing his hands together—anticipating revenge.

"Uh, next week, I think. Momma never goes anymore on account of Blanche turning everybody against her, but I'll find out for—"

"We need a plan. Does Clarence know Lucy is back at your house?"

My mind started spinning—running away with ideas for saving Lucy. Me and Daddy could camp out in the lean-to. Or I could take her to Arnie's farm.

"I *said*, does Clarence know where Lucy is?"

"I don't know, Thomas. How'd he find out she was in Junior's barn in the first place? Unless maybe Momma or Bessie told it at one of those meetings. I wouldn't put it past Blanche to go home and tell her good-for-nothing husband something like that."

"We need proof."

"Ann Fay's got a camera."

Thomas started shaking his head. "What's a picture gonna prove? Unless you get one of him hurting Lucy."

"Well, I'm not taking that chance, but still, a picture is something."

"What we *need* is to stop him in his tracks. A booby trap of some kind. Something that goes off when he opens the stable door."

"Like ice-cold water on his head," I said.

"Or wait! Not water."

Suddenly I knew what Thomas was going to say, and we both yelled it out at the same time. "Cow poop!"

"I can rig up a bucket." Thomas rubbed his hands together like he couldn't wait to get started.

"You can rig it up? Where'd you learn that?"

Thomas just shook his head. "Jackie, you don't know what you're missing—not having a big brother." He laughed then, so hard I thought he'd keel right over and fall into the river. "Oh, I do want to see old man Shuford with cow dookie dripping off his ears."

I laughed too. But we finally got ahold of ourselves long enough to come up with a plan. In the end, Thomas said I could let Junior in on our scheme because, after all, it was his barn. Not to mention we were going to need some extra muscle and a pickup truck to pull this off.

50

MAY 1960

"Yup," said Junior. "Sounds like Clarence for sure. And no matter who it is, they deserve a bucket of crap on their heads."

He stood back and watched while Thomas rigged a bucket above the door of Lucy's old stable. It was attached to a rope and propped with a stick so that when someone opened the door it would pull on the rope. The stick would fall out and the bucket would empty on the person below.

First we had to practice a few times with water in the bucket, once with me getting doused and once with Thomas. After all, we had to know if it worked. And it did—good as my alarm clock. But man, was it ever cold! Once I got done whooping and hollering and wiping the water out of my eyes, I said, "Thomas, you're a pure genius."

Thomas agreed that yes, he was, but then the bucket of water dumped on him and he squealed like a greased pig. "Maybe I'm a pure idiot," he said, but he laughed the whole time. "Boy howdy, I hate that I can't be here when that old man gets his comeuppance!"

He stopped laughing then and looked real serious. "But I could never. If that old man killed our cow over us playing ball together, I don't want to think what he'd do to my family over something like this." Thomas shook his head. "I'm counting on you, Jackie. Junior too. To get him and get him good."

"We'll get him all right," I said.

"When we're done with Clarence we'll meet you at the north corner of your property," said Junior. "We'll tell you all about it. Watch for my flashing headlights. Now Thomas, hop in my truck and I'll take you home. See *you* tomorrow night, Jackie."

It was hard to believe that in a little more than twenty-four hours we'd be giving Clarence Shuford a taste of his own medicine. I wanted in the worst way for Thomas to be there, but I kept thinking about what he'd said that day in his backyard—how his daddy couldn't defend him over getting hit with that bottle because his house could get burned down. Or worse.

I knew I couldn't breathe a word of this to anyone. Not even Wayne.

At school on Tuesday, Mrs. Cunningham sent me to the library to work on my speech. But my mind kept wandering from world peace to that bucket of cow manure. Somehow, I forced out two paragraphs about the relationship between the United States and Russia.

Mrs. Cunningham glanced over my paragraphs. "You're on the right track, Jackie. Now talk about how this applies to you and your classmates. Maybe recount some of our class discussions. And don't forget about hope."

"Yes, ma'am," I said. But I didn't work on my speech after school because my brain couldn't settle on writing. Instead, I found a small board in the woodshed and pulled out my wood-burning pen. First I lettered the board with pencil. Then I burned the letters to make it look real good. When I was done it said BACK DOOR FRIENDS ARE BEST. "There," I said. "I hope Thomas likes it."

I knew he would always feel more comfortable coming to the backdoor same as I did at the Hinkle sisters. For one thing, he'd think he should. But for another it just made sense, since the quickest route between his house and mine was through the woods and the pasture behind my house. I nailed the sign to the porch post where Thomas couldn't miss it, next time he came by. If he ever did.

At supper Momma said she wasn't going to the Home Demonstration meeting. "It's too nice an evening for sitting around talking about flower gardens when I can be right here working in mine," she said.

I had already known she wasn't going, but just the fact of her bringing it up made me think she wanted to. I felt sad that she missed her friends, all on account of Dennis's snooty grandmother.

But I had a feeling that things were fixing to change.

Soon as supper was over, Daddy said he was heading for his garden. "I've got to stake out rows for planting green beans. Jackie, you wanna help?"

"Uh, I can't. Junior needs me for some work at the barn," I said. Some people might consider that a lie, but I didn't. If you asked me, catching Clarence Shuford in a criminal act was work. *Important* work.

First, I had to feed and water Lucy. I tied her to a post in the lean-to. "We're fixing to catch the bad guy, Lucy. You did your part by providing the ammunition. Good girl!"

Junior was milking when I got there. He'd parked his truck up close to the south side of the barn where Clarence wasn't likely to see it. After he carried the milk to the house, we hunkered down in a dark corner of the stall next to the one Lucy used to be in.

"Now," said Junior, "I figure we've got thirty minutes or more until show time. Let's go over the plan. Once we catch him we'll throw him on the back of my truck. I'll hold him down while you drive us to the community building."

We went over it step by step, and when we had it all worked out in our minds, we got to talking about Clarence Shuford's drinking problem. "Know why my momma is sympathetic to Blanche?" asked Junior. "See, my pop was a drunk too. He embarrassed her in the eyes of the community time and again. According to

Momma, all Blanche's hoity-toity talk is just her way of trying to maintain some self-respect. We gotta be careful on account of I promised we wouldn't shame her in public."

I couldn't imagine how Junior thought we could avoid that—not with what we had planned. But there wasn't time to ask because we heard footsteps. Then the barn door creaked as someone slid it open.

I stopped breathing.

MAY 1960

That crazy old fool came in there singing.

"He's drunk," whispered Junior. "That makes our job easier."

We heard Clarence heading straight for where he expected Lucy to be. The door to our stall was unlatched, and we were ready to pounce.

Everything—and I mean everything—went just like we planned. Clarence turned the wooden latch and opened the stable door. Even in the near dark I could see that bucket tilt. And just that quick the air was full of the smell of cow poop and a whole wagonload of hollering and cussing.

Junior went out first. I was right behind him.

"Why, Clarence Shuford," said Junior. "Fancy meeting you here. In my barn, of all places."

He was practically yelling so he could be heard over all the noise Clarence was making, sputtering and cussing and kicking. Clarence wiped his face against his sleeve, but that just smeared things worse.

"Hmm," said Junior. "I expect we could help clean you up. But what's this in your hand?"

Sure enough—the man had brought some yew with him.

"Has Blanche not noticed somebody's been clipping her yew bush?" asked Junior. He was still yelling on account of Clarence making such a ruckus. "Because this is the third time I know of that someone has tried to feed yew to a cow. And in one case a cow actually died."

Clarence shook his head. "Not me. Water!" he sputtered. "Let me go!"

"Jackie, fetch a bucket of water. And get those rags in the corner. We'll wash him up. Not *too* good, though, because we need some evidence. Now Clarence, if you're smart, you'll hold still. Or we *could* just take you straight on up to the clubhouse and shove you in the door with your wife and all those other women."

Clarence held still. "No, please."

I got the water and Junior told me to set it right in front of Clarence. Then, with Junior holding Clarence's hands behind his back, I tied them together with some rope. Junior pushed his head into the water. He let him up and Clarence hollered and shook his head like a dog coming out of the river. Me and Junior got a poopy shower, but it didn't matter because we were having the time of our lives.

"Time to get this rattlesnake home," said Junior.

"Open the barn door." He pushed Clarence outside, preaching at him the whole time. "Listen here," he said. "I promised my momma I'd preserve your wife's dignity in front of her friends. But we *are* going to find Blanche right now." We shoved Clarence onto the bed of Junior's pickup, and Junior climbed on too. "Keys are in the truck, Jackie," he said.

Even with me up front driving, I could hear Clarence cussing and hollering the whole way.

The driveway and yard in front of the community building were full of cars, so I parked by the edge of the property. We had it all worked out what would happen next, but Junior told me anyway. Probably so he could torment Clarence.

"Jackie," he said, "you have the pleasure of inviting Blanche to step outside. Don't embarrass her. Just knock on the door. My momma knows to answer it. Ask for Blanche, and when she comes to the door, whisper that I've got something to show her. Momma will keep the other ladies distracted."

I could see Bessie through the window, not far from the front door. Women were scattered around the room, working at different tables. I knocked and then I heard footsteps and it wasn't ten seconds before Bessie opened the door. "Is Blanche there?" I said. "Junior needs to talk to her."

"I'll get her," said Bessie. Then she leaned in and

whispered, "Go easy on her. She's doing the best she can under the circumstances."

She pushed the door shut, and I waited about a minute for Blanche to come. Every so often, I'd hear a scuffle or some bad words coming off the back of Junior's truck. When Blanche opened the door, I said, "Can you come with me? Junior Bledsoe's got something to show you."

Blanche pulled back and covered her nose and mouth—like she couldn't breathe with me standing there. "What is that dreadful smell?" She started to close the door, but Bessie was right behind her, pushing Blanche's big pocketbook into her hands.

"Take this," Bessie told Blanche. "You'll need it."

"Oh, my! What is going on?"

"Please come," I said. "It'll be best if you hurry so the other ladies don't notice."

Bessie pushed against Blanche's shoulder, urging her outside, and then she closed the door. Blanche muttered all the way out to the truck. "Well, I never! Did she just send me out of my own club meeting? Bessie Bledsoe is going to regret this."

"Yes, ma'am," I said, even though Blanche would be the one doing the regretting. She was in for the surprise of her life.

And then the surprise sat up. Actually Junior pushed Clarence into a sitting position, and when he started ranting, Junior just let him go at it. But the sight of his wife stopped him.

Blanche shrieked and dropped her pocketbook. She threw her hands over her face.

"Blanche," said Junior. "We're trying to do this as quietly as we can on account of my momma wants to spare your feelings. Here's the thing—we caught your husband trying to kill Jackie's cow. He's killed one cow already."

"No!" said Clarence. "Wasn't me."

What a liar. Junior held up the branch he'd brought along. "With your yew shrub, Blanche. Tonight we caught him in the act. Now, Blanche, you *know* my daddy was a drunk too. He humiliated my momma in front of our family and friends more times than I like to remember. I don't wish that on nobody. So, we can leave here quietly. You take your car home while your husband rides in the back of this truck with Jackie. Or we can take him into the clubhouse and show all your friends proof of his wicked deeds. *Or* we could call the sheriff and show him. Do you have a preference?"

Do you have a preference? I had a hard time holding back the snickers on that one. It was like a multiple-choice test. A, leave quietly. B, show your friends. C, call the sheriff.

Long story short, Blanche picked A.

Junior explained that we'd need her to come up with thirty-five dollars to replace the cow her husband had killed. And on top of that, he told her to go to the passenger's side of the truck and find Ann Fay's camera on the seat.

"Since you're the one with clean hands, I want *you* to take a picture," he said. "We may need some proof of what happened tonight. Just in case we don't get our money. Or *if* for some reason we need to show the sheriff or send a letter to the editor. Ann Fay will have a copy made for you—as a reminder that neither you nor Clarence will be bullying anybody in this community ever again."

If I had thought fast enough I'd have jumped into the picture with Junior and Clarence. But it was too late. The flashbulb went off, and I knew Junior wouldn't tell Blanche to put in a fresh bulb and take it all over again.

Blanche took the camera and dropped it back on the seat of the truck. She started for her car, and then I reckon she remembered her keys, so she marched back over to where her pocketbook was on the ground and picked it up.

That's when I saw the tears running down her cheeks. And heard her sobbing all the way to her car.

52

MAY 1960

Junior parked by the side of the road and flashed his headlights a few times. He turned off his engine, and we waited for Thomas. I was in the back of the truck—that way I didn't smell myself so much. Besides, it's hard to think of a better feeling than driving through a warm night in the back of a pickup truck.

I hopped down from the truck and Junior got out too. "You don't smell too good," I said.

"Yeah. Ann Fay already told me I'll be bathing from a bucket in the yard tonight. And tomorrow my truck's gonna get some water and disinfectant."

From the sound of things, all the tree frogs in the county had come to cheer for us. I watched for Thomas's front door to open, but it didn't. Then I realized he probably wouldn't come that way or the rest of the family would notice him leaving. Most likely he'd been in the yard somewhere waiting.

But then I heard voices coming up the road. From the direction of Bakers Mountain. It was Thomas and his brother. We hurried to meet them.

"Thomas, Johnny—you should've see it."

"We did." They both said it at the same time.

"Me and Johnny were watching from the church-yard," said Thomas. "I wanted so bad to shout some *Hallelujah*s when you carried him up the road hollering and cussing. But we kept quiet. Don't nobody know we were there."

Of course Thomas and Johnny hadn't seen what happened in the barn, so we told them every detail and had ourselves some good laughs there by the side of the road. Then we got to the part about Blanche snapping that picture and marching back to get her pocketbook.

"We saw that," said Thomas. "We watched from behind those trees between the church and the community building." He slapped his leg and laughed like it was a real funny story.

"You better believe Clarence and Blanche'll be minding their p's and q's from now on," said Junior. "Jackie, you gonna give Thomas the money?"

"Oh, yeah. I almost forgot. Blanche got thirty-five dollars at her house." I reached into my pocket and pulled out the bills.

Thomas held his hand out like a stop sign. "No," he said. "My daddy won't take this."

"He's got to," said Junior. "It's not ours. And you need a cow."

"My brother-in-law Arnie will probably sell you

289

one," I said. "Or the Lutzes even. This money'll buy you a really good milk cow."

Thomas shook his head, but he took the money and fingered it ever so carefully—staring at it like it was some kind of miracle. "Daddy'll buy from Garland Abernethy," he said. He jerked his head in the direction of Garland's barn. "It's close to home."

I shrugged. "Suit yourself."

We heard a car coming then—from down around the curve. "Better shove off," said Johnny, and the two of them disappeared over the road bank and into the woods.

We headed for the truck and I climbed on the back. Junior cranked up the truck and pulled out into the road in front of the car that had slowed down—out of curiosity, I reckoned. Junior waved his arm out the window to signal that everything was okay, and then he headed for home.

Back at the house, I didn't know what to do first—take a bath or tell Momma and Daddy what happened. There was so much to say, starting with Thomas's cow dying and all the way up to us taking Clarence to his house.

"Son, what in the world?" asked Daddy. "Why didn't you tell us?"

I tried to explain that Thomas didn't want my family involved. And the only reason he let Junior in on it was because it was his barn and we needed his help.

Daddy stood there nodding just a little, but I could see from his face and the sag of his shoulders that he felt left out.

Momma just shook her head like she couldn't believe what she was hearing. In the end she held her hand over her mouth and said, "Oh, poor Blanche. She must be so humiliated."

I thought I understood why Momma, all of a sudden, felt sorry for Blanche. Revenge wasn't near as sweet-tasting as I'd expected. But still, I had a feeling Thomas and me both could sleep in peace now. That was one old man who wasn't likely to be doing any more treachery. Not after what we put him through. And not with Junior promising to use that picture against him.

Momma fetched my pajamas and put them in the bathroom just off the back porch. "Leave those filthy clothes out here," she said. She went inside so I could strip down and wash up with soap and warm water.

I thought I would never get to sleep for reliving it all.

Thanks to Thomas's genius idea, his family could buy a new cow. Clarence wouldn't be bothering them anymore. And maybe Dennis would leave me alone too. The cow manure prank wouldn't change what was in either one of their hearts, but it might keep them from doing hateful things—unless of course they wanted us to go ahead and humiliate them in public. I was pretty sure they didn't.

To help me settle down, I started practicing my

speech—whispering it in my head. I went to sleep talking to my imaginary audience about Russia and the United States working things out.

53

MAY 1960

When I woke up I could hear the radio in the kitchen. The news was that Russia had just shot down an American plane. The radio announcer didn't know why our plane was in Russian airspace, but he predicted that this incident would put the skids on upcoming peace talks.

At school, people said the plane was probably us spying on Russia. But no—according to the Eisenhower administration, one of our weather planes had drifted off course. That was all there was to it. Any peace deal was over. We simply couldn't trust the Russians.

That night while we ate supper we listened to more news on the radio about the plane. Afterwards Daddy and I helped with the dishes. Then I pulled out my binder so I could work on my speech.

But Momma wanted to talk. She had been sweeping the floor, but she stopped and grasped that broom handle with both hands and looked at me. "Your father and I have been talking. Son, we were wrong. *I* was wrong for letting Blanche scare me away from doing the right thing. I believed her when she said people would think we're communists. And she was always saying integration could bring violence. I was scared, Jackie."

Momma reached the broom under the table and pulled out crumbs. "But *now*, what do I find out?" she said. "That Blanche herself intended on doing violence— or whatever it took—to stop integration. Her husband was out killing cows, for heaven's sake! What would they have thought up next? Blanche wasn't warning me about other people doing violence. No sirree! She was *threatening* us." Momma swept the dirt onto the dustpan and dumped it in the trash.

She went to the phone and dialed a number. "I don't even *want* to go to her party anymore, but you can bet I will. Blanche has scared me away from my friends long enough. And I'm about to let her know that's over."

I could hear Blanche's phone ringing on the line. And then I heard Blanche's voice. "Hello."

"Good evening, Blanche." Momma's voice was friendly as could be. "This is Myrtle Honeycutt. I'm just wondering whether your magnolias are blooming yet. I'm sure looking forward to seeing them at your garden party in a few weeks."

Momma held the phone out so we could hear Blanche stuttering—something about not being sure who all was invited.

"Actually," said Momma, "I didn't receive my invitation this year. Maybe it got lost in the mail. But either way, I know I'm always welcome."

I couldn't hear what Blanche said next, but it didn't matter because Momma interrupted her. "Will Clarence be cleaned up by then?" She gave me a wink. "Because I'd hate for the other women to get a whiff of anything unpleasant that has happened to him lately."

I almost fell off my chair when Momma said that. And Daddy about snorted a mouthful of coffee all over the floor. Evidently she hadn't let him in on her little plan.

She said goodbye and hung up the phone. "So there!" she said. "I think this community is safe from that menace now. What do you think?"

"I think she understood your meaning," said Daddy.

"Woo-hoo! Momma, I'm so proud of you!"

"I'm proud of *you*, Jackie," said Momma. "For being brave—like Jackie Robinson. For speaking up and marching in Greensboro even. Through it all, you've shown me I was wrong to let a small-minded person like Blanche tell our family who we could be friends with. You go ahead and fish with your friend, invite him over here sometime so we can meet him."

"Really? Thanks, Momma."

I looked at Daddy to see if he agreed. He nodded. I reckoned he was thinking about his war buddy—the one who saved his life—because he reached over and squeezed my shoulder. "I know Jackie Bedford would be proud of you, son."

I thought how, when I first bumped into Thomas, he told me that between the two Jackies I had a lot to live up to. But he was probably thinking I was too lowdown to ever do it. Because somehow he knew I was the one who'd thrown that apple at him.

Maybe, all this time when I'd been hankering after Thomas and starting to care about things not being equal—well, maybe like he said, I *had* been trying to clear my conscience. But I preferred to think I was trying to do the right thing. For the right reasons.

I knew one thing. It sure felt good to have Momma and Daddy standing there feeling proud of me.

54

MAY 1960

What we heard on the news on Sunday shocked us all. Nikita Khrushchev declared that the plane they shot down actually *was* a spy plane. And to prove it, the Russians showed pictures of our pilot. They'd captured him alive!

So that meant President Eisenhower had lied to us about it being a weather plane! And here I thought he was going to make peace with Russia. If we couldn't trust our own president, who could we trust? On Monday morning I told Mrs. Cunningham I couldn't make the graduation speech. "It's a big fat optimistic lie," I said. "The audience will know we're not becoming friends with Russia."

Mrs. Cunningham put her arm around my shoulder. "I know, Jackie. I'm disappointed too. But don't make a fast decision."

At lunchtime she pulled me away from my friends so the two of us could sit alone. "How can you use this setback to reshape your speech?" she asked.

"You want me to write it all over again?"

Mrs. Cunningham smiled. "I want you to *revise* it," she said. "Nuclear disarmament *is* less certain now, but every relationship has setbacks. Do you always get along with your classmates?"

From the way her eyes twinkled, I could tell what she was saying. She knew Dennis wasn't exactly my friend, but she believed he might be someday. And the truth was, ever since that night we put Clarence in his place, Dennis hadn't said one cross word to me.

"Your speech is getting better and better," said Mrs. Cunningham. "That's what adversity does to us." She pushed her lunch tray aside and leaned forward, making her own little speech about knowing I could do this.

That woman was killing me. But I didn't even bother complaining. Mrs. Cunningham believed in me, and I'd do almost anything to make her proud. Besides, I really *did* want to be the graduation speaker.

"Okay," I said. "I'll see what I can do."

After lunch she sent me and Wayne to the library to work on the speech. Wayne read over it, then handed it back to me. "Looks to me like you just need to change the ending. Take out the part about Eisenhower's plans to visit Moscow in June. Or keep it and say that if he doesn't go, we'll all be disappointed."

"Of course," I said. "But then what? Mrs. Cunningham wants it to be hopeful."

"Ha!" said Wayne. "Tell everybody you hope he goes to Moscow."

"Very funny," I said. "I've got to come up with something that sounds impressive."

"Yeah, I know. You could write that good things take time and world peace won't happen overnight."

By the time we were done I had a speech about how Eisenhower and Khrushchev had made progress by *trying* to get to know each other. They both agreed that the safety of the world depended on reducing nuclear weapons. Disarmament could still happen.

And I said that peace starts at home and we could each do our part right here at the foot of Bakers Mountain. But I didn't know exactly what that meant, so the speech still felt like a lie to me.

55

MAY 1960

I kept thinking about that spy plane and how our government tried to hide the truth from us. Planning that speech had gotten my hopes up about world peace. Just writing it made me feel like maybe we wouldn't have to live with fear of bombs anymore.

But now I knew the truth. Russia and the United States would probably never trust each other.

There was something else churning in my mind too. Thomas.

Together we'd caught Clarence red-handed and taught him a lesson. Thomas had trusted me with that. But did he really and truly trust me? After all, I was still hiding the truth about that apple. It would always be nagging at the back of my mind. And his mind too.

I knew what I had to do. Confess.

I got up and went to church, and while the choir sang "What Can Wash Away My Sin?" I planned out what I would say. I'd tell Thomas I was sorry and I never intended to hurt him. It wasn't planned and it wasn't how I felt about Negroes and I sure wished I could take it back. And would he please forgive me?

That afternoon I grabbed my pole and headed for the river. I didn't even bother digging worms first. I could always find some in the woods.

I beat Thomas to the fishing hole, so I found me a spot of nice rich dirt away from the sandy riverbank and dug with a rock until I found a few worms. Before I was back at the edge of the river I heard Thomas coming down the path whistling a tune.

I met him at the fishing hole and that speech I planned in church flew right out of my mind. My belly felt like I had a school of minnows swimming around in there. So of course I started saying whatever came to my mind. "Tell me about your new cow. Did you get one? What'd your daddy say about Clarence and that bucket of poop? Or didn't you tell him?"

"That's a lot of questions," said Thomas.

"Yeah, I guess so. Did you get a cow?"

"Yeah, once we finally talked Daddy into keeping that money. He like to died laughing about Clarence and the cow poop."

"Did you go ahead and tell him about the bottle? Wouldn't it be safe now?"

Thomas put a worm on his hook. "No use stirring up an old pot." He threw his line into the water. "Don't you agree?"

I threw my line in too. "Yeah, I guess so."

Did he mean that? Or was he baiting me—giving me a chance to confess? I still didn't want to. All the arguments went in circles and picked up speed inside my head, just like someone was stirring them with a stick.

We could be friends without me mentioning this. After all, hadn't Thomas seen the black eye I took for defending Maribelle? Hadn't his momma seen me on television, marching with that sign about ending segregation? Not to mention how we'd fixed old Clarence real good. We did it together. Shouldn't that be enough? Why should I go messing everything up by telling him the truth?

I sat there staring up at the trees, feeling the breeze in my face and sucking in the smell of sweet bubbies on the bush beside me. I told myself how the weather was just right and it was a perfect Sunday in May and life couldn't get any better than this.

But that wasn't true. Things could be better. Because even with the day being perfect in every other way, the memory of that apple was hanging in the air between us. I couldn't keep pretending to be his friend without making things right.

So out of the blue I said it. "I didn't mean to lie when you asked if I was feeling guilty about something. This is the God's honest truth, Thomas—I didn't know what you were talking about. After Clarence hit you with a bottle—that's when I remembered. I dreamed about it, and the next morning it all came pouring over me. I

302

had done exactly what Clarence did. Well, not *exactly*, because what I threw was an apple. I didn't hate you. A big kid on the bus dared me to throw it. I'm real sorry, Thomas. It was bad. Terrible bad."

Maybe I was afraid of what Thomas would say. Because I kept on blabbering. He couldn't have squeezed a word in sidewise if he wanted to.

"You knew all along, didn't you, Thomas? How *did* you know? I'm sure you didn't see me, because I ducked down real fast. Right away I felt just awful about it, Thomas. I still do."

"Would you *stop* it?" said Thomas, and he said it real strong and forceful.

Now I'd made him mad. "Uh, sure. Stop what?"

"Talking."

"Oh. Okay. But Thomas . . ."

He threw up his hand and I clamped my mouth shut.

"Johnny knows people that ride your bus," Thomas said. "So he asked around. What'd you expect? He's my big brother. Someone told him it was Jackie Honeycutt. At first we plotted how to get you back. Johnny could've flattened your nose if he took a notion to. You know that?"

"Uh, yeah." I could see it all in my mind. And I pictured Thomas helping Johnny out. "But why didn't he?" I asked. "Why didn't you?"

Thomas shrugged. "Some things are worth fighting over. Like sitting down to eat at a lunch counter.

303

Getting a good education or a fair trial. Other things aren't worth the trouble. Like *you*, Jackie Honeycutt."

"Oh."

"You were a stupid little brat," said Thomas. "Not worth my brother's time or mine either. Not worth the trouble it could bring down on our heads. That's what we decided. What Johnny decided."

His words hit me like a bucket of cow poop. And sitting there on that perfect Sunday afternoon with the river running by us real quiet and steady, I felt just how dirty and lowdown I was. But at least I wasn't pushing it away anymore. I sat there and wallowed in my shame.

Then Thomas spoke up again. "It hurt real bad, Jackie. Not the apple so much as the humiliation. The way the kids on your bus laughed out the window at us. I was so mad I wanted to beat you up myself. But I couldn't. Because Johnny said if I did, things could get a whole lot worse."

Thomas was quiet for a minute and for once I couldn't think of a thing to say. Then he spoke up again. His voice was almost a whisper.

"Not being able to do a thing about it, that's always the hardest part."

I sat there on the riverbank listening to Thomas tell me about the hurt and humiliation. And I hurt too. I tried not to let him see the tears leaking out of my eyes. But I think he did.

"We were wrong about you, Jackie. Me and Johnny both agree about this. You're worth more than we thought. And you're not a brat after all. I accept your apology."

It took a second for his words to sink in. "You do? Really, Thomas? Because I'm very sorry."

"Yeah," said Thomas. "You said that already. Now, are you going to pull that fish in or not?"

My mind was so fixed on what he was saying that I'd totally forgotten I was fishing. But now I felt the tug on my line. I waited until I was sure that hook was in the fish's mouth, and then I gave my pole a yank. "Got him!" I said.

But wouldn't you know—when my hook came out of the water it was empty, stripped clean of my worm even.

For some reason that struck Thomas as real funny. I don't think I'd ever seen him laugh so hard. But truth was, I didn't even care. The sound of it was like a summer rain, washing all over me.

56

MAY 1960

Two weeks after Russia shot down our spy plane, Eisenhower went to the summit in Paris. Khrushchev was there, but he was in a bad mood. Evidently he demanded an apology from Eisenhower. He didn't get one, so he told Eisenhower he wasn't invited to visit Russia in June after all.

There was no way I was getting out of that speech, so all I could do was keep practicing it. I memorized what I wanted to say, changing some words here and there to make it sound as hopeful as possible.

Then something hopeful did happen. But not between the United States and Russia.

The telephone rang late one night, about a week before graduation. Daddy answered the phone, but Momma and I both got up too because late-night calls usually meant something bad had happened.

It was Ellie on the line, laughing and practically screaming. "They did it," she said.

"Did what?" asked Daddy. He was still waking up. "Is somebody hurt?"

"No," said Ellie. "Here, I'll let Maribelle tell you."

Then we heard Maribelle's voice. "The stores in Winston-Salem are integrating their lunch counters. And . . ." Maribelle stopped. I guess she couldn't go on because she started crying.

Ellie took the phone back. "We just got back from a very long meeting. Mr. Bradley and some others negotiated the agreement. It's really happening, Daddy. And tell Momma we're both fine. Couldn't be better."

Momma leaned in toward the receiver. "I can hear you, Ellie. I'm happy for you. For Maribelle."

"For all of us," said Ellie. "This is a victory for every American. Greensboro will follow suit, and soon all restaurants will integrate." Now *she* started crying. "We knew it would happen," she said, "but now that it *has,* we can hardly believe it."

Mama wiped at her eyes. "You did the right thing, Ellie, even when I was scared for you."

Daddy told Ellie he was proud of them both, and Maribelle asked if I was awake. I let out a loud "Yee-haw" so they'd know I was hearing the good news. And then the operator interrupted to say that our three minutes were up.

57

JUNE 1960

I sat onstage with my classmates—girls in white dresses and boys in our Sunday best. Every last one of us was scrubbed and nervous and sweating. The wooden auditorium chairs were so full that people stood around the edges of the room. They fanned themselves with the mimeographed graduation programs—except for a few people like Blanche Shuford, who was in the front row flapping a store-bought fan with pink flowers. As far as I could tell, that sorry husband of hers wasn't anywhere around. Dennis's mother was sitting beside Blanche but it appeared that his daddy hadn't shown up for his own son's graduation.

My family sat in the third row—Ann Fay and Junior. Ida and Arnie. Momma and Daddy. Everybody except Bunkie and Gerianne, who'd stayed home with Bessie and Miss Dinah. And of course Ellie was in Winston-Salem. She'd said she was sure sorry, but she couldn't make it.

Our class opened the program by singing "Getting to

Know You," and then Mrs. Cunningham made a short speech about how she enjoyed teaching each of us. We sang "I Whistle a Happy Tune," and Dennis's whistling was so good the audience started clapping even before he finished. Suddenly I realized why that was the perfect song for graduation. It was about being brave when you actually felt scared. In a few minutes I'd have to give my speech. My throat was dry and my armpits were wet. Sweat trickled past my ears.

After the song, Mrs. Cunningham introduced every graduate, calling us by name and bragging on our talents. She saved me for last. "Jackie Honeycutt has the gift of gab," she said. I saw Ann Fay and Ida back there snickering. "But Jackie has some worthwhile things to say, and he's worked hard on some wisdom he wants to share with us." She turned and motioned me forward. "Jackie."

I let out all the breath I'd been holding during the introduction. And for some reason, on my way to the microphone, I thought about Beth Lutz and how calm she seemed at the dairy show. At the speaker's stand I took a deep breath and held myself straight and still the way Beth did. I looked around the room, front to back and side to side.

Someone shushed their crying baby.

When the room was quiet I began to speak—barely glancing at the speech because I knew it by heart.

"When Mrs. Cunningham asked me to speak tonight,

she said that graduation speeches should be optimistic. So I chose a tiny topic that I was feeling hopeful about—world peace."

The audience laughed, so I figured I was off to a good start.

"My premise was this quote by Abraham Lincoln. *Do I not destroy my enemies when I make them my friends?*"

I told the audience that our eighth-grade class had discussed lots of current events in the last year, and we didn't always agree on controversial topics. I told them I *was* starting to feel hopeful about the relationship between the United States and Russia—until Russia shot down that spy plane.

Of course I had changed the ending—trying to be optimistic about world peace. But I hated the new ending because I wasn't feeling hopeful about that at all.

I stopped for a second and swallowed hard. I looked at the audience and started speaking again, but then I caught a glimpse of Maribelle Bradley. That stopped me right in the middle of a sentence. She was mostly a silhouette standing in the hallway against the light coming through the open doors of the school entrance. Still, I knew it was her. And Ellie was right beside her.

But for some reason I wasn't just seeing a silhouette of them in the hall. Instead, I saw Maribelle coming out of the Kress store in Greensboro. I saw her in handcuffs.

Most of all, I saw that thug's spit running down her face. I saw fear and bravery all at the same time.

Then I saw someone else. Thomas Freeman.

He wasn't there, of course. But I could see him in my mind—sitting on the riverbank with his fishing pole in hand. I saw him duck when that bottle came hurtling at him. And I think I even ducked a little myself just thinking about it.

While I stood there, probably staring into space, stuttering, and looking like a fool, I lost everything that was in my head to say about Russia and the United States becoming friends. I hated that speech anyway. And no wonder—because I couldn't control any of that. But I could do something about friendships right here at the foot of Bakers Mountain.

I thought about Jackie Robinson being brave enough to play in the major leagues when no other Negroes were doing it. About Maribelle's father putting his life on the line and coming back to inequality. And about Jackie Bedford, who sacrificed his life for Daddy during the war. If *he'd* taken the easy way, I wouldn't even be here. I thought about courage and that whistling song. And how I could fool myself into thinking I wasn't scared.

I folded up my paper. I wasn't going to give the end of that speech I'd written.

But I had to find something to say. People were shuffling their feet, and I could see Daddy leaning forward, nodding to me, urging me to keep going. After stuttering around for a sentence or two, I started talking off the top of my head.

"I've learned a lot during my eighth-grade year. I've learned about some things that Negroes go through and about freedoms and privileges I have that they don't."

In the back, Maribelle threw her hand over her mouth. Ellie clapped for a second or two before she caught herself and stopped.

People started whispering behind their programs. Others fanned themselves harder than ever.

"This year I made some new friends. Not just here at school, because this school isn't integrated. You see, this year I made some Negro friends."

Blanche Shuford dropped her store-bought fan. It slid to the floor, and I noticed she didn't bother to pick it up.

I told them about meeting Thomas on the riverbank and how he knew more about birds than anyone else I ever met. That alone would have made him perfect for the 4-H program. And besides, he had a cow. He would have loved to be in 4-H, except the state didn't hire many colored 4-H agents. "There was a law that says our schools should be separate but equal," I said. "But we've all seen on the news how colored schools aren't equal to ours.

"Things aren't equal," I continued. "But they ought to be. We should want them to be equal for everyone— even Negroes."

I saw how Blanche Shuford gripped the stiff handles

of that elephant-sized pocketbook, and I remembered her face when she picked it up out of the grass on the night when we humiliated her.

"This year I've gotten to know some people who are different from me. I've seen life through their eyes, and I like them better than I thought."

People shuffled their feet and whispered behind their folded programs. I heard some man clear his throat—and he wasn't quiet about it.

I looked around for Mrs. Cunningham. Maybe it was good that I couldn't see her, because I was probably ruining the whole graduation. For one thing, this speech was longer than the one we practiced. And I wasn't done yet. At least, I didn't think I was. I had no idea what I was going to say next. But I kept going.

"I can't make Woolworth or Kress stores serve Negroes sitting at their lunch counters. That's their decision. And I can't make our schools be integrated. I'm not even going to say that the best way to get rid of an enemy is to turn him into a friend, because I'm not very good at that myself. But Mrs. Cunningham says that graduation speeches should be optimistic, so I will just say that I hope it's true. I hope we'll try to see life the way others see it. And when things aren't equal, I hope we care."

I was finished. I don't know how I knew I was finished except that I had talked too long, and now that I paused, people were clapping. Some of them, anyway.

Daddy was clapping, and Momma too. I went back to my seat and Mrs. Cunningham came to the microphone.

"How about that?" she asked. "I learned this year that Jackie speaks his mind, and he has a lot going on in there too." She tapped her forehead. "Watch that young man. He'll do great things someday."

She invited Betty and Gloria to come to the front, and they sang "The School Song" from *The King and I*. The second time through they replaced the words "Royal Bangkok Academy" with the name of our school. When they did that, it was like the room lit up with smiles and laughter.

After that, we filed to the front of the stage one row at a time to receive our diplomas.

I took the rolled-up paper tied with black ribbon and the principal shook my hand and congratulated me. He looked real serious. Maybe I had just caused him a whole lot of trouble.

58

JUNE 1960

People poured into the hallways at the back of the auditorium and some slipped through the side doors. I glanced around for Mrs. Cunningham and saw her talking to some parents. She was smiling, so maybe they weren't fussing at her about my speech.

Ann Fay was the first member of my family to congratulate me. "Jackie," she said. "You waded right into that muddy wide river! I wish Imogene could've heard that, but you better believe I'm going to write all about it in my next letter. I'm feeling so proud right now."

Momma and Daddy squeezed through the crowd, heading toward me. They almost bumped into Blanche Shuford, except, when she saw them, she busied herself with something in her pocketbook.

Daddy pounded me on the back. "How do you do that?" he asked. "Getting in front of all those people and holding forth like that? It looked like you weren't even reading it."

"I sort of made up the last part as I went. Did I do okay?"

Momma gave me a quick hug, and then she leaned back and looked me in the eyes. "You're a real good speaker, Jackie Honeycutt. I think you just found your calling."

"No," I said. "Mrs. Cunningham is the one who found it."

Lots of people ignored me, but a few came to congratulate me. Ida and Arnie, Garland Abernethy, and a couple of people I didn't know. I still hadn't seen Ellie and Maribelle. But maybe they thought it wasn't a good idea to stick around.

"It's hot as next August in here," I said. "Can we leave now?" But I still needed to say goodbye to Mrs. Cunningham. She was talking to other parents, but when she caught my eye, she excused herself and hurried over.

"Mr. and Mrs. Honeycutt," she said. "This is one fine boy you've got here. And so much for insisting he write out a speech!" She laughed. "But Jackie, you got their attention and you held it to the end." She shook her head. "For a minute there, I thought there might not *be* an end."

"I'm sorry. I know it was too long."

"Maybe," she said. "Maybe not. Maybe we were

meant to hear every word of it."

Before we left, I stopped by the classroom. I found a Davy Crockett comic book with some other clutter in the bottom of my desk. I'd forgotten all about hiding it from Dennis. I started to put it with my other things to take home, but then I thought this was a good chance for me to practice turning enemies into friends. So I took the comic book over to his desk. "Here, Dennis," I said. "Some summer reading for you."

He just stared at me. Maybe he thought I was fooling with him. But I pushed it toward him, so he reached out and took it. He looked at the book and then at me and didn't say a word. I was starting to feel real awkward, so I said, "Guess I'll see you in high school."

"Yeah," he said. I walked away, and when I was halfway across the room he remembered his manners. "Thanks, Honeycutt."

I just nodded and kept going. I almost bumped into Pamela. She'd been crying. "I'll miss this place," she said. "And I'll miss you too."

"Uh. You've been a good friend," I said.

"I'm proud to know you, Jackie. That speech was terrific. I hope we have classes together in high school."

"If not, maybe we can have lunch together sometimes. Like we did this year."

"Sure. I'll save you a seat." Pamela leaned over, gave me a quick hug, and walked away. And that right there almost made me ready for school to start back up.

When we got home, Ellie and Maribelle were waiting on the front porch. And I declare they both snatched me up and held me so tight I thought they'd bust my ribcage.

"I thought you were going to talk about world peace," said Ellie.

"That was a stupid speech," I said. "There's not a thing any one of us can do about Russia. But I saw y'all standing back there, and well—I changed my speech right on the spot. It's your fault."

"No," said Maribelle. "You had it in you all along. Right here." She tapped her hand against her heart. "All you needed was a little reminder to let it out."

We went inside for cake and ice cream. Bessie and Miss Dinah had come with Gerianne and Bunkie, so we were all together again. All except Miss Pauline. That made me feel a little blue, so after a while I slipped outside to have a talk with Lucy. There on the back porch was a birdhouse made of twigs all tied together with twine.

And right above it, on the porch post, was the sign I'd made. BACK DOOR FRIENDS ARE BEST. I hoped Thomas would know that he was like the Bledsoes and the Hinkle sisters. At my house he could make himself at home.

A rolled-up paper poked out of the round entrance of that birdhouse. I pulled it out and unrolled it.

Jackie,

Happy Graduation!
Meet me at the river on Sunday? Maybe I
can teach you to catch a fish.

Thomas

I looked at that fine birdhouse and thought about things I'd learned from Thomas already. That life's not fair. That to earn his trust I had to face my past. And that enemies can become friends.

Maybe he'd even learned a thing or two from me. Like, I'd done some stupid things in my life, and there was a lot I didn't know about how unequal things were between us. But I was learning.

EPILOGUE

When I went into the new year, 1960,
I didn't expect to be snowed in with a colored family
who deserved freedom as much as I did.
I didn't know what all I'd learn from them
or that a personal enemy would make me care enough
to join their fight.

I still didn't know *how* to cross that muddy wide river.

When I went to graduation that night
I knew I wasn't happy with my speech.
I didn't know that Maribelle would show up and
I'd see Thomas in my mind's eye.
I didn't imagine that because of them,
and the two Jackies,
and all the brave people
who sat at lunch counters and marched in the streets,
I'd change my words midsentence
and wade right into that muddy wide river.

But I'm glad I did.

AUTHOR'S NOTE

In my novel *Blue*, the white protagonist, Ann Fay Honeycutt, goes into a makeshift polio hospital that is racially integrated. There she meets Imogene Wilfong, a Black girl who challenges Ann Fay to see life from her point of view. When their friendship is disrupted by a return to segregation in the hospital, Ann Fay begins to understand the injustice created by racism.

Blue led to a series (Bakers Mountain Stories), and I soon realized that I would eventually return to the theme of racial inequality. *Equal* is the Honeycutt family's continued journey into understanding and responding to the injustices of a racially segregated society.

TERMINOLOGY USED IN THIS BOOK

Throughout this story I've used the terms "Negro" and "colored," because those were the terms Americans used in 1959 and 1960. As the civil rights struggle evolved during the 1960s, Black pride evolved with it, and the term "Black" came into common usage. Later, as Black people continued to explore their identity and cultural heritage, many chose to identify as African American.

I also used the term "sit-down" to describe the lunch counter movement. Today we refer to such demonstrations as "sit-ins," but "sit-down" is the accurate historical term and expresses the intention of Black people to find a seat at the table in public spaces.

"SEPARATE BUT EQUAL"

In 1892, Homer Plessy, who was one-eighth Black, sat in a railroad car designated for white people only. After refusing to move to the "colored" car, he was arrested. He took his case all the way to the Supreme Court, where it was ruled that businesses *could* provide separate facilities for Black people and white people, as long as the facilities were equal. This doctrine became known as "separate but equal."

In the decades that followed, however, equality did not exist for Black people in America. The government provided far less money for Black schools than for white ones. African Americans were often denied their legal right to vote, were not given fair trials, and suffered countless cruelties by whites who feared they would gain too much power or want to marry their children.

Yet Black people served in each of America's wars. During World War II they fought and died for the freedom of oppressed racial groups in Europe. Those who returned alive were newly aware of how hypocritical we Americans were to proclaim "liberty and justice for all" while oppressing people of color here at home. They decided it was time to fight for their own freedom.

The civil rights movement that followed led to a 1954 court case known as *Brown v. [versus] Board of*

Education. In this case, the Supreme Court mandated that public school segregation would no longer be legal under the "separate but equal" doctrine.

Schools in both the North and the South did not immediately open their doors to Black Americans, however. Many communities resisted integration, and those who chose to integrate often experienced violence from angry citizens. Some brave Black students who first entered Southern white schools, a few at a time, were harassed or even viciously attacked by fellow students. But integration was slowly making its way into Southern society. In 1966, when schools finally integrated in Hickory, North Carolina, the process was relatively smooth and free of conflict.

Colleges across the United States were also slow to integrate. In 1959, some students and faculty at Wake Forest, the college that Ellie Honeycutt attends in *Equal*, started pushing for desegregation. A vote from the student body in 1960 rejected the effort. But student activists did not give up, and by the spring of 1962, Wake Forest was one of the first major private colleges in the nation to integrate.

Protest Movement and Lunch Counter Sit-ins

On January 1, 1960, a group of African Americans gathered at the airport in Greenville, South Carolina, to protest the treatment of Jackie Robinson and other Black friends who had used the main waiting room.

On February 1, 1960 four Black college students sat at a Greensboro, North Carolina, Woolworth lunch counter and ordered doughnuts and coffee. They were denied service but sat for a while and returned the following day. After that first sit-in Ronald Martin, Robert Patterson, and Mark Martin (pictured here) joined the movement.

This New Year's Day protest inspired other African Americans to stand up and speak out against humiliating treatment.

Exactly one month later, on February 1, four Black students from A & T College in Greensboro, North Carolina, walked into a Woolworth store, sat at the lunch counter, and ordered coffee and doughnuts. The manager would have been happy to serve them if they had stood to eat, but he refused to let them eat while sitting alongside white people. They stayed anyway, so he closed the lunch counter for the day. They returned the next day with twenty-seven friends. They came back daily with more and more students joining the protests, some at Woolworth and others at the Kress store nearby. Many counter-protesters showed up as well. There were often hundreds of people sitting down and milling about with strong feelings both for and against the protests. Police carefully monitored the volatile situation.

Eventually, rather than integrate, the store closed its lunch counter altogether. Students agreed not to protest if they could negotiate with store managers and city government. After more than a month of negotiations, however, they could not find an agreeable solution. The students resumed their protests, and some of them were briefly arrested.

News of the sit-ins spread rapidly, and suddenly Black people in multiple cities across the South were insisting on equal service at lunch counters. Some white people joined in as a show of support.

A few weeks after that first sit-in, students from Winston-Salem State Teachers College and Wake Forest College were arrested and jailed on trespassing charges when they sat at a lunch counter in Winston-Salem, North Carolina. Despite the arrests, the protests continued, as did negotiations with store owners. As a result, by May 23, 1960, multiple stores in Winston-Salem agreed to integrate their lunch counters.

The Woolworth store in Greensboro, where the first

sit-in took place, finally opened its lunch counter to Black people on July 25, 1960. It happened without fanfare or violence. Gradually other businesses followed suit.

In 1964, President Lyndon B. Johnson signed the Civil Rights Act into law. It outlawed discrimination based on race, color, sex, religion, or national origin. Since then, much has been accomplished in the struggle to equalize citizenship rights for people of color. However, the struggle for non-whites to experience equal opportunity and dignified treatment continues to this day.

THE COLD WAR AND RUSSIA

During World War II the United States and Russia were allies, but afterward they disagreed on how to divide and govern the countries that had lost the war. In particular they differed on who should control the city of Berlin, Germany. As tensions increased between the two superpowers, each began the buildup of nuclear weapons. The space race became a critical part of the competition because missiles were necessary to launch the weapons. This escalation of tension, which involved threats and spying, became known as the Cold War.

Both countries recognized the danger of amassing weapons and maintaining a warlike stance. Nikita Khrushchev, the Russian premier, set forth the idea of peaceful coexistence, and in September 1959 he visited the United States in hopes of improving relations

In 1959, in hopes of decreasing hostilities between the United States and Russia, President Dwight Eisenhower (center left) invited Premier Nikita Khrushchev (center right) to the United States. They are pictured here at the President's guesthouse in Washington, DC.

between the two countries. While he and President Dwight Eisenhower made progress in discussing peace, neither fully trusted the other. Both countries engaged in spying, and on May 1, 1960, when Russia shot down an American spy plane, peaceful coexistence experienced a serious setback.

The Cold War continued until 1991, when Russia's communist regime collapsed. The world continues to feel its chilling effects today.

Who Was Real?

In addition to President Dwight Eisenhower and Premier Nikita Khrushchev, I included several other real characters in this story.

In 1960, Dr. Martin Luther King Jr. was still rising in his role as America's passionate civil rights leader. Although he was not as well-known as he would become over the next eight years, civil rights activists were listening to his ideas about passive resistance. Over Easter weekend in 1960, in the midst of the lunch counter sit-ins, he spoke to several hundred students in North Carolina, inspiring them to continue the sit-down protests.

Jackie Robinson, famous for integrating major league baseball, had retired in 1957, but he went on to speak out for civil rights. The incident in which he was discriminated against in the waiting room at the airport in Greenville, South Carolina, inspired a protest by Black citizens. That protest led, one month later, to the beginning of the lunch counter sit-downs.

Reverend Carl McIntire was a radio preacher who taught that "racial brotherhood" was inspired by communists. He denounced anyone who promoted integration. With his radio program, which was broadcast over hundreds of stations, many of them in the South, he influenced countless Americans.

I've enjoyed dropping local characters into Bakers

After Rosa Parks was arrested for refusing to yield her seat to a white man, African Americans in Montgomery, Alabama, boycotted the bus system. Eventually, the courts outlawed racially segregated seating of Montgomery buses. Dr. Martin Luther King is pictured behind Rev. Ralph Abernathy (front left), a civil rights activist, legally riding at the front of a Montgomery bus for the first time.

Jackie Robinson broke baseball's color barrier when he joined the Brooklyn Dodgers in 1947. Prior to that, Jackie played one season in the Negro Baseball League for the Kansas City Monarchs.

Mountain Stories, and in this particular book I included several who are still living and who helped me shape this story. Mrs. Cunningham was my language arts teacher in seventh grade and again in eighth. She was innovative, nurtured the talents of each of her students, and held firm control of her classroom. I am a writer because Mrs. Cunningham planted that hope in me. I chose to include her because I wanted to honor her contribution to my life and to the lives of so many other students whose gifts she acknowledged and nurtured.

At the time at which this story is set, Ed Nolley was the assistant county agent responsible for 4-H in Catawba County. Nancy Hatley was an avid 4-H Club member. Barry Sigmon, Carolyn Lutz, Beth Lutz, and Rusty Lutz were also prominent 4-Hers in 1959.

The Lutz Dairy Farms have a long and respected heritage—extending back into the late 1800s—in the Startown community. For decades their superior cows and excellent showmanship dominated the competitions at local, district, and state fairs. Carolyn Lutz Miller and Beth Lutz Bowman, who won countless ribbons for their prized Jerseys, helped me understand what it would mean for my character to raise and show his cow.

4-H CLUB

The 4-H Club was formed in the early 1900s to develop self-sufficiency and leadership skills in young people. The club's logo is a four-leaf clover with the letter *H* in each leaf. The pledge explains the club's fourfold focus.

> *I pledge my head to clearer thinking*
> *my heart to greater loyalty,*
> *my hands to larger service,*
> *and my health to better living,*
> *for my club, my community, my country, and*
> *my world.*

Members of 4-H develop skills in various aspects of home and farm life, as well as personal growth, technology, caring for the environment, and much more. The 4-H Club held its first meeting (under a different name) in Springfield, Ohio, in 1902 and has since spread across the United States and to over fifty countries around the world.

RESOURCES*

BOOKS

A Glimpse of Jersey Cattle History in North Carolina and More, by W. R. Lutz (North Carolina Jersey Cattle Association/ Wallace Printing, 2013).

Mothers of Massive Resistance, by Elizabeth Gillespie McRae (Oxford University Press, 2018).

Social Reform Movements: The Civil Rights Movement, by Charles Patterson (Facts on File, 1995).

Step Into History: The Civil Rights Movement, by Olugbemisola Rhuday-Perkovich (Scholastic, 2018).

We Are Not Yet Equal: Understanding Our Racial Divide, by Carol Anderson and Tonya Bolden (Bloomsbury YA, 2018).

NEWSPAPERS

Catawba News-Enterprise, July 1959–May 1960.

Greensboro Daily News, February, April, and May 1960.

Hickory Daily Record, July 1959–May 1960.

VIDEOS

Black America Since MLK: And Still I Rise (PBS, 2016).

Eyes on the Prize, Episodes 1–6 (PBS, 2006).

February One: The Story of the Greensboro Four (Independent Lens, 2003).

Freedom Summer (PBS, 2014).

I'm Not My Brother's Keeper (Wake Forest University, 2001).

WEBSITES AND INTERNET ARTICLES

Cold War Roadshow: Khrushchev's Trip Itinerary. pbs.org/ wgbh/americanexperience/features/cold-war-roadshow-niki-ta-khrushchevs-trip-itinerary/.

International Civil Rights Center and Museum. www.sitinmovement.org/.

Moments in US Diplomatic History: Khrushchev Visits America: A Cold War Comedy of Errors, Act I. adst.org/2013/10/khrushchev-visits-america-a-cold-war-comedy-of-errors-act-i/.

Moments in US Diplomatic History: Khrushchev Visits America: A Cold War Comedy of Errors, Act II. adst.org/2013/10/khrushchev-visits-america-a-cold-war-comedy-of-errors-act-ii/.

National Civil Rights Museum. civilrightsmuseum.org/.

Books for Young People

Countdown, by Deborah Wiles (Scholastic, 2010).

Darkroom: A Memoir in Black and White, by Lila Weaver Quintero (University of Alabama Press, 1912).

The Enemy: Detroit 1954, by Sara Holbrook (Calkins Creek, 2017).

Freedom on the Menu, by Carole Boston Weatherford (Puffin Books, 2007).

Glory Be, by Augusta Scattergood (Scholastic, 2014).

The Lions of Little Rock, by Kristin Levine (Puffin Books, 2013).

Revolution, by Deborah Wiles (Scholastic, 2017).

Ruby Lee and Me, by Shannon Hitchcock (Scholastic, 2018).

The Watsons Go to Birmingham, by Christopher Paul Curtis (Yearling, 1997).

Yankee Girl, by Mary Ann Rodman Downing (Square Fish, 2008).

Nonfiction

Amazing Americans: Thurgood Marshall, by Kristin Kemp (Teacher Created Materials, 2014).

Birmingham Sunday, by Larry Dane Brimner (Calkins Creek, 2010).

Brown Girl Dreaming, by Jacqueline Woodson (Puffin Books, 2016).

The Cold War: The Twentieth Century, by Wendy Conklin (Teacher Created Materials, 2007).

Dwight D. Eisenhower: Thirty-Fourth President, 1953–1961, by Mike Venezia (Children's Press, 2017).

March Trilogy, by John Lewis (Top Shelf Productions, 2016).

She Stood for Freedom: The Untold Story of a Civil Rights Hero, Joan Trumphauer Mulholland, by Loki Mulholland and Angela Fairwell (Shadow Mountain, 2016).

Step Into History: The Civil Rights Movement, by Olugbemisola Rhuday-Perkovich (Scholastic, 2018).

Top Secret Files: The Cold War: Secrets, Special Missions and Hidden Facts About the CIA, KGB, and M16, by Stephanie Bearce (Prufrock Press, 2015).

Turning Fifteen on the Road to Freedom: My Story of the 1965 Selma Voting Rights March, by Lynda Blackmon Lowery (Speak, 2016).

Twelve Days in May, by Larry Dane Brimner (Calkins Creek, 2017).

We Are One: The Story of Bayard Ruskin, by Larry Dane Brimner (Calkins Creek, 2007).

*Websites active at time of publication

THANK YOU!

Every topic has its experts—people who have lived through a historical event, have studied a particular subject, or have experienced emotions that might help a novel writer create an authentic story. I am indebted to Shirley Cunningham, who remembers Mountain View School as it would have been in 1959 and helped me craft the school scenes. Working with her was like stepping back into eighth grade and being assigned to one of the world's best teachers!

I am grateful to Lynne Myer, Ashley Brodie, and Cozette Sinclair for their insights regarding cultural and racial aspects of this story. I owe thanks to my 4-H Club experts—Donna Mull, Carolyn Lutz Miller, Beth Lutz Bowman, Pam Nelson, Nancy Hatley Miller, Ed Nolley, Carolyn Branson Jones, Gary Jones, and Glenn Detweiler—for sharing their expertise and memories with me, and to Roberta Handlin and Alex Floyd at the Catawba County Library for helping me with research. Finally, I thank Carol Baldwin and my husband Chuck Hostetter, for listening, encouraging, and brainstorming at times when I simply didn't understand my character or know where Jackie's story was going.

PICTURE CREDITS

Harold Valentine / AP Images: 330 (top); Library of Congress Prints and Photographs Division, NYWT&S Collection, LC-DIG-ppmsca-08095: 325; LC-DIG-ds-07191: 328; Visual Materials from the NAACP Records, LC-DIG-ppmsc-00039: 330 (bottom)